THE GREENHOUSE MURDER

THE GREENHOUSE MURDER

SYBIL JAYNE BATH

Inspiring Voices®
A Service of Guideposts

Inspiring Voices books may be ordered through booksellers or by contacting:

Inspiring Voices
1663 Liberty Drive
Bloomington, IN 47403
www.inspiringvoices.com
1-(866) 697-5313

Because of the dynamic nature of the Internet, any web addresses or links contained in this book may have changed since publication and may no longer be valid. The views expressed in this work are solely those of the author and do not necessarily reflect the views of the publisher, and the publisher hereby disclaims any responsibility for them.

Certain stock imagery © Thinkstock.
Any people depicted in stock imagery provided by Thinkstock are models, and such images are being used for illustrative purposes only.

ISBN: 978-1-4624-0002-7 (e)
ISBN: 978-1-4624-0001-0 (sc)

Library of Congress Control Number: 2011935649

Printed in the United States of America

Inspiring Voices rev. date: 8/29/2011

I must first thank my loving husband Dale for putting up with a writing wife for years. His wonderful encouragement has filled my heart to overflowing. Thanks to Gloria Graham for her insightful critiquing. I must also thank all the wonderful women of the LAMBS group and those of the Adirondack Community Church who have encouraged me for years. This book is the culmination of years of thinking, "I can't possibly get a book published," followed by years of listening to encouraging Christian women who repeatedly said, "You can do it!" I finally adopted Habakkuk 2:3 as my mantra;

"Slowly, steadily, surely,
The time approaches when the vision will be fulfilled.
If it seems slow, do not despair,
For these things will surely
Come to pass,
Just be patient!
They will not be overdue a single day!"

I thank my Lord Jesus Christ for living up to His promise that He would stand by me if I only believed in Him. My commitment to Him has fulfilled my writing life in a manner that would have been impossible without Him. Thank you, Lord!

PROLOGUE

"Some trust in chariots, and some in horses;
But we will remember the name of the
Lord our God. (Psalm 20:7, NKJV)

Lake Placid, New York – 1922

The man's scream tore through the night air. Then the flash of gunfire shattered the night. The smell of sulfur and a halo of smoke were soon lost in the tall trees that surrounded the yard. A dapper young man dressed in the latest fashion of trim black suit and crisp white shirt returned his new 1922 Smith and Wesson into its embossed leather holster.

"You shoulda let me try to persuade him some more, boss," a huge man muttered. His lumpy pugilistic face leered at the dead body on the ground. He ground the brass knuckles on his scarred right hand into his left palm. "He woulda come aroun'."

"No, he was determined not to give away the location--Now we have to find it! It has to be on the property somewhere." The youthful boss spoke with conviction; he knew everything and expected everyone to agree with him. He pulled out a white handkerchief and swiped it across the white spats on his shiny black shoes.

"What about this no-good garden?" a thin man asked.

The boss glared at him, and said, "Notice how neat it is? Not a weed in sight. He's even got labels at the head of each row. He wouldn't of messed that up to bury nothin'. No, it's in the house. Let 's go. Too bad his wife ain't here. She might of been persuaded easy. Women got weaknesses." He headed for the house, and then paused to snarl at the other two. "Bring those crowbars. No telling how much we gotta tear this place apart." He entered the house. The other two shouldered the tools and followed.

The still night air resounded with the sounds of crashing wallboard, interspersed with the men's curses. They smashed dishes to the floor and wrenched kitchen cabinets from walls. Hammers pounded the floor, but they heard no hollow sound that would indicate a hiding place underneath. The boss didn't give gave up, but decided to search the cellar.

The small cellar contained only a cold coal furnace and a few shelves lined with glass pickle and vegetable jars. These were crashed wetly to the floor, their contents smashed into slime underfoot, as the three men futilely pounded the firm stone walls. Finally, the boss signaled that the hunt was over. "Guess he left them with someone else. We're done here." With the shallow vanity of youth, he fastidiously dusted off his trousers and climbed the stone steps to the first floor.

"How 'bout this glass place?" the big man asked. He peered at the greenhouse that was attached to the house as if staring at a structure from another world.

"Nuthin' to it. Just a table, crummy flowers, poured cement floor, glass walls 'n roof. No place to hide nuthin' in there." The boss sneered as he shone his flashlight around the long glass room. The delicate scent of orchids in bloom drifted from the dark room. None of the men noticed their perfume.

"We could smash it up good," the big man said. The boss noticed how his eyes lit with the desire for destruction, and decided not to allow him the pleasure.

"Why bother? We got liquor comin' in from Canada, an' I want to be on time to meet the guys runnin' it down Lake Champlain. No moon tonight. They should make good time, an' nobody can see 'em. I wanna be there before dawn. Let's go!"

They left the house, carelessly passing the body that lay near the garden. The boss shuddered superstitiously when he noticed the dead man's hand stretched out to the rows of plants as if even in death he wanted to be near his carefully tended garden. The three men approached the new Hispano-Suiza. Under the callow boss's gaze the two thugs each pulled a cotton handkerchief from a pocket and wiped their shoes. Their boss, Gentleman Jack Dennehy, gave an approving nod before they climbed into his newest kuxury car. Jack knew that his previous car, a Studebaker–Packard, had impressed the thugs, but he wanted them to salivate with envy. They sprawled on the soft leather seats in the back. When Jack nodded, one removed a bottle of their latest haul from the built-in bar. He poured a clear liquor into a cut-crystal glass and handed it to the boss in the driver's seat. Only then did the thugs pour their own drinks.

CHAPTER ONE

"I am the vine; you are the branches. If
a man remains in me and I in him, he
will bear much fruit; apart from me you
can do nothing." (John 15:5, NIV)

April 2006 – Manhattan, New York City

Wendy Bailey glanced up at her older brother Todd before they crossed the narrow street to the brownstone that housed the lawyer's office. Suddenly she heard the screeching of brakes. At the same moment, Todd caught her up in his arms and leaped across the street into the scant gap between two parked cars. A dark limousine with black tinted windows just missed them and tore down the block away from them.

"Phew!" Todd gasped. "That was close. I think he was trying to hit us!" Then he saw Wendy's white face and assured her, "I'm sure it was just an accident. Let's go in." Wendy pushed herself off the trunk lid of the sleek Cadillac that she was sprawled on. Todd held her trembling arm as they went inside the building. By the time they entered the elevator, she was no longer shaking. On the top floor, the elevator opened onto a lushly carpeted reception area decorated with large original scenic paintings. Ceiling spotlights were angled to show off the stunning paintings. The spots supplemented the light from the only window. Wendy caught a fleeting glimpse of a young man as he dashed through a door on the far side of the room. She wondered, *What's his hurry?*

Tony leaned against the door and tried to catch his breath. He hoped she didn't see him. *Don't make no difference anyway. Those hoods want to know she's here, that's all. They know she's inheriting. They paid me well for that info. Now, I got to find a private phone and call them, let them know she's here. I bet they already know. I'm sure I'm not the only one they have watching her. I wonder why they're so interested in her. That old place she inherited can't amount to much. Hardly seems worth the trouble. Oh well, who cares as long as they pay me.*

The siblings entered the office of their grandparent's old friend, Styvesant Powers. Wendy glanced around to see one wall covered with leather-bound books; another was solid glass with a view that overlooked spring-green Central Park. She was impressed, but clenched her hands tightly. She was nervous about the will they were about to hear read. She thought, *What might Gram have meant? In her last letter she said that I'd be excited to hear her new will, and that I mustn't lose courage. To believe in God and myself. What on earth?*

The lawyer smiled affectionately at the blond, blue-eyed young people. Only in their mid-twenties, they exuded an aura of calm and maturity. They sat in the chairs he indicated with a wave of his hand. He was aware they had no experience in dealing with wills and due to his fondness for them and his long friendship with their grandparents, he intended to make it as easy as possible for them. He adjusted his portly frame in his soft leather chair behind his desk. Wendy noticed his hand trembled as he brushed his sparse white hair from his forehead. She remembered that he was her late grandmother's age, which would make him ninety-six. The black and white photographs on the wall behind the desk pictured Mr. Powers with various New York State dignitaries and several U.S. presidents. The largest one showed a young Styvesant Powers flanked by an attractive young couple who bore close resemblances to Wendy and Todd. She was pleased that their grandparents' picture remained on their lawyer-friend's office wall long after their grandfather's murder during the Prohibition era and a year after their grandmother's death at ninety-five.

She said, "Mr. Powers, I appreciate your coming out of retirement to take care of Gram's estate. She spoke highly of you and was fond of you and your family."

"Thank you, I was close to her and your grandfather." He sighed and said, "That was a long time ago. I still miss going fishing with Charlie Bailey. We started fishing together about seventy years ago." He controlled his trembling hands and picked up two manila folders from an embossed leather folder that bore the legend "Bailey Estate".

He gave one to Wendy. "Your grandmother divided her estate between the two of you, but she also left a letter for each of you. Your letter, Wendy, gives information on the history of The Greenhouse Bed and Breakfast, which she left to you." Wendy nodded, her bright blue eyes and delighted smile indicating her joy in her inheritance. However, her quivering nerves made her hands shake as she accepted the envelope. She brushed a strand of blond hair from her forehead as the lawyer explained, "You're not obligated to keep the B and B, but she told me that it was her hope that you would follow your dream of owning your own business by running it as she did. You're young, but at twenty-four, you've had time to get a good education and see something of the business world here in New York."

The lawyer turned to the young man. "Todd, these investments were left to you." He handed Todd a manila folder. "I would advise you to line up a reliable investment advisor. Some of Mabel Bailey's investments are quite valuable, and not something for an amateur investor to play with."

Todd agreed. "I will, but I'm worried about Wendy taking on a B and B in the Adirondacks. As kids, we spent a month of each summer there when it was called the Greenhouse Guest House. Being out in the middle of nowhere was fun then, with our parents and grandmother on hand, but now..."

Wendy smiled at her brother. Todd had a calm, gentle manner, with a quiet humor that occasionally showed a sharp edge. Although he was only one year older than she, she had always known she could count on him, and now she was touched by his concern.

Mr. Powers smiled reassuringly at Wendy and said, "Your grandmother's caretakers, the Brewster family, is still in Lake Placid. I understand they're willing to continue to work for your family." Mr. Powers sat up importantly, and said, "The property isn't really in the middle of nowhere. The former logging road that connects the state highway to the property is open until snow blocks it. I'm sure you could have it plowed if you want to be open during ski season, which I guess would be your busiest time of the year. I suggest that you go up there, talk to the Brewsters, walk through the house and check its condition."

He continued to look at Wendy. "Lakefront property in Lake Placid is very valuable, but expensive real estate isn't selling now. I would advise you to wait and spend a summer at The Greenhouse to get a feel for it before making a decision."

Wendy pushed a strand of hair from her forehead, "I'll take your advice, and I'm looking forward to going back to The Greenhouse. I loved it as a child. I'm sure I'll love to run it as my own business, if I can! I remember Gram saying that your advice had been important to her even before Grandpa died. I will spend the summer in Lake Placid and I hope we'll see you and your wife up there as our guests. I'm nervous about running a business and I'm not sure I can handle it on my own."

Todd smiled at her and said, "I'll be with you, and I'd like nothing better than to relive my childhood summers. I'd like to restore Gram's vegetable garden. I'd be willing to be a junior partner, with you as," his fingers carved quotes in the air, the "executive senior partner". Does that make you more comfortable?"

She smiled and looked relieved. Then she said, "We'll talk about it, but in spite of my fears, I'm already convinced that I'm running the B and B." Her determination overshadowed her youth.

Mr. Powers looked delighted. "I'd like to see the place again. I'll get a fishing license before I come up to see you. The fishing in Lake Placid is excellent." He cleared his throat and looked at her intently. "Wendy, your grandmother's letter contains information that may sound unusual, even outlandish. I assure you that it is true. Goodbye now. I'll be speaking to you again soon, I'm sure."

The elderly lawyer walked Wendy and Todd to the elevator. He walked stiffly, but his old-fashioned manners didn't permit him to allow them to leave his office alone.

As the elevator door opened, Wendy suddenly said, "Wait, I thought of a question I want to ask Mr. Powers about the deed. Wait for me downstairs, Todd?"

"Okay, I'll be down by the front door."

Wendy hurried back to Mr. Power's office. She smiled at Alice, his secretary, and said, "I just have a quick question for Mr. Powers."

Alice knew of her boss's fondness for Wendy, so waved her in.

As soon as Wendy opened the door, she stopped, aware of a tense atmosphere in the office. Styvesant Powers was glaring at a young man who was hovering over Power's desk with the Bailey file in his hand.

The elderly lawyer asked, "What do you need, Tony?"

Wendy observed that Tony flushed, but then he drew a deep breath and said, "I hoped I'd have a chance to glance over the Bailey estate file. I don't know much about estates, and I thought if I looked it over..."

"No need for that," Powers said firmly. "That estate is unusual, and won't help you understand estates in general. You're close enough to your law school to take some evening classes. I'm sure there's one on estates. Understand?"

"Yes, sir. Thanks for the advice." Tony dropped the file and left the room.

Styvesant Powers glanced at Wendy, and shook his head, puzzled over the young lawyer's behavior. He walked to his desk, and picked up the Bailey file. "I'll put this away now. I shouldn't leave anything around until Alice has time to file it." He crossed the office to a file cabinet, unlocked it and placed the Bailey file inside, then relocked it. "There! That's put away safe and sound."

Wendy thought he looked satisfied, as if he had just accomplished something important.

"God only knows what that young man was up to, and only God knows the reasons why. Now, what brings you back?"

Wendy asked her question about filing of the deed; Mr. Powers answered her. He spoke plainly, without lawyer-speak, which she appreciated.

Then he took Wendy's hands and bowed his head. He prayed for Wendy and Todd Bailey's safety and well-being, concluding, *"Please Lord, let my friends' grandchildren prosper in this new venture in their lives. Keep them safe no matter what the enemy may throw their way. Guide them to live according to your Word. Amen."*

Wendy left the room as a warm feeling of safety enveloped her. She knew Mr. Power's prayer would stay with her as she ran the business that her beloved grandmother had entrusted her with.

CHAPTER TWO

"Commit your works to the
Lord, and your thoughts will be
established." (Psalm 16:3 NKJV)

Wendy curled up in her reading chair, the manila folder on her lap. Todd was rummaging through her apartment's tiny kitchen and she was sure that, as usual, he was looking for something to eat. Todd opened the refrigerator and her mouth watered when she heard the crackle of the wrapping of her favorite sourdough bread. She ignored thoughts of food and opened the folder. She removed the thick cream-colored envelope that bore her name in Gram's precise penmanship.

For a moment she was seized with grief as the pain of losing her last older relative swept over her. Then she drew a deep breath and reminded herself how fortunate she was that her grandmother had survived into her nineties. She leaned over the table to sniff the delicate pink phalaenopsis orchid in the center of the coffee table. It was her last gift from Gram, given to Wendy on her twenty-third birthday, along with a generous check.

Orchids abounded throughout the apartment. Wendy had always loved orchids. A table in front of the sunniest window in the room held an eclectic group of epidendrum, phalaenopsis and her favorite, an oncidium, commonly known as the butterfly orchid.

Wendy recalled her grandmother's tumultuous life. Gram was widowed in 1922, then outlived her son and daughter-in-law. In late middle age she had married her late husband's cousin, another member of the Bailey clan. He had been an affectionate substitute grandfather of whom Wendy and Todd had become fond.

Wendy breathed a prayer of thanks that when her parents had died in an auto accident while she was in college, her grandmother had stepped in to fill Wendy's mother's place. The summers spent at The Greenhouse Bed and Breakfast on Lake Placid, just outside the village of Lake Placid had been soothing to her spirit. She knew the same had been true for Todd.

She opened the envelope and called to Todd. "Come hear what Gram wrote to me. I'm sure she meant for you to hear it, also."

"Okay, I'm coming." Todd entered the room carrying a plate bearing an enormous sandwich. "Can I make you one?" he asked.

"No, I'm not hungry yet. I'd rather know what Mr. Powers meant. Gram lived such a quiet life. I can't imagine what he meant. Sit down, I'll read it."

She opened the folded pages and read, "'*My dearest Wendy, I know you are a brave young woman just from how you bore up after your parents' sudden deaths. I'll tell you what happened back during Prohibition. Please don't think less of your grandfather Charlie for what I will tell you, but during the twenties the times were wild and seemed to allow many kinds of excesses. The bootleggers made dealing in illegal liquor seem like a move for freedom from government interference in our private lives.*

Charlie managed to overlook that for a time of about fifteen years, Prohibition was federal law. I don't know all the details of his involvement with the bootleggers, only that arrangements were made to sneak liquor in from Canada by way of Lake Champlain. We had some Canadians staying at The Greenhouse the summer of Charlie's death in 1922. Charlie made private arrangements to sell them liquor. They paid in Canadian gold coins, which he was supposed to share with a dangerous bootlegger known as Gentleman Jack Dennehy. He did not share and I'm sure Jack murdered him, although the crime is still officially unsolved. I intend for you to have the gold.

Wendy stared at Todd and asked, "Can you imagine? The grandpa we heard about as an upstanding, honest man, dealing in illegal booze?" He just shrugged, took a big bite of his sandwich, and waited for her to continue reading.

"Charlie wrapped the gold in small oilcloth parcels. He joked to me that he had hidden it where it should grow, if only it could. He personally chose the orchids for the greenhouse to reflect the fortune they accompanied. Golden Sunrise is a lovely orchid and they are still available today. I had replaced several that died. I had made arrangements for them to be fed and watered, so who knows? I don't know how long orchid plants live. The pots they are in, handmade by Adirondack artisans, are probably also valuable.

When I closed the B and B last year after my first heart attack, I had the water drained from the pipes so nothing would be damaged from the severe Adirondack winters. If the house has been taken care of as I arranged, with the heat left on in the greenhouse, the B and B and its attached greenhouse should be in good condition.

One important caution, I understand that Gentleman Jack Dennehy (now in a nursing home, I believe) has a grandson who may be following in Jack's footsteps. If he should turn up-- BE CAREFUL! The senior Dennehy was a dangerous man and his grandson may be also. Every time Jack turned up in his flashy yellow Hispano Suiza sports car, my blood ran cold. He often had armed thugs with him, whom I am sure were capable of murder.

Remember that I love you and Todd dearly, and I hope that the good Lord allows me to watch over you from heaven. Keep the faith, my dearests.

Love, Gram

"Oh my, do you think she really believed that we'd be in danger from this Dennehy person?" Wendy dropped the letter and with one index finger, she wound a blond curl around her fingers.

Todd uncrossed his lanky legs and said, "I looked at my letter from Gram, and she seems sure that you will need protection. In fact, the bulk of the letter consists of instructions to have an alarm system installed in the house and to consult with the Brewsters about it." He waved his letter at Wendy, and then dropped it on the coffee table in front of her. "One of the Brewster relatives installs alarm systems, so she thinks we should talk to them. Typical of Gram's organizational mind, she even included a list of phone numbers to have the electricity and phone turned on. But how could there still be any gold from grandpa's dealings with bootleg booze?"

"Sounds like she thinks he hid the gold in the orchid pots. I'm not sure I believe that."

"We'll have to look when we get there, if you can bring yourself to uproot the plants." He laughed at her appalled expression, knowing her love for orchids. Wendy stared at the pink Phalaenopsis and remembered her Gram with fondness.

The door buzzer sounded and Todd got up to answer it. He pressed the intercom. "Who is it?"

"Liz, who else?" came the impertinent reply.

"Oh good, I really need to talk to Liz now," said Wendy. Todd groaned, knowing that Liz and he disagree about almost everything. Todd was not comfortable with Wendy's best friend. He felt her dramatic personality to be a strain. He tried to get along with her, knowing that she and Wendy were close in spite of their very different personalities.

When Liz entered, Wendy noticed that her friend was distraught. She threw herself into the easy chair near Wendy's. Liz patted tears from her reddened brown eyes with a colorful cotton handkerchief. Her long dark hair was pulled back into a casual ponytail, instead of her usual formal French twist. Wendy noticed that Liz was wearing her favorite tee shirt, advertising the ju-jitsu studio that she belonged to. Liz wailed, "What ever made me think I could survive as a chef in nasty New York!"

"Don't tell me that Salvio's isn't living up to your expectations," said Todd. Wendy gave him a sharp look, warning him to go easy on his usual caustic response to Liz's dramatic manner.

"He wants me to *cook faster,* can you believe it? He says we need a quicker turnover of diners, and he's even bugging the wait staff to hover over diners and whisk their plates off the table as soon as they've *almost finished*, so the table can be cleared for the next diners. Geez, I know the economy is bad, but why should we lower standards? Salvio's isn't McDonalds, for heavens' sake! "

She paused to draw breath and then noticed the legal papers and letters on the coffee table. "Ohh, I'm sorry, Wendy, I forgot. What happened at the lawyer's office?" She leaned toward Wendy and patted her arm. "Anything you didn't expect?"

Wendy handed her the letter from her grandmother and said, "Please read this, Liz, and tell me what you think."

Liz read the letter carefully, and then raised her eyebrows and said,

"Sounds like running an Adirondack B and B could be dangerous. What do you intend to do?"

"Gram was right about my wanting to run my own business. You know I haven't been happy at Exelt Insurance and although I love the museums and theaters, getting out of New York won't break my heart."

Liz glared at Todd, "I thought you were able to pave the way for Wendy at Exelt, Todd. What happened?"

"They're letting people go, and those still around are being hassled to work longer hours, with preposterous expectations. I can't expect to be there much longer."

"Then the two of you could run the B and B, right?" Suddenly, she sat upright in the chair. One thin arm shot into the air as punctuation as she exclaimed, "I can cook for your guests! I can't imagine a more laid-back atmosphere in which to work. I know I can't stay at Salvio's. This tiger can't change her spots."

Wendy started to laugh at Liz's mixed metaphor, but stifled her laughter when she realized that Liz was serious. "I think that would be an excellent idea, especially since I'm just a so-so cook, except for desserts. But the B and B might not make much money at first. Could you afford to work for a tiny wage plus room and board?"

Todd didn't wait for her reply. Instead he picked up his folder and said, "Gram even included advice on advertising. I could set up a web site with pictures. My new digital camera should work great for that. I hope the rooms still look retro twenties. That could be a big draw!"

"What kind of food would you want to serve?" Liz asked.

"I'll find Adirondack cookbooks on the web. There must be some available. Let me know when you have time, and we'll look together. After all, you're the chef!"

"This is going to be exciting!" Liz exclaimed. "Wow, Wendy, you're so lucky! A fresh start! You can really rock the apple cart! When are we going to Lake Placid?"

Wendy and Todd stifled laughter, and then exchanged a glance. He said, "Let's not get carried away. We need a business plan, not just excitement over doing something different. You've lived in New York for five years, Liz. You've become a city girl."

Wendy gave him an irritated glance, but Liz interrupted, "I graduated from Paul Smith's Culinary School, remember, so I spent several years in the Adirondacks. This will be like going home for me."

"Oh, that's right," Todd said, suddenly understanding Wendy's look. "I forgot that's where you went to school. Let's see how our schedules can be worked out, so we can drive up together for a few days. You haven't resigned from Salvio's yet, have you, Liz?"

"No, but I can see the handwriting on the wall. He wants a fast cook, not necessarily a good one! I'll tell him this weekend, when I'm scheduled to work."

Wendy jumped to her feet, "Okay, let's work on it. I'm going to resign from Exelt today! Adirondacks, here we come! I'm going to start packing. Can we leave tomorrow morning? That'll give us four days up there, until Liz has to give Salvio's the bad news."

Todd said, "I'll call the Brewsters and see if they'll turn the heat up in the house for us. According to Grams' letter, the heat was left on in the greenhouse to keep the orchids alive. The electricity has to be turned on, too. Maybe the Brewster's can do that. The phone connection can wait. We have our cells."

"I'm glad it's spring. I remember that Gram always said winter hangs on in the Adirondacks well into spring, but since it's April, we should see a taste of spring, though perhaps not much. I remember one year she complained about snow in June. She said it melted fast, but she had to cover her tulips to keep them from freezing."

"We can grocery shop when we get there," said Liz. "No point in hauling groceries all the way to the Adirondacks when there's the same stores up there."

"Good idea," said Wendy. "I'm looking forward to this. We can work on our business plan up there. That's your field of expertise, Todd."

Todd said, "We'll take care of details like phone service and fuel delivery when we get there. I'm feeling very optimistic about this. I guess your attitude is rubbing off on me, Wendy."

"I should hope so," said Liz caustically. "You're a natural pessimist, Todd."

"Come on, you two," said Wendy. "If we can't get along better than this, we shouldn't consider working together." When Liz and Todd stared at her, she explained, "You two are often at each other's throats. I don't like hearing it. I love you both and I'd like to see you get along better."

Liz admitted, "Yes, you're right. Todd tends to be possessive of you, and I over-react. Geez, I mean, aren't you allowed to have friends?"

"Okay, a truce has just been declared," announced Todd.

"Hear, hear, a truce!" declared Liz as she pumped a fist in the air. Both Wendy and Todd laughed, and then echoed her declaration, even copying her fist pump.

Then Wendy looked sober and reminded Todd of their grandmother's favorite advice. "She told us, 'Don't start anything without giving it to the Lord in prayer.' Remember?"

"I'll never forget it. I wouldn't have graduated from business school without that working for me." He dropped his head and with Wendy and Liz waiting silently, he thought for a moment, then prayed, "Dear Lord, let us never forget that in the business we are about to try to run, that we should work as if we are working for You, not ourselves. Please be with us as we consider this new venture. Protect us from those who may wish to do us harm. In the name of Jesus Christ, I pray. Amen."

Wendy sighed in relief, and said, "Thanks, Todd, that prayer was just what I needed. I'm still nervous about taking on a business, but if you'll help financially at first, as you said, I'm sure we can deal with it."

Todd agreed, "We're a team, not exactly the Three Musketeers, but a team, right?"

"You bet," Wendy and Liz agreed.

CHAPTER THREE

"Therefore do not worry about tomorrow,
for tomorrow will worry about its
own things. Sufficient for the day is its
own trouble. (Matthew 6:34 NKJV)

Wendy staggered to Todd's van, her arms loaded with boxes. The van was stuffed with suitcases, bags and a couple of boxes. Liz said to Wendy "It looks like we're moving permanently. This isn't just an exploratory visit, right?"

Wendy nodded and Todd explained, "Wendy and I will have to take care of some business while we're there, phone, electricity, fuel oil. We'll probably register with the Chamber of Commerce. Didn't you say you wanted to visit a bookstore in Lake Placid to look for Adirondack cookbooks?" When Liz nodded, Todd added, "If you finish your errands before we do, you could always take the bus back. When do you have to be back at Salvio's?"

"I was scheduled for Friday night. But I'm giving notice before that. No point in putting off the inevitable. We'll never agree on my belief in quality over quantity and his wanting the opposite. Wendy, I hope you packed cool weather clothes. April may be spring here in the city, but the Adirondacks have winter through May."

"I'm ready. Let's go!" exclaimed Wendy as she carefully placed a deep plastic tub of orchids in the back of the van. She climbed in the front passenger seat, knowing that long legged Liz preferred to stretch out in the back seat. Todd started the van and Wendy fastened her seat belt as a feeling of adventurous excitement coursed through her body. She was sure that this trip would open a new life for her. She didn't even mind having to take three days unpaid time off from work, just before her resignation took effect. She was fortunate to know someone who was looking for an apartment and would take over her lease, if she decided not to return. She was sure this trip was worthwhile. "I'm glad the Brewsters are willing to help us get settled into The Greenhouse," she said. "Having the heat on and hot water available is necessary as we find out what we have to deal with."

Todd said, "Jerry Brewster will see to it that the road is passable, so we can just drive right in, no matter how much snow may still be on the ground."

Liz said, "I called some old friends who are living in the Adirondacks, and they tell me there's a lot of snow this year. There's still skiing on Whiteface."

"Remember all the tulips that Gram planted the last year we were there?" asked Wendy. "The front of the house looked lovely from the lake, with so many flowers in bloom. Remember the apple trees that lined the old logging road? I loved to stand under them as the petals fell. It was like soft pink snow. My orchids are going to feel right at home in the windows of The Greenhouse Bed and Breakfast."

Todd said, "Liz, our grandpa found some old style apple trees in a local orchard, and planted them to give the place a genuine old-timey appearance."

"Gram did a lot of gardening with bulbs and shrubs, and she had a large vegetable garden in the back yard. I hope we can do that this summer."

"Fresh veggies, right from the ground?" asked Liz excitedly. "I'd love that!"

Todd said, "We're going to have fun with the garden, but the veggies can't be planted for a while. It's still too cold."

Liz suddenly changed the subject. "I want to know about this dangerous man that your gram mentioned. Could he know where the gold is? Or that there really is gold?"

"I don't know a thing about him, except for Gram's mention of him in her letter," Wendy admitted.

"I looked up the senior Dennehy on the internet," said Todd. "During Prohibition, he was really dangerous, running illegal booze as long as he could, then disappearing into Canada or Europe. He's reputed to have been a cold-hearted killer, but never served time. I guess he always had an escape plan in place, because he was never caught. That makes me think that he was smarter than your run-of-the-mill crook. Apparently Grandpa didn't know what he was getting into when he went into business with Dennehy."

Wendy said, "Well, if he's in a nursing home, as Gram thought, he's no danger. But if his grandson is following in his footsteps, illegal booze won't be his game. These days, drugs is the big illegal product, so who knows what he's doing. Cocaine, marijuana, Ecstasy, or knock-offs of pharmaceuticals. Those are selling for big bucks now."

Liz looked worried and said, "I can read the handwriting on the wind. If that guy turns up at the B and B, we could be in big trouble."

Wendy managed not to laugh at Liz's mixed metaphor, but Todd choked with laughter. Liz glared at him, "You're such a nit-plucker, Todd. So I don't always use correct grammar, so what!"

Todd roared with laughter. "Liz, I *love* the way you mangle the English language. You really make my day!" Liz looked at Wendy, unsure whether she should be offended.

Wendy smiled at her. "Liz, I love your mixed metaphors."

Liz sat up straighter in her seat, and smiled as she accepted Wendy's comment at face value. "Okay, I won't change, I promise. Like I could! English was never my favorite course in high school or college, except on the few occasions when we read a good author."

Changing the subject, she waved one hand in the air and asked, "Do you know that some straight-up ignoramuses banned "Huckleberry Finn" in high schools? That really hacks me to a crisp! Ol' Huck was my favorite character, and Mark Twain was the only writer I enjoyed in school. I *hated* Hemingway. What a chauvinist prig!""

Wendy and Todd were laughing too hard to conceal their hilarity. Wendy unhooked her seat belt, leaned over her seat back, seized Liz and hugged her. Wendy's laughter started Liz's laughter and the two of them clung together, barely able to breathe, they were laughing so hard.

Wendy and Liz howled at the sight of Todd gasping through his laughter, while struggling to concentrate on driving.

Finally, Liz sat up straight. "You know, Todd. You're really nuts." She hugged Wendy again and said, "How can anyone find it so funny to hear a few, what do you call them, mixed metaphers?"

Wendy said, "Metaphors, Liz. But it doesn't matter. We enjoy talking to you and even more, listening to you. You know you're my friend, and I'd love you, even if you spoke textbook English."

"Fat chance of that!" Liz exclaimed.

Wendy asked, "Do you realize we're going to have fun working together? I was a little worried at first, but now I'm not. We even enjoy each other's peculiarities."

Liz looked worried and asked, "I want to know if I'm going to have anything to say about what gets planted in the garden. Do I have a choice?"

Todd's voice was slightly muffled as he finished wiping tears of laughter from his face. "Of course, the cook has a lot to say about what we plant. Keep in mind, the weather is cold through spring in Lake Placid, so delicate plants probably won't survive. Of course, we'll have to buy tomato plants, instead of planting from seed."

"That's what some of my friends in college did," Liz said. "They covered the plants at night, too, because they knew that even if frosts weren't predicted, they turned up anyway. They used big plastic tubs."

Wendy looked serious. "We can deal with the Adirondack weather. Gram did, for years, and I bet Todd remembers what she did."

"Some of it." He glanced at Wendy and asked," Do you realize that we've just been speaking as if our staying at The Greenhouse is a done deal?"

She fastened her seatbelt and leaned back in the seat. She admitted, "I've been thinking that way ever since I heard Gram's will read. Just think, my own business! God willing, we can do it!"

The slim young man watched as his grandfather was wheeled into the nursing home's atrium. The old man exclaimed, "Jackie! It's good to see you!"

"Grandpa, please call me John. I haven't been called Jackie for decades. How are you feeling?"

"About as good as a ninety-five year old that's still breathing, I guess."

The young man shuffled his feet and shoved his hands in his pockets. "Look, Grandpa, I wanted to ask you about the gold that Bailey hid. Do you have any new ideas about where he might have put it?"

The old man hid his disappointment in his grandson's change of subject and said, "I haven't had a new idea for forty years, Jackie…uh, I mean John. Why do you ask?"

"I thought I'd follow up on it. I hear that Bailey's twenty-something granddaughter inherited the place, and she should be a push-over. I bet I can find the gold."

"That family was tougher than you know, Jack….uh, John. I bet she's just like her grandfather. Nice on the outside, tough as nails inside. And!" the old man struck a thin fist on the arm of his wheelchair, "They think they're blessed by God. Makes 'em stubborn as all get out!"

"That didn't keep Bailey alive when he met up with you, did it?"

"But I didn't get the gold. Good luck if you think you can find it, boy."

John grimaced at the term his grandfather used, but said, "I'm gonna try, and I bet I can do it. I'll find that gold, no matter what!"

The old man sighed, and said, "I wish you luck, J…John. You'll need it."

CHAPTER FOUR

"If we walk in the light, we have
fellowship with one another, and the
Blood of Jesus Christ His Son cleanses
us from all sin. (I John 1:7 NKJV)

Liz leaned over the back seat; her crop top rode up to reveal her flat abs. She rearranged the luggage so she could have a clear view out the back window. "Okay, creep, who are you?" she asked.

"Who are you talking to?" Wendy asked from the front seat.

"Somebody in a neat old Mustang who was parked across the street when we left your apartment just pulled a u-turn and is following us."

"Why would anyone want to follow us? It's just some guy who happens to be going in the same direction we are, the same time we are," said Todd firmly.

"Don't be naïve, Todd. I know the cars in Wendy's neighborhood. This one's a stranger. When I arrived with my luggage half an hour ago, he was parked across the street."

"Let's just wait and see how long he stays behind us," suggested Wendy. "If he takes the Thruway when we do, that still won't prove anything. But I admit that if he takes the Northway from Albany, as we'll have to, then I'll worry about him."

"That's some snazzy car," said Liz. "Looks like an original Mustang from the early sixties. Bet it has leather seats."

When Wendy stared at her, she said, "I love old cars, I mean not real old, like the twenties, but from the fifties and sixties. I hope he's still following us when we stop for coffee. Maybe he'll pull off too and I'll get a good look at it. It's hard to tell from here, but I think it has those new mag wheels."

Todd laughed. "Make up your mind, Liz. You just called him a creep, now you want a close-up of his car."

"Anybody who drives a car like that shouldn't be a creep. Probably rich, so that lets him out of creepdom."

"Creepdom?" Both Todd and Wendy chuckled. "That's a new one for me," Wendy admitted. "If he's following us, it's okay as long as he drives a neat car, is that it?"

"Not really. I mean, I don't like being followed – by anyone!"

An hour later, in spite of heavy weekday traffic, they were approaching the exit to the Northway. The Mustang stayed within several car lengths of them, until they took the Northway exit, then it continued on towards Albany.

"He's gone," Liz announced. "Headed into Albany."

"That takes care of your Mustang creep," said Wendy. "Of course, if his objective was to find out if we were going upstate, now he knows."

"Come on," said Todd. "You're not catching Liz's paranoia, are you?"

"No, but I'm unnerved about his staying so close to us, and following us right from my apartment door. I have a hunch that we haven't seen the last of him."

Liz said, "I wish we'd had a chance to see what the driver looked like, but the only time he was close enough, his hat and sunglasses didn't allow me get a good look at him."

"Oh, forget him," said Todd. "You're both imagining things. Now, do we want to shop for groceries in Lake Placid before going to The Greenhouse?"

Wendy said, "Might as well, and we can make a quick stop in the bookstore you suggested, Liz. Bookstore Plus, was that it?"

"Yes. I'm sure they'll have Adirondack cookbooks. We might want to pick up a book or two on Adirondack history while we're there.

Guests might have questions about the locale, and we really should bone up on our Adirondack history. Lake Placid history, in particular. Of course a lot of the recent history is about the 1932 and 1980 Winter Olympics. There's lots of information about that, because Lake Placid is still riding on its Olympic history. Oh, it's fun to see the competitions, like skiers jumping off the towers and landing in a pool."

"Yes, I saw that on the internet," said Wendy.

"Look, I'm getting hungry," said Todd. "How about stopping for a bite?"

"Well, what a coincidence!" said Liz. "There's a restaurant sign for the next rest area. Leave it to you to zero in on food, Todd."

"I'm getting hungry, too," admitted Wendy. "I didn't eat much breakfast this morning, I was so eager to get on the road."

"We're close to the Adirondack Park, but there isn't any place to eat once we get in the park until we're in Lake Placid, so yes, I think we'd better eat now," said Liz.

Later, in Lake Placid, the Bookstore Plus had two Adirondack cookbooks that met Liz's exacting requirements and she bought both of them. "It's a shame we have to grocery shop before I have a chance to read these, but they'll keep for later. Now, let's just get some food staples for the house."

Wendy agreed while she perused books on Adirondack natural history and those on local lore. She bought three, and Todd bought one on making Adirondack outdoor furniture.

In the grocery store parking lot, Todd swore when he caught a finger on his suitcase handle as he shifted the luggage to make room for the groceries they were going to purchase.

"Are you okay, Todd?" Wendy asked.

"Sure, just bent my finger back."

He pulled out his cell phone and was relieved to see three bars before he dialed. He identified himself and then asked Mrs. Brewster if the old logging road was clear. He grinned at her reply and said, "Then we'll be there right in a few minutes. Thanks, Mrs. Brewster...okay, Patty it is, then.

"Patty's husband, Jerry plowed the road after last week's snowstorm. Earlier this week, they turned the heat on. Jerry delivered stove wood in case we use the woodstove in the front room, the room Gram called the parlor."

Wendy smiled. "Sounds good. I remember Gram usually had a fire going in the stove when we had a cool evening. It comfortably heated the parlor and dining room. A woodstove makes such a toasty heat, so it's very cozy.

"That reminds me, I forgot to ask you about the kitchen stove. I guess I just assumed it was electric," said Liz.

"Yes, it is. It's a six burner stove, with two ovens. I'm sure you noticed I brought my microwave, too."

"We're all set, so let's go," urged Todd.

After they finished shopping, they started to pull out of the grocery store parking lot. Only Liz noticed the Mustang parked in the drug store lot next door.

"Look," she said, "That's the Mustang that was following us. How did he get here so fast?"

"Probably because we stopped for lunch and then went grocery shopping. Remember, Liz, when we stopped for lunch, you *had* to talk to the chef about everything on the menu. I admit the food was good, but we'd have made much better time if we had gone to McDonald's." He laughed as Liz shuddered at the mention of the fast food chain.

"What do we do, now that it seems he did follow us?" she asked.

Wendy said, "I just remembered I wanted to pick up a first-aid kit. We should have one on the premises, and anything Gram had will be seriously out of date. Pull over, please, Todd."

She started to walk toward the drugstore and Liz followed her. Todd shrugged and locked the van before tagging along behind them.

He called, "Don't forget we have frozen food in the van."

Wendy said, "This won't take long."

She walked alongside the sleek, dark car and casually glanced at the driver. He stared at her through the open window, eyeing her tee-shirt clad torso. A leer marred his attractive features. Wendy blushed, but Liz took her arm and marched her at a fast pace into the store. Todd paused and glared at the man, but he turned his head away, pretending not to notice Todd's presence.

Wendy bought the largest first aid kit she could find and she left the drugstore's parking lot quickly, flanked by Todd and Liz. The occupant of the car didn't look toward them.

Todd had no trouble finding the old logging road, as Mr. Brewster had cleaned the snow away from the four by five sign that read "The Greenhouse Bed and Breakfast -- established 1915." The firmly packed snow on the road supplied good traction.

"Springtime in the Adirondacks!" said Liz with a laugh "Snow and more snow!"

They drove a quarter mile through thick stands of darkly shadowed evergreens, and then passed the gnarled trunks of a dozen apple trees. They came upon the house clearing suddenly, and Liz exclaimed, "Isn't it pretty!"

The two-story white-clapboarded Victorian house rose gracefully from thick rhododendron bushes. The bushes stood in pale spring sunlight on the south side of the house. A dome-topped cupola with half-glass walls rose above a corner of the roof.

"An aerie!" exclaimed Liz. "How romantic!"

"Yes," Todd said, "I used to go up there and pretend I was an eagle in my nest."

Wendy said, "I remember I said I knew you were for the birds."

Todd laughed, "Remember though, you used to follow me up there. Gram said we had to share the space, but you said you had better things to do than hang around with a bird-brained brother." Liz shook her head at them while they both laughed at their memories of their childhood teasing.

A wide yard allowed a generous view of the house, and snow-covered shrub gardens bordered the yard's edge. Todd followed the drive to the front of the house in order to see the lake. A wide comfortable roofed porch looked east over the expanse of Lake Placid. The lake still held edges of ice where large trees hung over the water, but the main body of water sparkled silver in the afternoon sun.

"It's just like I remember it," said Wendy. "It's just colder. I've never been here this time of year before."

Todd backed up the car to where the driveway split and drove up to the back door. A small, enclosed porch sheltered the door. Todd and Wendy started unloading the groceries. Wendy glared at the rough, stone steps leading up to the porch, and promptly decided, *They'll be replaced with a wooden porch as soon as possible.*

Liz took over from there, carrying the grocery bags into the kitchen. She was pleased to see that there was a walk-in pantry in the kitchen, as well as many cupboards. It didn't take her long to get the groceries arranged to her satisfaction, so she started exploring the cupboards that held cooking implements. "Oh, good! Look at the cast iron frying pans and stew pot! I love cooking with cast iron."

Wendy plugged in her coffee grinder and ground enough of Liz's favorite Brazilian beans to make a full pot. Then she poured rich brown grounds into the gold filter of the European coffeepot, her grandmother's pride. She flipped the switch. "Thanks," Liz said. "I was just thinking that the coffee I had for lunch had worn off and I needed a caffeine jolt."

Wendy reassured her, "By the time we get our luggage upstairs, it should be ready. Now, we have to pick out our rooms. I'd like the Rose Room in the front-- that's where I usually slept when we were here for the summer. Come on, Liz, I'll show you the bedrooms. Let's go up the back stairs." She opened a door in the corner of the kitchen and revealed a narrow staircase lighted by several small lightly tinted windows.

The two women carried their luggage upstairs. Liz immediately noticed the Iris Room next to a narrow room that adjoined Wendy's Rose Room. "How nice, I love lavender and purple! Is every room done in a flower theme?"

"Yes," Wendy explained. "Gram loved flowers-- so she chose a different flower for each room. The Coneflower Room is right down the hall. That's the one Todd usually used. The Azalea and Daisy rooms are lovely, too. Gram looked everywhere for paintings, prints and knickknacks to match the rooms, and each bedspread has the room's flower on it. She said it took her years to finish each room just the way she wanted it." Pointing to a room to her left, she said, "The bathroom here is large because it was intended to serve the family." She showed Liz a bathroom containing a shower, a separate tub, a hot tub, two sinks and two mirrored medicine cabinets. A wide glazed window lit the room with a frosty light.

Liz asked, "What's this narrow room next to yours?"

Wendy said, "That's called a box room. Guests used to arrive with tons of luggage and Gram knew they wouldn't want their trunks cluttering up their rooms, so the luggage was put in here. We have no use for it now, but I told Todd I didn't want it filled with clutter. We'll find a use for it someday."

Back in the Iris Room, Liz said, "Wow, your Gram really must have worked hard on this." She picked up a delicate glass paperweight from the tiny curved-leg ladies-desk in the corner of the room. Engraved into the glass was a lovely purple iris.

"The other three guest rooms are on the other side of the house and are accessed by the stairs in the front hall. Only the largest of them has its own bathroom. The other two share a bath."

"Now, it's time for coffee," Liz announced, "and to sample my mocha-chocolate chip cookies I brought." Both went downstairs; Todd had already sampled the cookies. "These are great, Liz! Haven't I told you that you're a genius with chocolate?"

"You did, and I admit I agree. In fact, I brought my favorite chocolate cookbook with me. Want to bet The Greenhouse B and B will become famous for its chocolate desserts?"

"You'd win that bet!" said Wendy and Todd in unison. All three of them laughed at Wendy and Todd's unconscious trick of saying the same thing at the same time. It happened frequently and always amused them, as it had amused their grandmother.

Liz unpacked her cookbooks and arranged them on a wide shelf that seemed to her to be designed for them.

Wendy looked over the produce they had purchased. "Do you think bison belongs on an Adirondack menu? I saw some in the store and couldn't resist it."

"I'm game, pardon the pun," said Liz. "I'll cook anything." She took the package from Wendy. "Anyone could cook this. How about baked potatoes with bison steaks?"

"I'm hungry just thinking about it," Todd answered.

Wendy removed the broiler pan from the stove and noticed its gleaming cleanliness. "Looks like we're all set for our first meal at The Greenhouse."

Liz said, "Our snoop hasn't shown up, thank God. Did you see how he looked at you, Wendy? What a lech!"

"Liz, you don't think he was really the guy who followed us from our neighborhood, do you?" Wendy asked.

"I know that was the same car, no doubt. I was disturbed at his turning up like that, so I didn't really look at the car, like I'd thought I would. But he must have been following us really fast to catch up and be in the drugstore parking lot while we were grocery shopping. Of course, that Mustang *is fast*. And the van is poky, so he wouldn't have had any trouble catching up. But, what does he want with us? Why follow us? And was it just a lucky guess that we'd have to grocery shop, or is he smart enough to figure that out?"

Wendy shuddered, suddenly fearful of the idea that someone intelligent enough to forecast their moves might be following them.

CHAPTER FIVE

"He who has my commandments and keeps them, it is He who loves Me. And he who loves Me will be loved by my Father, and I will love him, and manifest Myself to him. (John 14:21 NKJV)

Liz and Wendy each ate a second cookie, and then Wendy pushed the Tupperware container to the end of the table, as if putting temptation out of reach. Todd looked at her indignantly and then helped himself to another cookie. When he finished his coffee, he rinsed his cup and placed it in the sink. He winced and shook his right hand, as if trying to rid himself of something.

"Does that sprain hurt?" asked Wendy.

"Yes, it's starting to swell. I think I'll use one of nature's remedies to take down the swelling."

Wendy followed him out the kitchen door and aross the back yard. At one of the snowbanks on the edge of the yard, he plunged his hand into the snow. Looking worried, she asked, "Do you think you should do that? You might get frostbite!"

"It's working, and it isn't cold enough to cause frostbite," Todd said. "The throbbing in my hand has stopped." He held his position for a moment, knowing he had to give the cold a chance to penetrate.

When he heard an abrupt sound of movement from the woods, he stood up and called, "Who's there?"

A figure dimly seen between the tree trunks moved closer, then pushed the bushes aside and stepped into the yard. Wendy shrieked in surprise at sight of the older man dressed in worn, but sturdy, outdoor gear and wearing old-style wooden snowshoes.

"Sorry, didn't mean to startle you," the man said. "I was just checking out a trail for a client. It runs across the back of your property, and I didn't realize it came so close to your yard. I'm Clive DuBois. I've been guiding around these parts for a good many years. You're opening the B and B again?"

Todd stepped forward. "Yes, I'm Todd Bailey. This is my sister Wendy. We'll probably open for business this spring." When Wendy glared at him, Todd amended his comment. "That is, Wendy will. I'm second in command. We're up here to look things over, and while we haven't officially made a decision yet, we love it so much here that I'm sure we'll open up for business."

'You're Mabel and Charlie's grandkids, then?" The old man pulled a red cotton handkerchief from his sleeve and wiped a sheen of perspiration from his face

"Yes, you knew them?"

"Sure did, great people, both of them. Awful, the way Charlie died, but he got mixed up with bad people."

Wendy asked, "Would you like to come in for coffee?"

"Be glad to."

Clive removed his snowshoes and Todd admired the neat webbing of rawhide that wove between the curves of wood. Clive noticed his attention and said, "I made these forty years ago, and never had to replace the webbing. It pays to use quality materials and take good care of them."

"I thought I'd get snowshoes, but I don't know what to look for. If Wendy decides to be open in the winter, we might need enough snowshoes for guests. But there's no hurry, this winter's over. Well..." He glanced back at the snow under the trees, "almost over."

Clive chuckled and said, "Showshoeing season can last far beyond ski season, because the trails in the woods usually keep their snow until late spring."

"Come inside and you can tell us about it," said Wendy.

Liz was at the kitchen table poring over the Adirondack cookbooks they had purchased. She was placing post-it notes on the edges of some of the pages of recipes. A grocery list lay beside the books. She looked surprised when Wendy and Todd brought Clive into the room.

After introductions were made, Wendy poured coffee for Clive and Todd. She placed the cookie container within Clive's reach. He tasted a cookie and then asked, "Who you made this wonderful treat?" Liz admitted that she had, but then said, "Wendy makes great cookies, also, but I'll be the chef for the B and B once we're open. Tell me, Clive, what brings you out here?"

He said, "I'm a professional Adirondack guide with over forty years experience and I'm concerned about the guy who hired me to show him the trail that loops around the back of your property. I can't imagine why he specifically asked me to show him that trail. It doesn't have the scenic views that others do. In fact, excuse me if I seem paranoid, but I'm wondering if he wanted to snoop on you. I can't imagine any other reason for wanting to be on that trail. In fact, I didn't think anybody else but us old-timers knew it was there."

"May I ask what your client's name is?" said Todd.

"Yes, he's John Dennehy, from New York City." Clive saw Wendy's hand fly to her cheek. He asked her, "That name mean anything to you?"

"Yes, but I should tell you some family history. That might explain it." She told him about her grandfather's fatal run-in with Gentleman Jack Dennehy. The guide nodded, already knowing the tragic story. Then she told him of the gold coins that were reputed to be hidden somewhere, probably in the greenhouse.

"I take it you haven't looked for this gold, or maybe don't believe it's really here, is that it?" Clive said.

Wendy shrugged, "We just arrived, and had to get settled in, so we didn't even think about it, but you're right. I have my doubts."

"I'll see what I can find out about Dennehy when I take him out this weekend. He calls himself John, maybe to distance himself from his rum-running grandfather's name of Jack. He's gone back to the city, but he'll be back tomorrow morning. He wanted to go out early. Do you want me to bring him by, or would you rather not see him?"

"Maybe we should meet him," said Todd. "Find out what he's up to. What do you think, Wendy?"

"Gram thought he was as dangerous as his grandfather, but I don't know how much she knew about him. But you're right, if she was correct about him, remember that saying, 'Better the enemy you know, than the one you don't' or something like that."

She turned to Clive and said, "Yes, we should meet him, if he's willing to do more than snoop on us from the woods."

"Okay, I'll bring him by tomorrow morning, prob'ly about nine. Thanks for the coffee and cookies. See you tomorrow." He shrugged on his coat and pulled his knit toque on his head. Todd and Wendy went outside with him and the two men talked briefly about snowshoes. Clive recommended against spending a lot of money on expensive snowshoes for guests. "They prob'ly won't spend a lot of time on snowshoes. Folks tend to come to B and B's to relax. Those modern plastic ones would be fine for them, but you might want to get a good pair for yourself. I'll keep my eyes open for some like mine, if you'd like."

"Thanks, I'd appreciate it." Todd watched as Clive put on his snowshoes at the edge of the woods, and then disappeared onto the trail.

Indoors, Todd asked the women, "What did you think of him?"

"I like him," Wendy said. "Don't you, Liz?"

"Yes, I do. But I'm concerned about letting John Dennehy on the property. Do you think that's a good idea?"

"What can he do?" Todd asked. "I'd like to do a close search of the greenhouse before he gets here."

"Yes," Wendy said. "I was going to do that earlier, but we got involved with the cookbooks and forgot. Let's do it now while it's daylight."

They were startled by a knock on the back door.

"I bet that's Mrs. Brewster, or Patty, as she said to call her," said Todd. He opened the back door and a smiling heavyset woman entered the room.

Patty Brewster greeted them cheerfully, and introduced herself, saying, "You must call me Patty. I'm so glad that there's family back here in the house. Every time I came by to water the plants and to keep an eye on things, it felt so lonely. Of course, I remember your grandmother being here. She was so cheerful and upbeat, she made it a pleasure to work for her. An' best of all, she was a good, loving Christian." Patty's chubby features were wreathed in smiles as she reminisced. "I'll never forget the year she gave away a big Thanksgiving dinner."

Wendy looked puzzled, so Patty explained. "The extended family who had arranged to be here for Thanksgiving cancelled at the last minute due to the kids getting the flu. The place was empty and she had the fixings for twenty-two people for dinner. She got in touch with the local Ecumenical Charity group and found out who didn't have any Thanksgiving dinner, and invited them here. What a spread she put out for them!"

Both Wendy and Todd were pleased to hear Patty's story. It sounded just like their memories of their grandmother.

Then Wendy remembered what she had wanted to know, and asked, "Do you know a guide named Clive DuBois?"

"Oh, yes, Clive's been around here for ages. Has he come by?"

"Yes, and we found out something that worries us. Let's have coffee," suggested Wendy. "I want to tell you about my Gram's letter and Gentleman Jack Dennehy."

"That nasty old hoodlum isn't still alive, is he?"

Wendy said, "Maybe, but it's his grandson, called John instead of Jack." She explained her grandmother's warning, and Clive's mention of his client as the same person.

"That guy must be up to no good," said Patty. Her smile was replaced with a worried frown. "If he's anything like his grandfather, he's dangerous. Do you want to let him in the house, even with Clive?"

"I don't think we'd be in any danger," said Todd. "We'll all be here, and if he intends to search for the gold, obviously, he can't. Which reminds me, Gram said you could recommend someone to put in an alarm system."

"Of course. My nephew can do that. I feel that you'd be safer with an alarm system. I'll have Dave call you to make an appointment." Her smile returned as she ate another cookie. "Yum, these are delicious." She noticed Liz's pleased expression and asked, "Did you make them?"

"Yes, I did. Apparently I'm going to have to keep a supply on hand, because they're popular."

Wendy said, "Thanks for lining up Dave to install the alarm system, Patty. Now, we haven't had a chance to work up a business plan, but I'm sure I'll be opening The Greenhouse for the summer season. Liz will cook for us, and Todd will set up the advertising and a web site, so there isn't much else for us to do to get ready. Thanks for following up on Gram's instructions to keep the house in good order. We don't even have to dust. The house looks perfect."

"I was glad to do that for your grandmother, and if there's anything I can do to help you when you get settled, just call me. It can be a big job to clean rooms, change the linens and do laundry after a houseful of guests leave. If I can help, just let me know. I'm retired and sometimes I have too much time on my hands." As she laughed, her entire body shook. She said, "I've worked hard all my life, and can't seem to settle into doing nothing but occasional babysitting."

"Thank you, Patty," said Wendy. "I'm sure we'll need you once the summer season gets under way."

"It's so good to see you here. I can't tell you how happy it makes me to have family back in the house." Patty hugged all of them with affection before she left.

Wendy said, "I'm glad to know there will be someone to help with the housework this summer. I can picture getting swamped with laundry and cleaning."

Todd laughed. "I'm the official lawn mower, so don't look at me for housecleaning."

"I can help, when I'm not cooking," said Liz. "You know, I think we're all set, and we don't have a business plan on paper at all. It's all in our heads."

"I'll write up a generic business plan, just to be sure we haven't overlooked anything. Then we can tweak it," offered Todd. "Now, I want to go up into the tower, revisit my childhood, you might say." He trotted up the kitchen staircase, with Liz's laughing comment following him. "You never left your childhood, Todd. You can't fool us." Wendy chuckled with her and then the two women returned to their perusal of the Adirondack cookbooks.

Liz opened a page at random, and then squealed, "Moose! Who would ever expect us to serve moose?"

Wendy said, "Forget that. Some of my grandpa's hunting friends used to bring venison, and Gram cooked such tender venison loins, they almost melted in your mouth. She said the trick was to cut the meat thin and cook them quickly in a very hot cast iron pan. I've never done it, but the taste is out of this world."

"Here it is — a whole chapter on venison! I'm going to read this in detail. If we can get some venison, I'll certainly try it. What fun!"

Wendy laughed at Liz's enthusiasm, and said, "I hope we can get some. I'd be willing to bet that Patty knows some hunters who might share their meat. For a reasonable price, of course."

"What price?" Todd asked as he returned to the kitchen. Liz showed him the pages of venison recipes and he repeated Wendy's rave review of their grandmother's deft hand with venison. "I hope we can get some. I'll remember to ask Patty when we see her again." He told Liz. "You realize that deer season is in the fall, so you'll have to wait a while."

"A good recipe is worth waiting for," Liz said importantly.

"You bet!" said Todd and Wendy in unison.

"Hey, you two. Cut the twin routine. This saying the same thing at the same time is too much."

Wendy admitted, "There's nothing we can do about it. Being born eleven months apart may not make us twins, but we were brought up that way, so we just got used to tuning into each other's thoughts. You're stuck with the Bailey almost-twins, Liz."

"Oh, I'll get used to it. I'm just not used to being with the two of you at the same time, but I think that's the way it's going to be here at The Greenhouse."

"Right!" said Wendy and Todd, again in unison. Liz threw up her hands in defeat, and the three of them laughed together.

Wendy threw her arms around both Todd and Liz and hugged them. She felt as if she was wrapped in a warm blanket of family and friendship. She realized that her concerns that Todd and Liz might not get along had vanished.

At dinner that evening, Liz was happy with her first effort at cooking bison. She was pleased that the stove had a built-in grill, and after she lightly dusted the meat with lemon pepper, she grilled the meat to a tender deliciousness that had Todd raving over it. They were sure that bison had become a favorite meal for all of them.

Before they went to bed that night, Wendy reminded them all that her Gram's recipe for success included prayer. They held hands and waited for Wendy to speak. She prayed silently until she felt she had the appropriate thoughts in mind.

"Lord, I want to stand up for you in my lifetime. Give me the courage and the insight on how I may do this." After a brief pause, she went on, "Please protect us from those who may wish us harm. Thank you for those you have already sent to help us, and may we always be grateful for your love and your ever-present assistance. We love you and are ever grateful for your presence in our lives. In the name of Jesus Christ, amen."

Both Todd and Liz repeated, "Amen."

CHAPTER SIX

"The Father of mercies and God of all
comfort, who comforts us in all our
tribulation, that we may be able to comfort
those who are in any trouble, with the
comfort with which we are ourselves are
comforted by God." (2 Corinthians 1:3-4)

Immediately after breakfast, Todd said, "Now, let's get into that greenhouse and uproot some orchids." With a flourish of one arm, he led them to the parlor.

Liz slid an arm over Wendy's shoulders and said, "I'm sure they can be repotted without damaging them."

Wendy smiled at her, "You're probably right. We can be gentle with them."

Todd stopped in the parlor. "Is this blue thing on the floor your ju-jitsu exercise mat, Liz?" he asked. If so, why is it the parlor?"

"I didn't think we'd be using this room today, and I do have to keep up with my exercises. When I don't have anyone to practice with, I lift weights and do exercises."

"Oh, I see. Our warrior woman has to keep herself prepared for our protection," said Todd, smiling to indicate that he wasn't being sarcastic.

Wendy took her brother's arm and gently squeezed it. "Come on,

Todd. You know she's good at ju-jitsu. She might as well keep it up while she's here."

He understood the importance of their getting along, so he shrugged and said, "Well, there's no harm in it. I probably feel that my male status as protector is being usurped." Both women were relieved that Todd was willing to accept Liz's expertise.

They entered the greenhouse and inhaled the warm, slightly damp air. Liz said, "Ohh, I love all the light in this room." She held both arms out to the sunlight streaming through the windows. Over twenty glass prisms were hung from the ceiling. They caught and reflected the light, bathing all three of their bodies in brilliant rainbow colors

"Yes, it has a magical atmosphere," agreed Wendy. "I love the prisms that Gram hung. I must have been about eight years old then. Do you remember, Todd?"

"Yes, I was impressed, too. Gram had such a great imagination. Did you notice the clay pots the orchids are in? They have Adirondack motifs carved into them. Pine trees, swirling water and mountains."

Wendy had arranged her orchids around the house, placing them where they would receive filtered sunlight. She put her butterfly orchid in her bedroom. It sat on an east windowsill where she would see it bathed in early morning sunlight every day.

They lined up the dozen orchid pots on the metal table in the center of the room. The flowers were in bloom, some a delicate pink, which Wendy knew was her Gram's favorite color. Others were a rich, golden color.

"The table has holes in the middle," said Liz. "Is that to water plants here?" She peered overhead. "There's a series of pipes overhead, with sprinklers attached."

"Gram used this table when she started seedlings for the vegetable garden." Wendy explained. "She wanted them to get a good start before putting them outdoors. As I'm sure you know, spring can be tricky here, with frosts wiping out early gardens."

"Good idea," said Liz. "Your Gram must have been a practical person."

"She was," Wendy said as she rooted in one of the closets. "Here, I found several trowels. I can lift the plants out without disturbing the roots. I'm glad Gram had Patty water and feed the orchids. Maybe we should have something like sheets of plastic underneath so we don't lose the potting mixture.."

Liz hurried to the kitchen and returned with a roll of plastic trash bags. She peeled off a few and laid them on the table. "These should do it. What is that stuff in the pots?

"It's something that's especially for orchids," said Wendy. "It lifts out easily with a trowel. I hope I interpreted Gram's letter correctly and I won't be uprooting these plants for nothing. I'll start on the gold colored ones." She eased the tangled roots of the plant out of its pot. "Oh, look," she cried, "there's a little package in here, wrapped in…I don't know, is this oilcloth?"

Todd peered over her shoulder, "It sure is. Open it quick, let's see what you have." Wendy carefully peeled the crumbling wrapping away, and said, "They're coins, all right. I don't know if they're gold or not. They'll have to be washed before I can tell."

Todd took the seven flat disks from her hand and took them to a sink. He put a stopper in the drain, and turned on the water. The disks were a dull gold until Todd scooped some dry cleanser from an old metal pot on the counter. After he'd scrubbed them between his palms, they gleamed brightly in their true colors. "Wendy, come look!"

She quickly moved to her brother's side. She cried out, "Yes, that's gold! They're still shiny, after all these years! I can hardly believe it!"

Liz said, "Let's get them done, so you have time to run to the bank and rent a safe deposit box. We can't have this gold lying around here. That could be dangerous!"

"Right," said Todd. "Back to work." He started on another pot, while Liz and Wendy worked on two others. Within half an hour, they had a pile of gold coins on the counter by the sink, all having had the detritus of decades washed away. Wendy concentrated on watering the repotted orchids.

"What'll you put them in to carry them?" asked Liz.

"We should put them in doubled plastic grocery bags, so the package will be pliable," suggested Wendy. "Then they should fit in a small safe deposit box at the bank."

"Good idea," said Todd as he laid the coins out on paper towels. Liz said, "I'll get the plastic bags."

"How many coins are there?" Wendy asked.

"I count thirty. I'd like to weigh them, so we know how much they're worth. I'll get the scale from the kitchen."

He returned with the scale, and piled the coins into the shallow pan on top. He shook his head in amazement. "There's two pounds of coins here. Look, will you two put them into the plastic bags? I'm going online to find out what gold is worth today."

He retrieved his laptop from his room and within a few minutes, he had an answer. "Gold is gong for one thousand ninety four dollars an ounce, but that's not taking into consideration what they might be worth to a numismatist." At Liz's puzzled look, he explained, "That's a coin collector, especially someone specializing in antique coins. Are we ready to go to the bank?"

"Yes," Wendy answered, showing him Gram's canvas grocery bag that she had placed the plastic bags of coins in. "We have to open a bank account for the business, so we can do that at the same time. We'll need a post office box, since I didn't see a box at the end of the lane. I don't suppose there's mail delivery out here."

"You got all the orchids replanted and back in place," said Liz admiringly. "You really intend to take good care of these orchids, don't you, Wendy?"

"Yes, I do. We should get other plants before our first guests arrive. The greenhouse looks bare with only orchids. Let's stop at a greenhouse and pick up a few colorful plants on our way back."

"Good idea, we have to maintain the greenhouse aura, don't we?" said Todd.

Liz muttered, "Two pounds is thirty two ounces, times one thousand ninety four dollars…"

Todd scribbled on one of the paper towels and said, "Thirty five thousand and eight dollars."

"Wow," said Wendy. "Now, let's get out of here and get these into the bank."

They all froze as they heard a knock at the kitchen door. Todd hurried to the kitchen. The women heard Clive's voice and another voice they didn't recognize. Wendy whispered, "You don't suppose that John Dennehy is here already?"

"We'd better find out," said Liz as she hurried from the greenhouse. Wendy tucked the canvas bag containing the gold into a cabinet and followed, closing the glass door behind her.

They entered the kitchen and found Clive there with a slender man dressed in what the women recognized as expensive outdoor clothing. Wendy thought, *Is he trying out as a model for L. L. Bean?* She forced a smile onto her face as Clive introduced John Dennehy. "Sorry to surprise you," Clive said. "I thought we'd come by tomorrow, but John asked to come by today and be introduced."

"May I ask why?" Todd asked coldly, as he stared at Dennehy.

John turned his attention to the women. He smiled warmly at both, and then said to Wendy, "I believe we have a history in common. Your grandfather and mine knew each other well and did business together."

"If you consider murder to be business, yes, they did," Wendy answered.

Clive looked uncomfortable and said, "I don't think we should stay, John. I'm sure these folks have a lot to do to get The Greenhouse ready for business." He edged toward the door, but hesitated when John didn't move.

John said, "I think there's been a misunderstanding." He focused his attention on Wendy. He leaned toward her and said, "When ordinary folks got mixed up with bootleggers during Prohibition, some terrible things happened. I hope you won't hold me personally responsible for what happened over eighty years ago." His smile seemed practiced, but Wendy had to admit that his warmth appeared genuine.

"No, I don't hold you personally responsible, but I don't want to have anything to do with your family," she said firmly. Liz stepped closer to Wendy and said, "Goodbye, Mr. Dennehy. Bye, Clive."

"Glad to have met you folks." John took Wendy's hand and pressed it firmly, then turned to go out the door. Todd followed only long enough to shut the door behind them.

"Wow!" Wendy said. "He really tries to be charming, doesn't he? I'm not impressed. I can't quite put my finger on what I find wrong with him." She sank into a chair at the table. "He's too sleek and too well tailored for going out hiking or for meeting us. And, under that fake warmth, he's the coldest person I've ever met."

Liz asked "Do you think it's safe to go into the village now?" she asked.

"Wendy and I can go," Todd said, "We have to do the bank business. You'll be safe here alone, Liz. Clive's with Dennehy, so he won't be coming back right away."

"Liz, you're not afraid to stay alone, are you?" Wendy asked.

"No, I'll practice ju-jitsu while you're gone. I have a feeling I'm going to need to be in good form." She left the kitchen, and climbed the stairs to her room. By the time Wendy and Todd had retrieved the bag of gold coins and had their coats on, she had returned, wearing a navy blue form-fitting ju-jitsu practice outfit and was carrying a pair of eight-pound weights.

"Hey, you look great in that outfit," Wendy said. "It shows off how trim you are."

"Come on, let's go, Wendy. Let's let muscle woman practice."

Both women glared at him and he went outside to start the Jeep. Wendy clasped both of Liz's hands on top of the weights. "I'm praying for our safety, Liz, for all of us." She closed her eyes and said, "Lord, I feel that John Dennehy may be up to no good. Please protect us." Liz echoed her prayer, "Yes, Lord, please protect us from all harm. In the name of Jesus Christ, I pray."

Liz had been doing her exercises for about ten minutes when she heard a knock on the back door. She opened it to find a tall, slim young man in a Department of Environmental Conservation Forest Ranger's uniform. At her surprised expression, he laughed lightly and said, "My friends the Brewsters said I should stop by to meet you folks. I'm just going off duty now, so please excuse the uniform. I'm Dan Picard." The man's square jaw set off an attractive, tanned face. She invited him in.

She introduced herself, explaining that she was the chef for The Greenhouse Bed and Breakfast. "It's owned by my friends, sister and brother Wendy and Todd Bailey."

"This must be quite a change for you from New York City. Do you like it?"

"I love it. The quiet and being able to cook the best food without being rushed is what I wanted. I'm not new to the Adirondacks because I graduated from Paul Smith's College."

Dan's warm brown eyes were admiring as he glanced at her practice outfit and asked, "Ju-jitsu or yoga?"

She explained her history in ju-jitsu and mentioned her awards won in New York. "I've no one to practice with here, yet, but I hope to find someone, or a group."

"I do ju-jitsu and I'd like to have someone to practice with. May I call you?"

Liz said she'd be delighted and gave him her cell phone number. He grasped her hand warmly before he left, each pleased to know a friendship had begun.

Liz returned to the parlor and picked up her weights. "Don't get your hopes up, girl," she scolded herself. "This guy might not be as great as he seems on first meeting. But I sure hope so!" She looked forward to telling Wendy about Dan Picard. She lifted her weights, but didn't start her exercises. Instead, she looked up. *"Lord, we're counting on you for a lot here in our new home, protection from John Dennehy and success in our new business. Now, I'm asking you to guide me in what may be a new relationship. Please don't let me be led astray or trust a man who doesn't deserve my trust. Thank you, Father. Amen."*

CHAPTER SEVEN

"God has sealed us and given
us the Spirit in our hearts as a
guarantee." (2 Corinthians 1:22)

Liz continued her loosening-up exercises in the parlor. She was feeling limber and was enjoying the familiar routine when she heard an erratic tapping sound from the greenhouse. She looked through the glass door. Against the west wall she saw a tiny brightly colored bird beating itself against the glass.

She entered the greenhouse and looked closely, Thanks to Wendy's insistence that they should know the local birds, she recognized a rufus hummingbird. Wendy's new Adirondack bird book had an article on the tiny bird and Liz sympathized with its confusion. An orchid in bloom just inside the glass had drawn its attention.

"Get lost, little hummer, you're too early for flowers." She tapped on the glass and moved the orchid pot away. The tiny bird flew away. "We could put up a feeder. I'll call Wendy now, so she can buy one." She grabbed her cell phone and called; her friend promised that she'd buy a feeder on their way back. She asked Liz to make the sugar-water feed so it would be ready when she returned.

Liz went into the kitchen and picked up the bird book, which Wendy had left on the table. She found a recipe for hummingbird food. She poured the sugar, water and red food coloring into a saucepan and put it on the stove to cook. It had come to a brisk boil when she heard a car pull in. She set the pot off the burner and removed the lid so it would cool. She heard a knock, but knew it was too early for Wendy and Todd's return.

She opened the back door and was upset to see John Dennehy and another man on the porch. Her heart raced as she wondered if she was in danger. John pushed his way in and although she tried to close the door, an ugly, heavyset man forced his way in.

John waved a hand at the other man and said, "I'd like you to meet Stan Gubinsky. He's worked for me for years." The man nodded in her general direction, but didn't offer to shake hands. His deepset, hooded eyes glanced around the room, but didn't meet hers. Liz decided to put on a bold front and asked John, "What do you want?"

"I'd like to have a tour of the place. How about it?" He chuckled and leaned back against a cabinet with both hands in the pockets of his designer jeans. Stan edged behind Liz, standing where she couldn't see him.

Liz said, "No, I'm expecting Wendy and Todd back any minute, and I want to finish something before they get here."

John smirked and said, "They'll be in the bank for a while. These small-town banks make a big deal about opening accounts for new businesses. Besides, the locals all knew their grandmother, so they'll want to talk a lot about her, reminiscing and all that sentimental garbage. You won't see them for an hour."

He noticed her surprised expression, and sneered as he said, "I keep an eye on what you folks are doing. In fact, that cloth bag your little blond friend carried into the bank probably held the gold." He laughed at her open-mouthed expression. "Yeah, I figured you must have found the gold by now. And I intend to get my cut." When she started to protest, he cut off her indignant remark, saying, "I'll take half. I figure that's what my old grandpop shoulda got from his deal with Charlie Bailey in 1922. Tell your friends that unless they come up with half – in the original coins -- by July four, there's gonna be fireworks at this place that'll level this house to the ground!" He tossed a card on the table and said, "Call this number before July four. If you don't, I'll be back with some friends who specialize in fireworks." He chuckled.

"You might say they're incendiary specialists." His face hardened and he said, "Remember…July four, no later."

Liz still hadn't decided what to say or do when both men abruptly left the house. When the door slammed, she collapsed into a kitchen chair and dropped her face into her hands. *Some protector I am! I all but fell apart!* She lifted her head and cried out, "We asked for your protection, Lord. Please look after us. Tell us what to do before he blows us to pieces!"

At one-thirty, Wendy and Todd returned, carrying flats of plants. Liz needed something to get her mind off Dennehy's threat, so she helped carry the plants into the greenhouse. She collapsed into a chair and drew deep breaths to calm herself enough to be able to tell of the threat. Finally, she was able to explain what had happened.

Todd said, "I'm concerned about how Dennehy knew we were going to the bank this morning. He must have followed us, or had someone else follow us."

"He must have been close," Wendy said. "Liz said he even described the bag we were carrying and jumped to the conclusion that it contained the gold. I'm glad you didn't let on that he was right, Liz."

"I figured he less I said the better, but *he knew!* When is Patty Brewster's nephew going to come to see about the alarm system?"

"I'll call her now," said Todd. "She should know about the threat, too, since she'll be working here this summer." Within a few minutes, he had informed Patty of Dennehy's threat and made an appointment for an alarm system to be installed.

"He'll be here tomorrow morning, and Patty said she'll recommend that he bring a friend, a forest ranger, with him."

"What can a forest ranger do for us?" Wendy asked.

"We'll have to wait and see," said Todd. "Now, where are you going to put that?" He pointed to the hummingbird feeder that Wendy was filling with the cooled nectar.

"I'll put that cast iron pole we bought into the ground on the side of the greenhouse near where Liz saw the hummingbird. I remember there are day lilies there."

Liz said, "There must be, I saw some spear-shaped leaves coming up near the spot where the hummingbird hit. Too bad he's too early for them right now. Let me help you with that feeder, Wendy. I'll feel better if I'm working."

"I like sprucing up the lawn with a hummingbird feeder," said Todd. He didn't look at them, but was staring into space. Wendy knew he was worried and trying to think of how to handle the situation.

The women left the house and Todd sat at the table and looked over information on alarm systems that he had downloaded recently from his computer. He winced at the cost of the best systems and made a note to ask if a motion detector could be placed at the area of the driveway where it split.

Then he laughed at himself and crossed it off. *According to Gram, the biggest driving hazard around here is white-tailed deer. Just what we'd need — an alarm every time a deer goes across the driveway. Now, I'd better start to work on some newspaper advertising. We have to get some paying customers in here.*

The phone rang and an eager young voice introduced himself as Bob DiNunzio from an Albany newspaper. "I'd like to come up and interview you folks before you open for business. I'll bring a photographer. I'm sure our readers will be interested in hearing about hidden gold from the Prohibition era in an Adirondacks bed and breakfast."

Todd said, "We'd welcome you for an interview, but with the focus on our business. Mention of gold might bring snoopers who would interfere with our guests."

"Oh, no, the gold's the big draw. I don't want to write about just another bed and breakfast." His tone had changed unpleasantly as he asked, "Have you found it yet?"

"If we do, we won't announce it to the media," said Todd curtly. "If you want to do an interview and take pictures of the house and greenhouse, we'll arrange it. But we don't want snoops looking for imaginary gold."

"My source says it's for real. If you haven't found it, maybe I'll have better luck."

"No, no gold hunting on The Greenhouse property. Just forget it!" He hung up without waiting for a response.

Wendy and Liz entered the kitchen, enthused about their hummingbird feeder. Wendy glanced at Todd and asked, "What's wrong? You look upset."

He explained about the phone call and, still angry, he asked, "Who would his source have been? And why would anyone think they could come here to look for the gold? Don't people have any sense of private property or personal ownership?"

"Could Dennehy have put him up to it?" asked Wendy.

"No, he's sure we already found it and put it in the bank!" Liz answered.

Todd admitted, "There are more people who know about the gold than we knew. He may not be the last gold-seeker we hear from. Now, look at these ads I made up. I included the digital photos I took of the bedrooms and the outside of the house."

"That's impressive," said Liz as she peered over Todd's shoulder at his laptop. "Come look, Wendy. If I didn't know about this place, these ads would draw me to come here. The lighting in the rooms is just right. Each room looks distinctive, just as they are." Todd clicked from one ad to another.

Wendy looked at the ads and agreed, "Yes, they're great!" The phone rang and she jumped to answer it. "The Greenhouse. May I help you?" She listened for a moment and then said, "We'll be pleased to accommodate you this weekend, Mrs. Hart. I'm pleased that Mr. Powers recommended us. What time on Friday do you and your husband want to arrive?" She scribbled on a desk calendar placed on the counter near the phone. "Yes, that's fine. Dinner will be at 6:30. Be sure to bring a sweater or light jacket. Spring in the Adirondacks is cool. We look forward to seeing you."

She hung up the phone and pumped one fist in the air. She and Todd exclaimed together, "Our first guests!"

Wendy said, "Mr. Powers told them about us. Mrs. Hart said she and her husband are looking forward to experiencing spring in the Adirondacks. Now, speaking of spring, I have to find out what's coming up in the gardens." She raced for the front door, with Todd and Liz's laughter following her. When they heard her excited squeal they trailed after her. She cried, "Look at all the crocuses! I didn't know Gram planted all these. I only knew about the tulips. And look, they're coming up, too."

Liz looked at the tall green spears critically. "Will they bloom by the weekend?"

"Not a chance," Wendy said "Mr. and Mrs. Hart will have to settle for crocuses. And the flowers in the greenhouse, of course. I'm glad Patty kept the greenhouse clean. A cement floor, even with coats of paint, doesn't look too elegant."

"Not too elegant?" said Liz sarcastically. "It doesn't even lok okay. Some colored grass mats would look nice on the floor."

"We bought a few azaleas in some pretty pots."

"A few!" Todd exclaimed. "I had to drag her out of the garden shop before she cleaned the place out. Let's arrange the plants we have, see how much room is left. Liz, did you see that "Orchid Girl" here bought some Cattleyea orchids?"

"I saw half a dozen plants on pieces of bark. Are they Cattleyeas?"

"That's it, and I'm going to have to put hooks on the house wall."

"How about draping swags of a light gauzy fabric around them?" said Liz. "Silk would be good because it doesn't mildew if it gets damp."

"Great idea!" said Wendy. "Silk swags and grass floor mats. We'll be all set!"

"Hello!" called Patty from the back door. "Do you know who's sitting in an old car at the top of the lane? He looks like a hood. He stared at me when I drove in."

Todd raced toward the Jeep, calling over his shoulder. "I have my cell and I'll call if he's trouble." Patty joined Wendy and Liz on the tiny back porch and asked, "Do you think we should call the state troopers?"

Wendy ran into the house for her cell phone, calling back, "No, wait until we hear from him, five minutes, at least." When she returned, they stood close together. Wendy stared at her watch as the seconds crawled by.

Finally, she announced, "Five minutes, let's call the troopers."

Just then, Todd returned. He said, "Whoever he was he left, but I saw tire tracks near the entrance to the lane. Must be someone who's keeping track on us for Dennehy."

Patty observed their worried faces. In an effort to distract them, she asked, "Would you like some Burning Bushes? I have to divide mine. They would look nice near those big balsams in the side yard."

"Patty, you're an answer to prayer," said Todd. "These women were about to buy out the local plant farms." Wendy, Liz and Patty went into the house, all talking about plants that would brighten up the yard. Todd heard the words "rhododendron" and "burning bush" and "azaleas". He was relieved that they were distracted from their worries. He wondered if it was too early to call the state troopers. After all, he thought, *Dennehy hasn't actually done anything yet. He could deny he'd said anything that could be construed as a threat. No, we'd better wait until and if he actually does something--and hope it isn't too late.*

Todd drew a deep breath and then said aloud, "Lord, we need help here. This is obviously beyond our capabilities. We don't know how to deal with a potential threat. Please keep the potential from becoming actual. We love you and depend on you. Thank you, Father. Amen."

CHAPTER EIGHT

"We, being many, are of one body in
Christ, and individually members of
one another" (Romans 12:5 (NKJV)

When Todd returned to the house from his inspection of the vegetable garden, the three women were at the kitchen table enjoying coffee and cookies. He pointed to a large sheet of paper that was spread on the table. The outline of the house was apparent, but the single rectangle, various circles, triangles, and swirling outlines were meaningless to him.

Patty explained, "Your grandmother said she was a visual planner. She needed to have things down on paper before she would make a decision. This is her gardening planner. I kept it for you. Here's the vegetable garden," she pointed to the rectangle. "The deciduous trees are the triangles and the maples and apple trees are the circles."

"I remember seeing this," said Wendy. "She would study this every spring, before she made any changes in the plantings."

Patty pointed to one area filled with a large triangle and swirling designs. "This is where she wanted to plant more rhododendrons, where that big white pine is. But she had her last heart attack before she could have the tree removed and the rhodies put in."

"Then we should do it!" said Wendy. We'll have Gram's rhododendron garden."

"Wait a minute!" said Todd. "Taking a tree of that size down will be expensive."

"I know someone who will give you a good price to cut down the tree and remove it." said Patty.

"What? Another of your relatives?" asked Todd. His sister glared at him and he knew he'd hear from her later about his rudeness.

"No, just an old family friend. After your family's lived in Lake Placid for a few generations, you know everyone. My nephew, Dave will be here tomorrow at nine to see about your alarm system, okay?"

"You bet!" said Todd. "I'll feel more at ease when that's done."

Suddenly the house shivered with a blast of wind. They all stared at one another, until Patty said, "We're supposed to have a storm tonight. Wind and rain, fairly mild as Adirondack storms go. Just don't leave anything outside that you don't want blown away. It's a good thing I don't use my clothesline any more. This wind would take it down. But Wendy, you might like to put a clothesline someplace where it's not visible from the house. Air-dried sheets would be a treat for your guests. Well, think about it, I have to go now, and see what I have to put under shelter at home. Bye now." She hurried out the kitchen door, struggling to close it firmly against a gust of wind.

"We don't have anything outside, do we?" Wendy asked. "How about the lawn rake you were using on the front garden beds, Todd?"

"I put it away. Gram taught me well. Remember when you left the trowel out, Wendy?"

"Do I! I had to go out as soon as the sun came up before breakfast and find it."

"Wow! She must have been fussy!" said Liz.

"No, she was right. If you don't lose things, you don't have to pay to replace them, see?"

"I get it. Now, you said you found something you wanted to show me in a greenhouse closet, Wendy, but you were leaving in a hurry to get to the bank."

"Yes, come see. We were talking about sprucing up the greenhouse and I found something that might help." She led the way to the greenhouse and to Liz's surprise, she opened an almost invisible narrow door that blended into the outside house wall. A six foot tall narrow form was propped in the back. Wendy removed it from the closet and when she leaned it against the house wall, Liz realized that it was a cross made from raffia. They studied it and Wendy said, "It looks handmade and it's in good condition. Maybe it could be mounted on the wall near the Cattleya orchids."

Liz suggested, "You could tie it in to the orchids by draping a strand of silk over the horizontal arms. It probably dates back to the twenties. It's stunning. At six feet tall, it would be a focal point for the wall. I'm glad you found it."

Todd entered the greenhouse and Wendy asked, "Do you remember this, Todd?"

"No, but it looks like something Gram would have." He studied the effect as Wendy held it against the wall between the orchids whose wiry tendrils clung to rough slabs of bark. "I like it! I'll hang it right away. I'll get the hammer and a nail. Then I want to photograph it. It gives the greenhouse the kind of spiritual quality it needs. Its earthiness offsets the prisms hanging from the ceiling."

"Earthiness?" Liz asked.

Wendy smiled at her. She realized that Liz had not noticed Todd's artistic side and knew that her friend would now see Todd differently.

When he left, Wendy said, "While I have this closet open, Liz, let me show you something." She reached into the dark depths and pushed a knot on the back wall. A door opened, revealing a narrow staircase that led upstairs into the dark. "This goes up to the Azalea Room closet and was in the house when my grandparents bought it. No one knows why it was put in.

"You know, thinking of the silk, we'd better order it on line. I haven't seen a fabric store locally, and we don't have time to shop in Plattsburgh or Albany, especially since we're having our first guests next weekend."

Liz agreed. "Good point. I think I'd better do it now. The way the wind's coming up, we might lose the electricity tonight. By the way, I'm planning on cooking salmon for dinner tonight. If the electricity goes out, we can grill it in the fireplace."

"I'm glad I have you to think about food, Liz, because I don't usually give it a thought until I get hungry." Then a blast of wind shivered the greenhouse and Wendy dashed for the door into the house. Liz laughed at her alarm, but she followed.

Neither of them noticed a dark, heavyset figure at the edge of the woods. The figure shook a fist at the darkening sky, but his curses could not be heard over the storm. Still snarling, he turned into the deep shade of the trees and onto the trail.

The electricity stayed on until after they had eaten their dinner. It went out while they were sitting in the parlor, each curled up with a book. "We might as well go to bed," Wendy said. "We sure can't read any more tonight. I'm glad this storm is going through the area tonight, instead of next weekend when we have guests." They each picked up a flashlight, which Todd had made sure they had ready. They made their way upstairs.

Wendy's room was in the front of the house and she couldn't resist watching the storm, illuminated by lightning, as it tore across the lake toward them. She had never seen whitecaps on Lake Placid before, but the entire lake was covered with them now. They seemed to dance with each lightning bolt. Her usual pleasant view of Shelter Strait, the narrow strip of water between Buck Island and Moose Island was invisible in the storm. In half an hour, Liz knocked on her door and asked if she could stay with her. "Yes, of course," Wendy said. "Come look out the window, and see the whitecaps on the lake." They both watched the storm, dressed in warm nightgowns and curled in a large easy chair. They shared a blanket draped over their shoulders. As soon as the lightning started, Wendy started to count. "One one thousand, two one thousand…"

A huge explosion of thunder drowned out her words. Then another lightning bolt smashed nearby, and they heard a huge rending crack, which they knew meant a big tree was destroyed. Moments later, Todd, dressed in pajamas, tapped on the door and asked to come in. They called for him to enter and he said, "We won't need anyone to cut down that big white pine for the rhododendrons. It's blown to bits."

They continued to watch the storm, each of them wrapped in a blanket. They watched until a faint, hazy sun began to make an appearance over the tops of the mountains on the east side of the lake.

Liz said, "That rain came down like gangbusters last night! Now it's time for coffee, waffles and bacon. I'm glad we bought some Adirondack maple syrup. Today is a day for maple syrup! It'll probably warm up later, when the sun comes out, but for now, let's just eat!"

Wendy and Todd agreed and, throwing on robes, followed her downstairs. They didn't even dress for the day, planning on doing so after they had finished eating their delicious hot breakfast. Without having to hurry, Liz had it on the table promptly.

Todd glanced around the table and said, "You know, eating breakfast together like this, we look like a family. Two sisters and a brother." When Liz gasped, he asked, "Don't you think so?"

"I do," she admitted. "But I didn't think you'd see me as a sister. I mean…" she hesitated and Todd finished her thought, "You didn't think I liked you, right?"

Liz only nodded, so Todd said, "We haven't been working together long, but I already see how well we three fit together, as a working team and as Christians."

Both Wendy and Liz smiled in delight upon hearing Todd's thoughts.

A tap at the kitchen door revealed Dan Picard, dressed for a ju-jitsu workout with Liz. Instead, he was invited to sit down and eat waffles with them. Later, he admitted that he was so full he couldn't exercise, but would appreciate having a tour of the house. Liz asked him to wait until she dressed and then she took him on a tour. The two of them, tall, lean and fit, looked so good together that sentimental Wendy had to smile.

Todd glared at her, and scolded her for what he called "matchmaking." She denied being responsible for the pairing of Liz and Dan, saying that they had taken care of it themselves. Todd said, "You're wishing them together, though, aren't you?"

"Of course I am, some people are obviously meant for one another." He laughed at her remark, but didn't deny that it could be true.

Soon, Patty showed up to ask how they had weathered the storm. They told her that they had enjoyed watching it from an upstairs window, and she laughed, calling them, "True Adirondackers." They told her of the lightning striking the white pine. She promised that her old friend would come by and give them a price on removing the tree's shattered remains and roots.

They went outside to look at the tree and were amazed at the extent of the damage. The tree was split down the middle and the lawn was strewn with so many wood shards that Todd claimed it looked like a toothpick factory.

"Wow," said Wendy. "That was some lightning strike."

Patty said, "That's why there's lightning rods on the house. That was the first improvement your grandmother said they did. She had asked locally if it was necessary, and was told not to let it go. Some of our Adirondack storms are really powerful. You don't want to take chances."

"Good thinking," said Todd.

"Look, what's this?" Wendy asked. She was peering around the base of the shattered tree. She picked up a worn, soaked rain-hat and showed it to them.

"A man's rain hat? What's that doing here?" Patty asked.

"More important, who was here?" Todd asked. He looked around the tree and peered at the trail that approached it before curving off in another direction. "Someone was caught here in the storm and left in a hurry, I bet. That's not a pleasant thought." Wendy had to admit that she didn't like the idea that perhaps someone was spying on them. She firmly put the thought from her mind, realizing that she would probably never know who had lost the hat on their property, so there was no point in worrying about it.

Later, Wendy reminded Todd of Patty's suggestion that they put up a clothesline on which to dry the sheets. He thought that was a good idea and he knew of a clearing where a line would be out of sight of the house and promised he'd put it up soon.

CHAPTER NINE

"But whoever listens to me will dwell
safely, and will be secure, without
fear of evil." Proverbs 1:33 (NKJV)

Wendy sat at the kitchen table, but the cup of coffee Liz had poured for her grew cold as she turned the rain-hat over in her hands. She said, "It's a cheap thing, not something that John Dennehy would wear, judging from the way he was dressed when he was here with Clive DuBois." She tipped her head back in thought, then said, "That guy Stan you described who came here with John, Liz. This seems more like his kind of hat."

"I was just about to say that," Liz said. "He wore old, crummy clothes and this seems to be more his style than Dennehy's."

"What would he be doing here?" asked Todd, as he paced the floor. "Do you suppose he's spying on us for Dennehy? But why? He knows the gold's locked up in the bank. What else could he want?"

The phone rang and Todd answered it. His face lit up, "Hello, Mr. McAfee. It's good to hear from you." He listened, and then looked at Wendy, catching her eyes. "Oh, you're planning on coming up here to look the place over to update our insurance coverage. Yes, I'm sure we need to do that, but I hope that won't increase our insurance premiums." He paused, then asked, "Excuse me, what did you say about gold?" He scowled and asked, "How did you hear that story?" His scowl deepened. "He did, did he? I'm sorry to hear that because it might mean we'll have gold hunters up here interfering with our guests." His expression lightened. "Yes, we have rooms for next weekend and we'll be glad to reserve one for you and your wife. Thanks for calling, Mr. McAfee. Bye."

He hung up the phone and slumped into a kitchen chair. At Wendy's puzzled look, he explained, "Mr. McAfee needs to check out our insurance coverage, as Gram's letter said he would. McAfee said that Mr. Powers has been, what he called 'riding the story of the Prohibition gold at every cocktail party in New York'. You know Mr. Powers likes his cocktails and considers himself quite the raconteur, so I'm sure a lot of people know about the gold by now."

"Oh no!" said Wendy. "I thought we could trust him, but I recall Gram saying that Sty, as she called him, had 'a fondness for a drink now and then.' She claimed it was the Irish in him. He said he wants to come up here to fish, but I wonder if he really wants to look for the gold."

Liz commented, "The sooner we let him know that it's found and tucked away in the bank, the better."

Wendy agreed. "You're right, Liz. Then maybe he'll stop spreading that story. But, I'm afraid the harm's been done. Who knows how many people he's told. When is trout fishing season, anyway?"

Todd said, "It started April first, but Lake Placid is usually still iced in by then. This spring has been unusually warm, so there's enough open water for fishing. The season lasts until mid–October, so I expect we'll hear from Mr. Powers soon. Or as you said, Liz, we should call him and let him know the gold is securely in the bank. If he still wants to come up to fish, fine, let him. We said he could. In fact, we said that we expected him, didn't we, Wendy?"

"We did, and like you said, since the lake's ice is almost melted, he shouldn't have any problem putting a boat in to fish from. Now, let me update the reservations book. You didn't write down Mr. McAfee's reservation, did you, Todd?"

"No, and he wants to come up next weekend. I see you have someone listed here for then, Mr. and Mrs. Hart, no children. You wrote down that they're staying in the Rhododendron Room. Where should we put the McAfee's? How about the Peony Room, since it's a corner room and looks out on both the lake and the forest?"

Liz laughed and asked, "Do you think he'll give you a break on insurance premiums if he had a nice room?"

"They're all nice rooms, Liz. Nobody gets short-changed around here."

A series of metallic rattles and a loud backfire made them all jump to their feet. An old Ford pickup drew near the back door. It stopped with a shudder and the driver's door squeaked open. A heavy-set man with a gray head of unruly hair and a bushy mustache got out and approached the back door. "Hello!" he called when he saw them observing him from the small porch's door. His wide, cheerful grin put them at ease and they hurried out the door and met him on the lawn.

"I'm Terry Johns, and my friend Patty says you need a porch." He approached the back door and tapped the worn wood. Then he tipped his head back to observe the flaking molding above the door.

"You need a door first, and it looks like we'd have to start by pulling out the door frame. Not too secure, that frame." He turned back to them, holding out his right hand to Wendy. He firmly shook her hand, and after she told him her name, he turned and shook hands with Liz and Todd. "Patty says security is your big worry, and I can see why. You gotta let me measure before I can tell you what I can do." His torrent of words stopped as he returned to his truck and pulled out a large toolbox. He removed the largest metal measuring tape they had ever seen and walked up to the door. Then he turned to Todd and asked, "What size did you have in mind?" Instead of waiting for an answer, he asked, "Plan to put any furniture on it, like a picnic table or chairs?"

Wendy answered, "No, we just want to have a wider, more secure spot from which to enter the house."

Liz interrupted, "Maybe a bench to put bags of groceries down while we're unlocking the door and disarming the alarm." Wendy nodded and Todd said, "Good idea, and I want to put motion sensor lights above the door, for security reasons."

"Gotcha! I can do that, too." At their surprised expressions, he said, "I'm a jack-of-all-trades, but I enjoy woodworking most. Now, about the size." He handed one end of the metal tape to Todd and instructed him to walk out to the distance he thought the porch should be. Terry stood against the house, holding the tape. He said, "I'd suggest you have it eight feet wide. That would give you enough room and it's cheaper and more efficient to use conventional size lumber. I can use eight-foot lengths and there'll be no waste." Todd stopped at eight feet from the back of the house and said, "This is enough. After all, it isn't intended for entertaining."

"Good thinking!" exclaimed Terry. "I can have lumber delivered tomorrow and pick up the lights at Aubuchon's this afternoon. We'll be all set to go tomorrow morning." He pulled a small spiral notebook and a stub of pencil from his shirt pocket and scribbled some figures. "Based on last week's cost of wood, but not including the light fixtures, this is what it'll cost you." He tore off the page and handed it to Todd. "Okay?" he asked.

Todd's eyebrows rose as he stared at the figure. Wendy looked worried until he said, "This isn't very much for the amount of work you'll do. Are you sure this is all you'll charge?"

Terry grinned and said, "There's one more fee, and it's one you'll enjoy. Come with my family and me to the Adirondack Community Church at either the nine or ten-thirty service Sunday morning. You'll enjoy it, I promise. There's even a coffee hour with home-baked goodies between the two services. You know where the church is, don't you?"

Wendy said, "Main Street, right across from the post office, isn't it? Stone gothic church on a lake?"

"You got it! I always figure that new folks in the village need to meet other folks and the best way is to go to church. We're pretty casual in dress, for the most part, because folks come up here to ski, play hockey, or other sports, and they don't plan on fancying up for church, see?"

"Yes, I see," said Wendy. "In fact, when we were arranging for our post office box, I saw the church and told Todd it was so pretty that I wanted to see the inside. We don't have guests until next weekend, so we can make it." She glanced at the other two and said, "Well, I can at least."

Liz said, "I'll go with you, and Dan mentioned that church also. He often has to work weekends, so he can't attend very often, but if he's free, he'll join us."

"I'll stay here and keep an eye on things," said Todd. "After Dave gets the alarm system put in, oh well, that'll be after the back door is replaced, but then I can go to church. Say, Liz, I forgot, did you call Salvio's and give your resignation?"

"I emailed them yesterday and the manager said he had a list of chefs looking for jobs, so I'm sure it's already filled. I also called a girlfriend who's looking for an apartment. Mine isn't much, but it's better than the dive she was living in. I've cut my ties to nasty New York."

"Don't blame you!" said Terry. "I've only visited New York a couple of times, and enjoyed what I went for, and then couldn't wait to leave. It's the Adirondack Mountains for me, any day! By the way, if you get the chance, you should go on the gondola up Whiteface Mountain. It starts up in June. Right now, you can go up to the top of the ski jump towers in an elevator. You really shouldn't miss that view!"

"Thanks, Terry, I'm sure we will," said Todd. Terry put his toolbox back into his truck, waved goodbye and left.

"Wow, he's a cheery fellow," said Liz. "I was thinking of making more cookies, now I know I will. Someone that upbeat must love chocolate chip cookies."

They went inside and had just sat down at the kitchen table, when there was a brisk knock at the door. Todd got up to open it, saying, "Wow, we're busy today". He saw a young man wearing a sweatshirt bearing a logo that read *Security Systems for Home and Business*. "Oh, you're Dave. Come in, we were expecting you."

The young man introduced himself to all of them as Dave Brewster. He asked if there was an outside entry to the basement. Upon being assured there was not, he said, "That's good, because basement entries are often difficult to wire an alarm to, especially in older homes. Now, let's see the place." He pulled out a clipboard, with an outline of the floor plan. "Aunt Patty drew this for me, so I'd have an idea of what you might need, but I have to see everything anyway."

Wendy waved a hand at Todd, so he took Dave on the tour. Both women stayed in the kitchen to talk about the food they would serve the following weekend. They had prepared menus and a shopping list by the time the men returned. "What do you think, Dave? What do we need to do to protect ourselves from break-ins?" Wendy asked.

"Todd said you were advised to replace the kitchen door and put a larger porch outside. I agree, and I agree that you also need good lighting out there. That would be the first step. That back door is in poor condition and the glass pane would allow anyone to get in. The front door is solid and could be wired with an alarm as is. Of course, not many burglars use the front door, even out here away from close neighbors." He put a check mark on his chart. "The downstairs windows should be wired, and the greenhouse will be a challenge."

At Wendy's worried look, he assured her, "It can be done, and the wires won't be obvious. You should have a separate alarm panel for the greenhouse, so that means for now, you'll need one for the front door, one for the greenhouse, and later, after the back door is replaced, one there. I'll go over some figures and let you know what it'll cost." He chuckled at Todd's concerned expression, and assured him, "Aunt Patty said I was to treat you like family, so it won't cost you a fortune. And I promise," he held up his right hand in a Boy Scout salute, "It'll be the best job I can do, and that's top of the line."

"Thanks, Dave. We appreciate your help," said Todd. Wendy added her thanks. Then Dave said, "I saw Uncle Terry's old clunker going out the road as I was coming in, so I guess you've been talking to him about the repairs."

Wendy said, "Yes, he was and we enjoyed meeting him."

Dave explained, "He's not really an uncle, just an old family friend, and a top-notch wood-worker. He'll love working on an old house like this. It's really his style. Well, I'll go now. Thanks for the tour. This place is beautiful. It was worth it coming out here just for that." He waved and went out.

Todd sat at the table and said, "I like him, and feel that Patty steered us right when she recommended him. Now, do you have us ready to feed a few more people next weekend?"

"You bet," said Liz. "They're going to love the food here."

That evening, Wendy called Styvesant Powers at home and asked if he was ready to fish Lake Placid. She was informed that he had purchased his fishing license and his wife, Eleanor was shopping for what she called, "country clothes" He laughed with Wendy and said, "It's going to cost me a fortune, but she's really looking forward to this trip. Eleanor loves good clothes. You know she used to be a top model when she was young, don't you?"

Sty didn't wait for Wendy's reply, but kept speaking. "Last year we went to a posh resort in the Carolinas and it was too fast-paced, where the recreation director was always trying to talk us into doing things that were beyond our capabilities. I promised Eleanor that our time with you would have an easier pace. Maybe she'll visit the Lake Placid Center for the Arts and local clothing and antique shops. That's her style. How about the week after next? That'll give me time to clear up a few matters."

Wendy was so pleased that they were coming, she didn't ask about why he had been talking about the gold. When she reported to Todd about the conversation, he admitted, "I'd like to talk to him face to face, anyway."

Then the phone rang, and Todd answered. His face went white as he listened, then he suddenly hung up. "What is it?" Wendy asked.

"Just that Dennehy creep, trying to scare us. Forget it, he's all hot air."

"What did he say? Did he mention his July Fourth deadline?"

"Yes, but we'll inform the state troopers and make sure that his so-called incendiary specialists are nowhere around us."

Liz said. "Dan's coming over this afternoon and we're going for a hike. He might have some ideas on how we can protect ourselves." She ignored Wendy's smile on hearing about the date.

"We'll have the alarm system in long before Dennehy's deadline, but that will only let us know if someone tries to break into the house. Oh, Dave agreed that we should have motion-sensor lights at the back door. It might deter anyone sneaking up to the door if a spotlight suddenly came on."

"Good idea," chorused both women. Wendy went on, "What do you think he meant by 'incendiary specialists'? You don't suppose he's going to have someone set fire to the house, do you?"

Todd suggested, "We'll have to talk to Dan and see what he might recommend. I know the State Troopers can't patrol the property as our personal guards. They have enough territory to patrol. But it might be more in a forest ranger's line to patrol the access road, since it leads to hiking trails. Maybe Dan can recommend someone who could be hired to patrol the property around Dennehy's deadline, but I hate to think of the cost."

Wendy said, "We need more information before we make any decisions."

"So we do," said Todd. He observed Liz pulling a tin of cocoa and several bars of baking chocolate from a cabinet. "There's nothing that takes my mind off my worries like chocolate, so go right ahead, Liz! Say, what are you making for the McAfee's next weekend?"

"We decided on Beef Wellington with twice-baked potatoes and whatever vegetables strike my fancy at the moment. That's a big meal, so I'll make lemon meringue pie for dessert. It's nice and light, not too filling after a big dinner."

"Great!" said Todd "That's one of my favorite dinners." He turned toward the driveway, and said, "Look, Dan's here."

They immediately shared their news with Dan about the alarm system, the porch and new door. He expressed relief, but when told about the "incendiary specialist" that John Dennehy had threatened them with, he shook his head.

"I'll arrange my vacation so I can stand guard here the weekend of the Fourth. If you don't mind, I'll line up some friends to spell me, so there's always someone here."

At eight-thirty the next morning, a lumber truck delivered the eight-foot, two by fours, new door and framing wood that Terry had ordered. He accompanied the delivery and went right to work. Wendy and Liz were surprised at the speed with which he worked and remarked on it when they brought him coffee and cookies.

"It's all a matter of doing what I'm familiar with. I've had decades of practice, so I should know what I'm doing by now." He wolfed several cookies and a cup of coffee and went right back to work.

By four o'clock that afternoon, the new back door, motion sensor lights and the porch were finished, except for paint on the door and on the new framing. Terry told Todd that the porch should have a coat of preservative stain. He said that he would come back the next morning, "after the dew evaporates", to do that after painting the door and trim.

Both the Baileys and Liz thanked him and looked forward to seeing him the next day.

Wendy waved goodbye as Terry left. She said, "He's such a cheerful person, and the speed with which he works! I've never seen anyone get so much done so fast."

"He's an amazing person," Todd agreed. "I just realized that since we moved here, I've met the most interesting people I've ever known."

Wendy agreed with him, "First Clive DuBois, Patty and Dave Brewster, and now Terry Johns. I wonder if it's the mountain air that brings people with such interesting personalities here."

Liz exclaimed, "No. It's the air that makes them become interesting. It affects their outlook and makes them cheerful and helpful."

Wendy and Todd laughed, but both agreed that she could be right.

Liz continued her thought, saying, "Besides, between the mountains, the lakes and the rest of the scenery, it's obvious to me that God lives here, so why wouldn't the residents be cheerful?"

"Good point," said Todd and Wendy in unison.

CHAPTER TEN

"By faith we understand that the worlds were framed by the word of God, so that the things which are seen are not made of things which are visible." (Hebrews 11:6 NKJV)

Dick and Carla McAfee enjoyed their dinner of Beef Wellington and twice-baked potatoes. After eating, they went for a walk in the dusky evening air along the lakeshore. Carla shrieked in delight every time a fish jumped, and she was thrilled by the mallard ducks that winged across the lake and splashed to a landing near the shore.

Dick McAfee was pleased to report that he could allow a substantial discount on the B and B's insurance due to the alarm system, once it was installed the next week. He also approved of the updated fire extinguishers that Todd had purchased and installed.

Todd commented, "They're not the prettiest things to have on our walls, but I'm sure our guests feel more comfortable knowing they're available, just in case."

The weekend was very pleasant, and the subject of the gold wasn't mentioned. Both Wendy and Todd felt it would spoil the lovely weekend with their grandmother's old friends if they mentioned it.

Sunday morning dawned bright and clear. Wendy and Liz decided to go to church with Dan, who had the day off. The McAfee's declined to accompany them, saying they wanted to walk some more and take the rowboat out on the lake. "Not to fish," said Carla. "We just want to enjoy the view. It's so beautiful from shore, I imagine it's even lovelier from the lake." She requested and received a cushion to place on the wooden boat seat.

Liz and Wendy returned from church before the McAfee's were ready to leave, so Liz prepared a hearty lunch of roast beef sandwiches. She said she didn't want them to get hungry on their return trip to the city. Both Dick and Carla sported tans and said they felt fit from all the walking they had done. They promised to recommend The Greenhouse B and B to their friends. Wendy didn't mention that the Powers were due to come up the next weekend, but wished the old friends could have vacationed together.

Patty turned up early on Monday and announced that when she washed the sheets, this time they would be hung in the sun. "They'll smell like the mountain air. Your guests will love it. Look, Wendy, let me run your personal laundry with the sheets. You can wear the scent of mountain air. Won't you like that? "

Wendy agreed that she would and her blouses and underwear were washed and joined the sheets on the line in the sun.

Wendy stood beside tall, elegant Eleanor Powers at the end of the dock from which Styvesant Powers had launched the small aluminum rowboat. They watched Sty row well out into the lake, his fishing guidebook claimed there was a deep hole. He determined to find where the cold-loving lake trout lived. He cast his line and settled back against a cushioned backrest to wait for a strike.

Eleanor laughed lightly and said, "There's a happy man. If he actually catches a few fish, he'll be in seventh heaven. As for me, I'm counting on you, Wendy, to suggest where I should shop in Lake Placid village."

Wendy admitted she hadn't had time to shop. The B and B preparations took most of her time. "The only shop I've been in, other than The Bookstore Plus, is Ruthie's Run. They have nice clothes, and some lovely imported wool sweaters, both pullovers and cardigans. Maybe you'd like to start there.

"Sty said he thought you'd like to see the Craft Shop at the Lake Placid Center for the Arts. The carvings and paintings are stunning. I'm hoping I can eventually add to my Gram's collection of Adirondack art, which I'm sure you noticed in the parlor and your bedroom."

"I did. The flower paintings are lovely, I'm really taken with them. That wood carving of a buck on the mantle in the parlor took my attention as soon as I walked in the room. So majestic!" Eleanor started to walk back toward the house, and Wendy followed her, realizing that she was drawing herself up as tall as her five toot four would allow, in emulation of the tall, lovely, white-haired woman in front of her. Wendy thought, *No wonder she was a famous model. She's beautiful and just look at the way she walks, or glides, really. I couldn't do that if I practiced the rest of my life.*

At Eleanor's suggestion, Wendy accompanied her on her shopping trip, first to buy a wool sweater at Ruthie's Run, then to the craft shop where Eleanor bought several beautiful woodcarvings of trout that she wanted to give Sty for his birthday in the fall. Wendy took mental notes of the other artwork on display. She particularly wanted to buy some wood carvings of deer to add to the one in the parlor. *Maybe I can put them on my birthday wish list,* she thought. The opportunity to stroll at leisure through the spacious craft store was a pleasure and she reminded herself to bring Liz here when they had time.

As Wendy pulled into the lane that led to the driveway, she could see a car almost hidden in the trees just ahead of the turnoff. *Anyone wanting to hike the trails up the hillside beyond us is supposed to park by the road. Is someone watching us, and why?*

Eleanor interrupted her thoughts by asking, "Wendy, are you worried about something? You look concerned." Reluctantly, Wendy told her about John Dennehy's threat, specifically that if they hadn't made arrangements to pay off Dennehy, there would be trouble by the Fourth of July.

"You must tell Sty about this. He knows the history of your grandfather's run-in with the senior Jack Dennehy. In fact, I know he was worried about young John, thinking his grandfather may have influenced him. Do tell him."

As they drew near the house, Wendy saw Dan and Liz approach. She parked the car near them. Eleanor carried her packages to the house and was met by Sty on the wide back porch. He carried her packages indoors. His wife met his questions about the bags from Lake Placid Center for the Arts with smooth evasions.

Wendy stopped to talk to the two young people. "Dan, I need some advice. There's someone parked at the end of our lane, on our property, but he seems to be trying to hide his vehicle. At least, he's in the trees just beyond the beginning of our driveway."

Dan replied, "It could be a hiker who didn't want to leave his car by the highway and decided to cheat by a half-mile and park on your property. Let's walk out there and see who it is. I'm off duty, but I'm always carrying my Ranger ID, so if he's illegally parked, I'll ask him to move."

"What if it's that thug, Gubinsky?" asked Liz.

"The same rules apply to him," said Dan calmly, as they walked down the drive. When they approached the car in the trees, it started up and, tires spinning, it pulled out, passing them at as fast a speed as could be managed in such a short space. The tinted windows prevented them from seeing the driver, but Dan wrote down the license number. "I don't know if this will tell us anything, but I'll run it by my supervisor and see if he'll permit me to find out whose car that is. Illegal parking isn't a big deal, but the threat against you changes the picture."

He admitted, "I hope you don't mind, but I told him about the threat. I knew he'd want to know of any threat of violence. That's State Police business, of course, and he'll pass it on to the troopers in Ray Brook barracks if he thinks the situation warrants it."

Wendy said, "Thanks, Dan. I appreciate your interest. It's nice to know that somebody in a position of power is taking an interest. Now, Liz and I had better get back to the house. It's time for our afternoon snack."

They walked quickly to return to the B and B, knowing Sty and Eleanor would be hungry. Liz smiled as she remembered from yesterday that Sty had loved her double chocolate chip cookies and, no doubt, would want more.

Todd was waiting for them, and after he was informed of the car that left so suddenly, he said, "While we eat our cookies, I'm going to ask Sty about his mentioning the gold at cocktail parties on New York.

The timing is probably good, since I understand that people are more accommodating when they have food than at any other time."

Wendy, Todd, Liz and the Powers relaxed in Adirondack chairs on the sunny lawn overlooking the lake. Sty wore a satisfied expression, which the others were sure was due to his catching his limit of five trout that morning. He had suggested that they eat them for dinner that evening, which offer was gratefully accepted.

Todd watched Sty eat his third cookie and drink a big gulp of lemonade, then he asked, "Sty, we had heard that you often mentioned the Prohibition gold at parties in New York. I wondered why you would mention it so publicly, knowing it could draw unwanted attention from fortune-seekers." He then mentioned the Albany newspaper reporter who claimed to have a source and said, "I hoped it was not you, or your office."

Sty flushed and said, "I have a confession to make to you. I had several reasons for wanting to come up here. One was to see you and return to this lovely place." He waved a hand that encompassed the house and lake. "The other is that I knew you were not planning on serving liquor, unless guests requested it for a special event, as was your grandmother's habit." His flush deepened and he glanced at Eleanor. "I've come to realize that I drink too much and at my age, that's bad for me, so I'm trying to stop drinking any liquor. I realize that only by cutting myself off from alcohol can I stop drinking too much. When I drink, I talk too much, and carelessly, as well."

Eleanor reached over and patted his hand. "I'm not drinking either, since that will make it easier for my dear Sty to avoid liquor."

A deep voice behind them said, "How noble of you!" They spun around in their chairs to see John Dennehy just a few feet away. The smirk on Dennehy's face betrayed that he was pleased to have been able to sneak up on them. He was dressed in casual, but fashionable clothing, light tan slacks and a green cardigan sweater over a stylish green and tan striped shirt.

Todd got to his feet. "What are you doing here?" He took several steps toward John, but the other man held up a hand, palm outward. "I don't want to talk to you, Bailey. You're as hard to get along with as your stupid old grandfather.

"I thought you ought to know how this old coot," he waved a hand at Sty, "got his money. Enough for a poor kid to pay off his loans from attending a top law school and pay for this lovely lady," he glanced at Eleanor, "to go to the best modeling school. Top drawer, all the way."

He looked at Todd, and then glanced at Wendy. "Did you know your grandfather had a partner?" Wendy's eyes widened. "Yes, but he got his cut early, leaving your grandfather to deal with my granddad alone. Why do you suppose he represented your grandmother for free all those years? Guilt!"

John's smirk widened and he said, "Sorry to mess up your lawn party, but I thought you wouldn't want to have anything to do with this old cheat, once you knew the truth."

Eleanor rose gracefully from her chair and faced John. "It's *you* who doesn't know the truth! Sty represented Charlie and Mabel when they bought this place. The family they bought it from had problems, with all of them claiming rights to the house. Sty spent months tracing deeds, title searches and contracts before the deed could be cleared and the property sold. All for free, for the sake of friendship! And what's more, when Charlie began to suspect that Jack Dennehy, your grandfather, was a dangerous man, Charlie paid off Sty and told him to stay in New York, preferring to face the risks himself. Again, for the sake of friendship! You wouldn't understand anyone working that hard for a friend, or running a risk for a friend."

She clasped her hands in front of her and asked, "You don't have a friend in the world, do you, John Dennehy?"

John snarled and took a step toward Eleanor, but Sty leaned forward in his chair and pushed the other man away. Taken by surprise, John stumbled and went down on his knees, but scrambled to his feet. There were grass stains on both knees. "Look at this, you jerk! These pants cost me a fortune."

John began to step forward, but Liz and Todd, who had circled around in back of him, seized him, each grasping an arm. They fast-marched him up the slope of the lawn to where his car was parked, about fifty feet down the driveway. They dumped him in the driver's seat, high-fived one another and waited until Jack drove away. Then they returned to the others.

Eleanor and Wendy applauded them when they returned and Sty stood up and clasped both of them in his arms. "You two are all the protection anyone could need! That was a great move, the two of you grabbing him at the same time and marching him off. What a team!"

Liz and Todd were released from Sty's embrace, only to be hugged by Wendy and Eleanor. "You are a great team," Wendy said. Liz admitted, "I guess we are."

Wendy took Eleanor's hand. "I'm so sorry for this rude interruption."

Sty said, "Sometimes you can't escape history. It sneaks up on you."

At the sound of rustling under the trees on the other side of the lawn, Wendy drew away from the others. She saw a hulking figure leaving the area. Liz asked, "What is it, Wendy?" Wendy held one hand to her forehead to shade her eyes. "There seemed to be someone over there. By the lightning-hit tree stump, maybe heading toward the trail. A heavy-set person, not too tall."

"Gubinsky?" asked Liz. "Do you think he's still hanging around?"

Todd said, "I wonder if Gubinsky's in business for himself. No honor among thieves, as the saying goes."

The Baileys had to remind Sty who Gubinsky was, and that he had accompanied Dennehy on his first visit. Sty was worried and urgently reminded them that they should report Dennehy's July Fourth threat to the State Police in Raybrook. "You should tell them that he threatened to blow up the house."

Todd assured him that he would do so, but reminded him that so far, no crime had occurred, and the threat couldn't be proven. "It's our word against his, and I'm sure he'd deny that he made any threat. I'll report it, anyway."

Sty said, "You should write a statement and turn it in to a local judge. Of course, Dennehy will probably ignore the summons the judge should issue, but if there's trouble in the future, it'll be on record."

Todd took both Wendy and Liz by one arm and said, "Come on, let's go in the house and write our statement on my computer. We'll use that little room next to the kitchen that Gram used as her office."

Wendy said, "I was most impressed that Gram, always prayed out loud before she even opened her books. I loved to pray with her because I felt her prayers were so deep!"

"Yes," said Sty. "The depth of her devotion to Christ is what got her through Charlie's murder and then the renovations that were necessary after Dennehy's men trashed the house looking for the gold. They made a mess in the kitchen, even smashing the dishes."

"Why the dishes?" asked Wendy.

"Probably from frustration because they couldn't find the gold. They apparently had no imagination, or they would have thought of the orchid pots, where you found it."

"Let's go, Wendy and Liz," said Todd. He headed to the house with the two young women trailing behind him. Sty and Eleanor waited, preferring to stretch out in the lawn chairs until the statement was finished. The three young people took their time drafting their description of Dennehy's threat. Liz recalled his comments word-for-word, so Todd wrote the statement exactly as she described it. He mentioned Stan Gubinsky's presence and even Liz's description of him as a 'thug'.

After the statement was printed, Todd said, "We'll all sign this with Sty as a witness to our signatures, then I'll deliver it to the troopers in Ray Brook, first thing tomorrow morning. The sooner it's on record, the better."

Liz chuckled and reminded him, "Don't forget you have to clean Sty's trout before I can cook them for dinner."

Todd groaned, but admitted that the delicious trout would be worth the effort of cleaning them. He headed for the kitchen, where the trout had been left in cold water.

CHAPTER ELEVEN

"You shall not be afraid of the terror
by night, Nor of the arrow that flies by
day, Nor of the pestilence that walks in
darkness, Nor of the destruction that lays
waste at noonday. (Psalm 91:5-6 NKJV)

Wendy carried a basket of sheets and towels downstairs to the laundry. She told Patty, "One more load from the other side of the house, and we'll have everything down here."

Patty placed the sheets in the washing machine, poured in detergent and assured Wendy, "I could've carried them down. You don't have to do it all."

Wendy laughed, and said, "I have an ulterior motive. I ate so much of that lovely coq au vin at dinner last night and then had seconds of the lemon meringue pie. That was after having two helpings of the trout the night before! How can something that tastes as light as lemon meringue be loaded in calories? I have to work it off. It isn't fair!"

Patty laughed, and then admitted, "I gave up trying to lose weight years ago. I'm round as a barrel and that's the way I'm supposed to be! As long as I still have a lap for my grandchildren, the family won't complain. By the way, did you take some of your clothes off the line from the last wash I did?"

"No, I brought all my clothes up here with me, so I haven't run out of clean things yet, why?"

"I brought the last load of sheets in and put your things in your room, but I thought you had more than that."

"Yes, I did. I wonder if I put them away and then forgot. I'm sure they weren't stolen off the line by the birds to line their nests."

Patty chuckled at the idea of Wendy's clothes used by their wild neighbors. Wendy went upstairs to get the rest of the laundry. Tourists who saw the sign on the highway had stopped, giving them a full house for the past week, and their guests had been good company. Everyone had enjoyed Liz's food, the ambience of The Greenhouse Bed and Breakfast and shopping in Lake Placid village. Todd had easily persuaded Clive DuBois to take a group on several hikes up Mount Colburn, the rounded mountain that rose behind them. The hikes, with different participants, were spread over a period of two days. Both the guests and Todd had returned exhausted the second day, but Clive took it in stride as if it had been just a leisurely stroll. Knowing that Clive's seventy-two years sat lightly on the experienced outdoorsman didn't help Todd's ego. To Wendy's amusement, he refused to admit that the hikes had worn him out and insisted on going fishing with several guests the next day

Wendy had developed the habit of walking the length of the driveway to see if anyone was hiding where they had seen a car concealed earlier. Now that it was early May, she began to relax, hoping that John Dennehy had decided to forego his plans for vengeance. The B and B had been busy, with guests every weekend, and some through the week. She was sure that the number of guests coming and going, as well as Dan leaving his Forest Ranger vehicle at the house while visiting, was sufficient to keep them safe. *There's safety in numbers*, she thought.

. While she was making beds, the phone rang and the caller identified himself as Joel Greene, the personal assistant to Madame Olga Stravizinky. When Wendy asked who that was, he indignantly informed her that she was *the* primary soprano with the New Orleans Opera Company. Madame was planning on spending a long weekend in the Adirondacks, the weekend after next, "for the fresh air." He commented that *of course* Madame had to stay someplace where the cuisine was excellent. "Not just good, mind you. Madame is an epicure and insists on eating nothing but the *finest cuisine.*"

Wendy assured him that the food at The Greenhouse Bed and Breakfast would meet her exacting requirements. He went on to inform her that Madame liked to sleep late and then eat a sumptuous breakfast. Wendy described the waffles served with local maple syrup they often served, "with maple smoked bacon or local home-made sausage", she added.

"Ohh, that sounds wonderful. She can go for gentle walks in the forest glades nearby, can't she?" he responded. Wendy was glad she had her back to the dense forest behind the house when she answered, "Of course she can." *Forgive me, Lord, it's only half a lie. There must be some gentle walks out there.* Aloud, she said, "We'll walk with her, if she wants company. Are you coming with her?"

"Yes, and I'd like to have a room next to hers, so she can talk to me any time she needs to. She likes to discuss her upcoming roles in depth before the new opera season begins."

Wendy assured him that the rooms were available She thought, *I hope Madame knows what walks in the Adirondacks are like. Oh well, she'll find out.*

She finished making the beds and went downstairs to enter Madame Stravizinky and Mr. Greene in the reservations book-- with a note in red for Liz to read, "haute cuisine!" Then she and Patty sat down with cups of coffee and discussed the problem of John Dennehy's threat. Wendy twirled strands of hair and admitted, "I don't know how we can protect the place. It would take a small army to patrol the lawns around the house to make sure that someone like Stan Gubinsky wasn't setting up illegal fireworks aimed at our house."

They jumped when they heard a knock at the back door, and then Dan stuck his head in and said, "I just stopped by for coffee, but come out here and look at what I found on your porch."

As if drawn by an invisible magnet, Liz appeared, ready to invite him in. First, she stepped out onto the porch to see what he was referring to. She screamed, her voice resonating with fear. Wendy and Patty, followed by Todd, raced out the door. All of them shrank back at sight of the object at their feet.

"Those are your clothes, Wendy," said Patty, her voice shaking. A bloody squirrel wore Wendy's powder blue sleeveless tank top. Her underpants, streaked with blood on the crotch were also on the body.

"Wait here," ordered Dan. He hurried to his truck and returned with a digital camera. He took a few close-up pictures of the animal, and then stepped back to include the setting of the porch and the back door. Then he asked if Wendy had a plastic grocery bag. When she brought it, he placed the animal, with the clothes, in the bag. "I'll report this to the troopers as soon as I leave here. This is certainly a threat." He put the bag in his truck.

Inside, Dan washed his hands thoroughly. Once seated with a cup of coffee in front of him, the young Forest Ranger pulled his notebook from his pocket and said, "I checked the license plate of the car that was hidden and then beat it out of here. It belongs to a Stan Gubinsky." When they looked alarmed, he asked, "Who is he, and why would he be here?"

Wendy explained that Gubinsky appeared to be a "muscle man" who worked for John Dennehy. "I think he's dangerous, a thug who follows Dennehy's orders. I wonder who thought of killing the squirrel and taking my clothes off the line to dress it in."

"It looks like either Dennehy or Gubinsky are likely," said Dan. "You're going to need all the help you can get on the Fourth of July. I'll do what I can to line up volunteers. Patty, did you know about this?"

Patty ran the fingers of both hands through her hair. "Yes, I do, and I'm worried."

"Will the Brewsters and your clan, the Halseys, make themselves available to do guard duty?"

"I don't know why not. They always pitch in whenever someone needs help. This situation certainly qualifies. We'll be here!"

Liz glanced at the calendar and said, "The Fourth of July is on a Sunday this year. Why don't we have several barbeques through the weekend of the Fourth? We could feed everyone who is willing to come by. We'll make a Fourth of July party of it, all weekend long!"

"Great idea!" said Wendy. "I was just thinking we'd be beholden to Dan's friends and other people who might be willing to stand guard. Now, I'm thinking they'll have a good time. Let's start on Saturday and keep going, as long as there are people to feed. Okay, Liz?"

"Okay! This sounds great! I'll make my famous potato salad, and cook spare ribs on the outdoor charcoal grill."

Wendy told everyone about the famous opera star Madame Stravizinky, who would be with them in two weeks. Liz and Wendy made up menus for that weekend, making them as lavish as their budget allowed. Liz almost glowed, apparently in her element with the elaborate meals.

Then Liz and Dan left to walk the trails behind the property; Wendy and Todd went outdoors and lounged in the sun on the front lawn's Adirondack chairs. They discussed Dennehy's threat and how best to handle it. Both admitted they were nervous.

Wendy was relieved that they had delivered their statement to a local judge and decided they should give her an addendum concerning the squirrel. Judge Andrews had assured them that a summons would be issued, but she had admitted there was no means of forcing Dennehy to respond to it. Patty joined them and distracted them as she verbally made a list of who to invite to the "guard party barbeque", as she called it. Wendy reminded Patty about Madame, as she had begun to refer to their operatic guest. She said, "Liz and I made a menu that would be suitable for a queen, even an operatic queen."

Patty said, "I can't wait to meet her. If she looks like the opera stars I've seen in magazines and on TV, she'll make me feel skinny!" They were laughing at Patty's remark when they heard a piercing scream from the back of the house. The three of them hurried to the top of the driveway, where a teenaged girl stood trembling, both hands over her face. Patty trotted up to her and threw her arms around her niece. "What is it, Kinsey? Come on, tell Aunt Patty. What's the matter?"

The girl's quaking fingers pointed to the thick wild blueberry bushes that grew along the driveway. "There's a d…d…d…dead…b…b…body in there. I was checking the…the b…b…b…blueberries to see if they were g…g…g…gettin' ripe, and I saw him!" She threw her arms around Patty and gave up trying to speak through her sobs.

Todd strode in the direction she had pointed, peered into the thick bushes and said, "There's a body here, all right, looks like two bullet holes in his chest."

"I'll call the troopers," Wendy hurried to the house.

Within five minutes, two troopers arrived with an investigator from the New York State B.C.I. He identified himself as Tom Decker and after looking over the body, he asked all of them to sit together so he could talk to them. Patty and Wendy quickly set up folding chairs on the back porch.

They observed one of the troopers studying the tires on Todd's Jeep. He even pressed a piece of blotting-type paper over the treads, apparently to obtain a match to some other treads.

A half hour later, an exhausted Wendy, Todd, Patty and Kinsey had explained for the third or fourth time that they did not know the man, nor did any of them own a gun. Investigator Decker stood up and asked. "Do you expect any guests in the next forty-eight hours?" he asked.

The trooper who had looked at Todd's tires approached and whispered in Decker's ear, then withdrew.

When Decker glanced at Wendy, she answered his question. "No, no one's expected until the weekend. That family has had reservations for several weeks. There won't be any problem with their coming, will there? We can't afford to turn guests away."

"We need to check a few things. I can't make any promises, but if you all check out, we should be wrapped up by the weekend. Now, I'd like to see all your driver's licenses." Todd pulled out his license, but Patty had to go into the kitchen for her purse, and Wendy had to go upstairs for hers. Kinsey blushed and told the trooper that she didn't yet have a license. Upon being handed the licenses, he peered at each one and then the person it belonged to, seeming to check the pictures with the person. He started to fill out the license numbers on a page in his folder, but Wendy asked, "Do you want me to make copies of them for you?"

"Yes, thanks. That'll save me time." He handed her the licenses and she went into the house to use the copier in the office.

As soon as she returned, Decker repeated, "I want to ask you again, do you remember ever seeing him before?"

Kinsey let out a fresh wail, so Patty put her arms around her niece and hugged her. Kinsey's tee-shirt was rumpled, so Patty pulled it down, smoothing it over the girl's back. The gesture seemed to calm Kinsey, and she bravely tried to smile at her aunt.

Todd spoke out, "No, we didn't. He was obviously dumped here after being killed somewhere else." At a glare from the investigator, he continued, "He wasn't bleeding onto the ground where he lay, so apparently he bled out somewhere else. There wasn't even much blood on his shirt, just a little around the bullet holes."

The trooper threw his hands in the air. "Another CSI fan, I see." Todd stared at him, eyebrows raised, and the trooper admitted, "You're right, it looks like that, and fresh tire tracks in the dirt at the edge of the road near where he was found indicates that someone stopped there recently, probably last night. That's why I had the tires on your Jeep checked. They don't match, lucky for you."

Wendy leaned forward. "We should tell him about John Dennehy, and the statement we gave the judge. If Dennehy's been served with the summons, this could be his way of telling us that he means business. After all, what could be worse for a bed and breakfast that caters to families, than to find a dead body on the grounds? Also, Mr. Decker should know about the dead squirrel dressed in my clothes."

'What's this?" the trooper asked. He pulled his chair close to Wendy's and signaled to Todd to move closer. They told him about the dead squirrel and that Dan Picard had pictures. Wendy said she'd get a copy of the statement and went into the house. She gave it to the trooper and he read it carefully. He asked if he could keep it and without waiting for an answer, put it in his folder.

Just then, an ambulance pulled into the driveway. There were no lights flashing, and hey had heard no sirens, so they assumed the ambulance personnel must have been informed they were picking up a dead body, so had no need to hurry.

Then Trooper Decker asked, "Could the dead guy be this Gubinsky thug?"

"I only glanced at the face," Todd said. "I didn't look close enough to be sure." He tried to look away as the trooper gestured to him to come with him, but he had to follow. The light in the ambulance was dim, but Todd looked closely at the pallid face. "No, that isn't him, another thug of Dennehy's, maybe? A falling out among crooks?"

"Who knows? We'll pick up this Dennehy and find out where he was this afternoon. We'll also ask if he shoots squirrels. By then, we should know what caliber bullet was used on the squirrel and we can ask if Dennehy owns one of that caliber..." He accompanied Todd back to the porch. "In the meantime, none of you are to leave town." He addressed himself to Wendy and said, "Thanks for copying everyone's driver's licenses. That'll save time."

"Will you keep in touch and let us know what you find out?" asked Wendy.

"If you want to call me in about a week, I'll let you know of any developments, but don't expect details." He handed Wendy his card and after his gaze lingered on her for a moment, he said goodbye.

Kinsey asked, "Aunt Patty, do you still want me to help you wash the windows?"

"Yes, hon, but let's start that job tomorrow. You've been through enough today."

Liz announced, "It's time for chocolate chip cookies. Let's go inside."

Kinsey said, "I don't know if I can eat anything, but I'll come with you." Once the cookies were in front of Kinsey, the enticing aroma persuaded the girl that she could eat. "Maybe one," but Wendy was pleased to see that she ate several even before Patty poured lemonade for them.

"Do you suppose we could ask Mr. Decker if the crime scene tape around the blueberry bushes can be removed by the weekend?" Wendy asked as she and Todd returned to the porch. She peered at the three troopers crawling on their hands and knees in the bushes.

"Let's wait a few days before we bother him," said Todd. "He's got enough to think about right now. I'm sure that B.C.I. will concentrate on identifying the body. Besides, the crime scene guys are still poking through the leaves in the blueberry bushes. I don't think they'll find anything, but they have to follow procedures."

Wendy glanced at him with a smirk, and he admitted, "Yes, I follow CSI, so I know the general routine, but that's it. Decker doesn't have to worry that I'll play detective. I can't help wondering what Dennehy will think of next. If he was responsible for the body!" In answer to Wendy's raised eyebrows, he admitted, "Yes, I believe he's responsible. This could just be the next step in a harassment scheme. I'll go in and write an addendum to our original statement, and file it with the troopers."

He went in the house, but Wendy remained on the porch. Now that she was alone, she knew she had to give the problem to God. Tipping her head back to the clear blue sky above, she pleaded, "Father God, we ask again for your protection. We don't know just what we're up against here, but this doesn't look good. Please protect us, our home and all those who live under our roof, those who live here permanently, or our guests. Thank you, Father."

CHAPTER TWELVE

Be strong and of good courage; do
not be afraid, nor be dismayed, for the
Lord your God is with you wherever
you go." (Joshua 1:9 NKJV)

Wendy looked over the menu she and Liz had planned for Madame Stravizinky's visit. She said, "I know she'll love the food here, but I hope she doesn't expect The Greenhouse to be sophisticated."

Liz shrugged. "All we have to do is feed her well and take her for gentle walks. That's the impression you had from her personal assistant, right?"

"Yes, and I see no reason why she would expect anything else. The weather is lovely now. But rain is expected for tonight, but clearing tomorrow."

Todd groaned, "The TV forecast is usually correct for Vermont, but with the mountains surrounding us, weather in Lake Placid is so variable, there's no telling what we'll get."

"Before I get involved with other things and forget," Wendy said, "I want to call the editor of the local paper and see if he was planning on running an article about the body found here." She pulled the phone book toward her and looked up the Adirondack Daily Enterprise's number. As she dialed, she muttered, "Good thing we advertise with them. I'm sure they don't want to offend an advertiser."

When she was connected with the editor, she introduced herself and asked how much attention the paper was going to pay to the presence of a body found on the premises. "Of course, it would be bad for business if it got much attention." She listened for a minute and then said, "Yes, I know the police blotter is listed, but we'd appreciate it if there was no further press coverage about the body found here. I understand from a recent conversation with the troopers that they don't yet have an identity, but they feel it isn't a local." She listened again, then thanked the editor for his time and said goodbye.

"Okay, he said that they didn't have anything to report beyond what would appear in the police blotter, which is a bare-bones statement of who, what, and where. If an identity is made and especially if it's someone with local ties, he feels they would have to run an article. So far, they don't know any more than we do, which is very little".

"Good!" said Todd. "Not that I think that city papers would pick up a local article mentioning it, but we're better off if little is printed about it. Oh, here she is..." He went to the back door, followed by both Wendy and Liz.

A glossy black BMW with rental plates had just parked in back of the house. A thin, spry young man hopped from behind the wheel and opened the passenger door. A tall, portly woman got out of the car. She moved with a dignified grace as she made her way to the porch.

"Welcome to The Greenhouse," said Wendy. The woman smiled at the three young people. Speaking with a slight middle-European accent, she said, "How lovely." She gestured around the wide yard and stared at the tall white pines that bordered the yard. "This is stunning. How fortunate you are to live in such a beautiful place." She approached them, and then seized one of Wendy's hands and one of Liz's. She said, "I am Olga Stravizinky, tell me your names." Wendy introduced herself and Todd, and then introduced Liz as the chef. "I am so pleased to meet you." Her slight accent gave a pleasant lilt to her words that intrigued Wendy.

She asked, "You are family?" Wendy explained that she and Todd were brother and sister, and that Liz was like a sister to them.

"How wonderful, that you work here together. That is the way it should be, that friends and family work together! Yes?"

"Yes, you're right," answered Todd. "It couldn't have worked out better, that we each have the talents that we need to run this place."

Wendy noticed the man had emptied the car of a huge amount of luggage, so she suggested, "Let me show you to your rooms. Todd will help with the luggage." Madame Stravizinky introduced her personal assistant, Joel Greene. Wendy led them into the house. Todd and Joel made two trips each to place all the luggage in Madame Stravizinky's room. Joel's luggage amounted to only a small suitcase and a laptop computer. Wendy suggested, "When you're settled in, please come downstairs to the parlor for tea and muffins." Madame looked delighted at her suggestion and promised that she would be with them shortly.

True to her word, ten minutes later, Olga appeared wearing beige linen slacks and a long-sleeved magenta silk blouse. She admired the paintings and the carving of a buck on the mantle. Joel personally served her a cup of tea and offered a plate of maple-walnut muffins. Then he excused himself and, taking a muffin with him, he went out onto the front porch, where he settled into a chair to admire the view of the lake. Madame told Wendy how pleased she was with the elegant décor of the Azalea Room.

Madame finished he muffin quickly. "It was very delicious, Liz. Do you find the maple syrup locally?" she asked.

"Yes, there are a number of locals who make their own maple syrup. We're lucky that our housekeeper knows them all, so we had fresh maple syrup delivered as soon as we set up in business."

"How fortunate! I now consider you my friends, so you must call me Olga. My last name is too difficult to manage on a daily basis. Is that to your satisfaction?"

"Yes, we're honored to be on a first name basis with you and very pleased that you are our guest," answered Wendy. "Tell me, what is the season of the New Orleans Opera?"

"We perform from October to April. We are a satellite group of the Brooklyn Opera Company, so I had to be in Brooklyn to discuss business. I could not resist the idea of the few hours' drive up here to Lake Placid. I am so pleased to be here in this lovely place."

Wendy asked Olga if she would like to finish her tea on the front porch in order to enjoy the fresh air and the lake view. Her suggestion was met with enthusiasm and the three women moved to chairs on the front porch. Todd excused himself to do some gardening and Joel commented that he was stiff from the long drive and asked if he could accompany him. Todd invited him to come with him.

When there was a lull in the conversation, Olga surprised Wendy and Liz by asking if they were upset by the recent event of the body found on the property.

Wendy looked startled, and asked, "How did you know? I didn't think it was in the papers. I…I mean, I hoped it wasn't."

"I saw a small article in a New York City paper, one that implied it was a gang killing, related to a drug dealer in New York." She looked intently at Wendy and said, "I hope you are safe here, that local police are watching out for villains who may invade this lovely place."

"Yes, we've met some New York State Troopers and we're friends with a New York Forest Ranger." To her surprise, Wendy felt that she could trust Olga enough to tell her about the threat from John Dennehy. She went on to explain that a group of friends, including forest rangers, would spend the Fourth of July weekend at the B and B for a two-day barbecue.

"How marvelous! Your Independence Day celebration spent with friends who will protect you! How American!"

That evening's dinner of fresh-caught trout was a great success. The lemon/rosemary sauce that Liz invented caused Olga to extravagantly praise the food. She ate with gusto. After dinner she asked if Wendy would walk with her and Joel. Wendy agreed and suggested the gentlest close by trail. Once she was on the trail behind the B and B, Olga looked at the trees and wildflowers with appreciation. She clasped her hands together in delight as a sparrow trilled its song from a branch.

Wendy smiled at Olga's dramatic enthusiasm at the sight of lush tender ferns, delicate trout lilies and sturdy hellebores. She was ecstatic when she was shown a small shady glade carpeted with the broad leaves and flowers of brilliant red trillium. "To think you live with this every day! How wonderful!" She was overcome with delight and hugged Wendy. Wendy returned her hug, but didn't admit that her indoor work to run the B and B allowed her very little time to enjoy the out-of-doors.

However, she vowed that in the future she and Liz would make time to walk the trails close to the house. She thought, *this is surprising.*

I'm learning more about the beauty of this place in the last two days than I have in the months I've lived here...

The narrow trail necessitated that Wendy walk in front of Olga. At a point where the trail dropped into a hollow and the ground was still damp from the last rain, Wendy noticed several heavy footprints. They were of large smooth-soled shoes, unlike the lugged soles that Todd and Clive wore while hiking. She looked around so she could remember the place later and warned Olga to walk around the damp spot. She decided she would mention the footprints to Dan when he came by that evening to see Liz.

Once they were back at the B and B, Olga accepted Liz's offer of lemonade and joined Wendy and Liz. On the front porch, she sat on a rocking chair. She looked out over the lake and watched the shadows of the trees lengthen in the water. She sighed in contentment. "This is so lovely. That villain John must not be allowed to interfere with your beautiful home. When I was younger and living in Bosnia, there were many villains, some posing as politicians. Some were ruffians who would kill anyone just because of their ancestry. This one seems to be only interested in money. That is often the most dangerous person, one who feels he is entitled to whatever he wants."

Olga stretched her legs and arms. "I think I would like to go to bed early. This fresh air has tired me." She hugged both women and went indoors.

Wendy smiled at Liz. "I'm so pleased to know Olga. She's nothing like I expected. I imagined a more formal personality. She's a delight to have here."

Liz agreed. "She must be brave. Hearing about John Dennehy didn't scare her at all. Her history in Bosnia must have something to do with that. She probably lived through some dangerous times."

Joel Greene crossed the yard to the house, having walked along the lakeshore after dinner with Todd. "I must go to bed early, all this walking has worn me out. So good night. Thanks for the lovely evening."

They said good night to him, aware of their own tiredness.

Wendy noticed dark clouds moving their way from the mountains. "Look, Liz, it seems that we'll have rain tonight. I won't complain.

Todd said that if it didn't rain soon, he'd have to water the gardens. The tulips are done for this year, but the hellebore are coming out. I had to look them up in one of Gram's garden books. I've never seen them before. They're very pretty. I really like the pink ones."

She laughed as Liz yawned widely. "Okay, so you're not a gardener. Sorry for going on so about the flowers. Well, I'm ready for a good night's sleep, too. Goodnight." They went indoors and Wendy set the alarms. Then, knowing that she had much to thank God for, she spent a half hour in prayer before going to bed.

CHAPTER THIRTEEN

Search me, O God, and know my heart; Try me, and know my anxieties; And see if there is any wicked way in me, And lead me in the way everlasting. (Psalm 139:23-24 NKJV)

Wendy fell into bed. The walk on the trail and the extra work in the kitchen to help Liz prepare elaborate meals for Madame Olga left her exhausted. She fell asleep.

A piercing scream jolted her awake. She sat up in bed, but rain drumming on the roof and a strong wind shuddering the house was all she heard. She was sure she had not dreamed the scream, so she jumped out of bed and put on her robe. She hurried into the hall, where she found Todd and Liz waiting.

"Did you hear a scream?" she asked. Both had heard it, but were unsure where it came from. Then again, a scream ripped through the night air, from the other side of the house.

"Olga?" asked Wendy, as they raced for Olga's room. "What could have happened?" They found her door open, and Joel Greene sitting on the edge of her bed. He was speaking soothing words, while stroking her forehead. Olga lay with her eyes closed, her pale face appearing ghostlike in the light from the hall. Joel glanced at them, and shook his head. They withdrew, knowing the situation was under control. After several minutes, Joel appeared at the bedroom door, closed it and motioned to draw them away.

"Is she all right?" Wendy whispered as she followed him.

"Yes, she'll be all right now. I'm sorry you were awakened. She hasn't had a nightmare in months. We hoped she was over it."

"Over what?" Wendy asked.

"During Hurricane Katrina, Madame was trapped for hours on the second floor of the opera house. She saw the water rising around the building and felt the wind shaking it. She was terrified, sure that she was about to die, but then the police arrived in a motorboat and rescued her. She had nightmares about it for months, until she had professional counseling. We thought she was over her fear. Tonight's wind and rain, in an unfamiliar place, well," he paused to wipe a handkerchief over his narrow, perspiring face. "As you heard, it started again. But she's all right now. I gave her a prescription sleeping pill, and I'm sure she'll sleep through the rest of the night. She might not even remember it in the morning."

Wendy said, "We'll take our cue from her and not mention it it if she doesn't."

"Thank you, I appreciate it," said Joel, as he returned to his room. His feet were dragging and his shoulders slumped tiredly.

"What an awesome responsibility he has," said Wendy.

"I guess you can never know what burdens other persons are carrying," said Liz. "I hope she doesn't remember this. She might be embarrassed. I'm preparing maple-walnut pancakes for breakfast tomorrow, with her favorite coffee. I hope she feels well enough to enjoy it."

The next morning dawned with watery sunshine, but there was little evidence of the storm. A few broken branches littered the lawn. Todd picked them up before breakfast, hoping that Olga wouldn't be reminded of her nightmare.

She came down to breakfast wearing a lovely peach-colored silk shawl over her shoulders and both hands clutching it at her chest. She looked tired, but greeted them with a smile. "I woke you last night, didn't I?" she asked. "I'm so sorry, I didn't expect that to happen."

Wendy hugged her and said, "It was no problem for us, Olga. I hope you got back to sleep all right."

"Yes, I have sleeping pills that I take if I have a nightmare. My therapist didn't want me to get addicted to them, so she was stern about taking them only at such times. They knock me right out, so it's just as well I don't take them often. I'll be groggy all morning unless I get some exercise."

"Perhaps we could take a walk after breakfast," suggested Wendy.

"Good idea," said Olga. "What is that heavenly scent? It smells like maple syrup, but there's more to it. What delight do you have for me this morning, Liz?"

"Come sit down, we're having maple-walnut pancakes this morning." Wendy led her guest to the dining room and Liz followed with pancakes, bacon and a pitcher of warm maple syrup.

Before they said grace, Olga told Liz that the lovely aroma that filled the room made her more eager than usual to thank God for his goodness. Both Liz and Wendy smiled, pleased that their guest was a practicing Christian and fit into their small family.

They all ate their fill, but over their second cups of coffee, as they were discussing which trail they should walk, Todd came in the house through the back door and suggested they walk down to the lake. "The trout might be really jumping this morning, and that's always a pleasant sight." Olga agreed with him.

Wendy noticed that Todd looked strained, so she sent Olga, Joel and Liz out the front door and asked Todd if there was a problem.

He said, "Let me call the troopers. Then I'll talk to you." Wendy listened as he told the troopers that another animal dressed in Wendy's clothes had been left on the back porch. "No, not a squirrel this time, it's a white-tailed fawn. It's a good-sized one, but it still has some of its spots. I didn't see any bullet holes, and from the way it's bleeding from the mouth, it looks like road-kill. …. No, I won't move it. I'll just cover it up so our guests can't see it Thanks, see you soon." He turned to Wendy and said, "Let me get one of those old sheets that Patty put away for dust clothes." He went into the laundry and returned with an old sheet, then went out the back door.

Wendy followed him, and burst into tears at the sight of the bloody long-legged fawn dressed in one of her blouses. She knelt by the fawn's side and asked, "How, uh, how did someone catch it? Gram always told us that the does hide their fawns so well that you could almost fall over one without seeing it."

"That's true, so I suspect this one is road-kill. There's a lot of broken bones, and I think its neck is broken. I'm no expert, but I've seen enough road-kill to know how their bodies get broken up. It must have been following its mother across the road and didn't run quite fast enough."

"Poor little thing, and then to be used for such a vicious purpose. Oh, here's the troopers." She stood up and stepped away from the fawn as a trooper's car pulled up. B.C.I. investigator Ted Decker got out and approached them.

He nodded to Wendy and said, "I heard the call, and I decided to take it." He approached the fawn and pulled back the sheet. He put on latex gloves before examining the body. "No bullet holes and a broken neck. I think your brother's right, Miss Bailey. Looks like road-kill to me. Tell me, how many articles of your clothing were missing from the clothesline?"

"This is the last item, Mr. Decker. I hope this means that whoever's doing this has run out of ammunition, so to speak, and it'll stop."

"I hope so too," he answered. "Now I'll see if they found anything." He nodded at several troopers who were approaching them from the road.

A trooper said, "There are tire tracks similar to the ones we found when the body was dumped." He looked at Wendy and said, "We took a cast, so we can compare them." The B.C.I. investigator moved out of Wendy's hearing to talk to the troopers, and then they all left, taking the dead fawn with them. They left Wendy's blouse with her. She held it between two fingers, knowing she wouldn't ever wear it again.

"Ready for breakfast?" Wendy asked Todd. "Liz put some pancakes in the warming oven for you."

"Thanks. I think I will eat now. Are you joining Olga and Liz on their walk?"

"Yes, Olga is leaving later this morning, so I'd like to spend some time with her before she goes." Wendy went into the kitchen and dropped the stained blouse into the garbage can.

Todd had just sat down at the kitchen table with his pancakes, when the phone rang. He answered the phone and Wendy saw his face turn red, apparently with anger. He covered the mouthpiece with his hand and whispered "Dennehy." She was proud to see that he was controlling his anger. He remained politely silent when John claimed he had an offer for him.

Todd held the phone so Wendy could hear. She was surprised when John said, "How does it feel to be working for your little sister, Todd? Wouldn't you rather be in charge? Isn't that what being a man is all about, being in charge?"

Todd answered, "That's none of your business, Dennehy." Suddenly Todd lost control of his temper. Wendy jumped away as he shouted, "You can quit leaving those dead animals on our porch! That's sick, just sick!"

Dennehy sounded puzzled as he asked, "What dead animals? I don't know what you're talking about." He sounded sincere, and Todd didn't respond for a moment. Then Dennehy said, "Look, if someone's leaving dead animals on your property, I hope you're talking to the police."

"You bet we are, and they're going to be talking to you!"

"I'll see what I can find out, but I can assure you, I wouldn't touch a dead animal under any circumstances. They're full of germs! You couldn't pay me enough to carry one to your porch or anywhere else. Look, I'll stop by and talk to you. I can make you an offer that's much better than anything your sister can offer."

"Don't bother. I want nothing to do with your offer!" Todd hung up abruptly, and then finished his breakfast. He chewed the bacon with such ferocity that Wendy had to chuckle at him.

Todd nodded at her and said, "There's nothing like taking out your anger on your breakfast. I'd better find something physical to do this morning, and burn off my mad at Dennehy."

Wendy was pleased so see that he spent most of the morning working on the flowerbeds, then dumped the broken limbs from the storm in a heap at the back of the property. Then, when Olga was ready to leave, he helped Joel carry Olga's luggage to the car. Olga hugged each of them and promised that she'd be back at the first opportunity. She gave Wendy her card with her address and phone number and exacted a promise that they would keep in touch. "Don't forget to tell me about your Fourth of July barbecue. I want to hear about all the fun!"

Wendy promised and she, Todd and Liz stood together to wave goodbye as the car left. They had just turned to go back in the house when another car pulled into the driveway. They stared as the bright yellow, sleek, antique vehicle drew close. Then Wendy whispered, "Oh, no! It's Dennehy."

In a tone of awe, Todd said, "It's a Hispano–Suiza. I've only seen pictures of them before." Wendy was amused to see that Todd was conflicted, desiring to see the elegant automobile, but not wanting to let Dennehy see that he was impressed. The top was down, exposing elegant leather seats. John Dennehy, dressed in a 20's duster and matching driving cap, slid from the car. He stood by it, one slim, leather–gloved hand resting casually on the door. "It's really something, isn't it? They knew how to build cars in France back then, didn't they?"

Wendy asked, "Was this your grandfather's car?"

Dennehy looked surprised and disappointed, then asked, "How did you know?"

"Gram mentioned it in her letter to me, saying that her blood ran cold when your grandfather turned up in his Hispano–Suiza. I'm not surprised. Are you responsible for the dead animals?"

"No! As I told your brother, I wouldn't touch a dead animal. I have a hunch who might be responsible, but I'm not going to say anything now. Would you like a ride? This old girl still rides as smooth as when she was new in 1915. Come on, I'll show you."

"No!" Wendy said sharply. Todd echoed her, saying, "No, we want nothing to do with you. Please leave the property."

"Okay, okay. I'm going," said Dennehy as he slid back in the car. He glanced at Todd and said, "Remember what I said. You oughta be working for me or for yourself, not for your little sister. Don't forget we have a hot date on the Fourth of July."

He drove away laughing, with Wendy staring openmouthed at Todd. Liz asked, "What did that jerk mean? Did he offer you a job?"

"No, but he hinted that he wanted to make me an offer when he called this morning. I told him off then, but he obviously wanted to show off his car."

Wendy shook her head, and said, "He really puzzles me. I think he was sincere when he said he wouldn't handle a dead animal, but of course, that doesn't mean he wouldn't hire someone to do it for him."

"Right, we don't know. But I doubt that he was responsible for the dead animals. It doesn't seem to be his style. He wants to impress us with how successful he is. You notice he only briefly mentioned the Fourth of July. I guess he thought that the threat of violence didn't fit with his elegant show-off antique car, and the clothes he wore to go with it."

"Show-off is right!" said Liz, her voice high in anger. "Well, we'll show him what the Fourth of July is like around here. We'll be cooking on all cylinders and it won't be his style!"

Wendy and Todd laughed, then applauded her tirade. They all went back inside.

The evening seemed almost too quiet without Olga's bright, cheerful chatter over dinner. They realized that they had become accustomed to her company and Wendy admitted that she would miss Olga's presence in their lives.

"We must keep in touch with her," she said to Todd and Liz at dinner. "I think she's going to be a regular guest here at the Greenhouse. I hope we'll have more people like Olga, those who want to come back year after year."

"I like that idea," said Todd. "There's nothing like repeat customers."

Wendy said, "Have you noticed that most of our guests are Christians? I thought at breakfast this morning that Olga fit nicely into our family."

Liz stared at Wendy and said, "Me too. I had the same thought. And our guests never said no when we asked if we could say grace before a meal. That young family with two children seemed relieved. They would have said grace, if you hadn't asked."

Todd said, "Is that because word is getting around, maybe through Sty and Eleanor, that we're a Christian household?"

"For some people, yes," answered Wendy. "But those who came here due to our web site, maybe picked up on something subtle in the ads you wrote, Todd."

He said, "The photo of the parlor shows the wooden cross on the wall. I thought I included it because it's hand carved Adirondack art, but maybe my subconscious wanted to tell people we're Christian."

"Good thought!" said Wendy. "In that case, your subconscious is working to our benefit, Todd. I mean, drawing the people we're comfortable with. I hope it continues."

Liz said, "God willing, it will!"

CHAPTER FOURTEEN

"Deliver me, O Lord, from evil men; preserve
me from violent men, who plan evil things
in their hearts. (Psalm 140:1 NKJV)

Dan didn't knock, but entered the house wearing a concerned expression. Wendy and Liz looked up from the Adirondack cookbook they were studying. Both noticed his expression and Liz asked, "Is there a problem, Dan?"

He looked at Wendy and said, "Yes. You mentioned seeing a footprint on the trail when you were walking with a guest and heard sounds when a guest was leaving. Since then I've been looking at the trail every time I've been here. I don't want to scare you, but," he pulled out his handkerchief and wiped perspiration from his forehead, then said, "There's tracks, large male footprints, enough of them that I think someone's watching you from the trail nearest the house."

Wendy said, "I thought I heard someone on several occasions, when I was in the back yard. In fact, last week, when Terry Johns was here to roto-till the vegetable garden, he thought he glimpsed someone on the trail, but when he looked closely, no one was there. I'm sure someone has been watching us, but he apparently doesn't stay long, because any time I heard a noise, I looked, and no one was there."

Liz asked, "What purpose could it serve for anyone to spy on us? It doesn't seem like something that John Dennehy would do, so who is it?"

'Good question," Dan said. "I would set a trap if it was my property."
He shook his head at Wendy's alarmed expression. "No, not to catch
someone, just to be sure that someone human is there. The deer are
always around, but their sharp hooves leave obvious tracks. If you were
in the habit of running water on the trail from your garden hose, tracks
would show up easily."

Liz said, "It might also let a snoop know that we're aware that he's
there. After all, why else would we water the trail?"

"True," agreed Dan. "Just put a trickle hose along the ten feet that
border your back yard, and let it soak in good."

"Good idea," said Wendy. "Todd got a trickle hose when he picked
up garden materials. He's using our grandmother's hand tools for the
most part. Patty's husband kept them oiled, so they haven't rusted
since they were last used. Did you see the tomato plants he put in last
week?"

"Yes, and that's a sturdy wire fence he put around the garden.
That was a big job, but it'll keep out the rabbits, since he buried it so
they couldn't dig underneath. Of course, the deer will jump right over
it. You can pick up some aluminum pie plates at the dollar store and
hang them from the fence. If there's any breeze blowing, they'll rattle
and keep the deer away. It'll work best if he can hang them at a slight
distance from the fence. Give them some room to bounce around in a
breeze."

Wendy said, "We usually have a breeze off the lake, so we'll do that.
Too bad getting rid of our snoop isn't as easy. Oh, look who's here."

B.C.I. Investigator Tom Decker approached the back door and
Wendy let him in before he had a chance to knock. He smiled warmly
and said, "I just have a quick question for you." He nodded at Todd who
came in the door immediately after him. Tom asked if they could sit
down, so Wendy gestured for them to enter the dining room. Decker
asked, "Do you know the name Otis Cleary?" They all shook their heads
negatively, so he passed around a grainy black and white photograph,
which apparently was taken when Cleary had been arrested. Again they
all shook their heads.

"He's the dead guy?" asked Todd.

Tom said, "Yes. He's had some work history with Dennehy, running drugs, doing some dirty work for him. I'm assuming he got in an argument with Dennehy, maybe shortchanged him on drug sales. That's only a guess, though." Then he pocketed the picture, said goodbye. He paid special attention to Wendy by shaking her hand and reminding her to call him personally if she had any problems. Wendy responded by inviting him and his family to attend the Fourth of July barbecue. He was pleased at the invitation and said he'd attend. Then he left, leaving the four people around the table shaking their heads in puzzlement.

Wendy told Todd about Dan's suggestion that they soak the portion of the trail that bordered their property. He agreed that it was a good idea and promised to run the soaker hose out to the trail.

He said, "Our snoop will get wet feet, at least, but I wish I knew who that is. Look, the next time you hear a sound from the trail, yell for me, and I'll get right out there." He laughed, and said, "I'll probably just scare some deer, but I can't think of anything else. Anything legal, that is."

"What could we do that is illegal, and would work?" asked Liz urgently.

Todd shrugged, and then said, "A snare trap, perhaps, but I'm afraid we'd catch an animal in it."

Dan and Wendy spoke at once. "No, don't do that," said Wendy. Dan said, "You'd get yourself in more trouble than it's worth. Don't do it. If you caught someone, he could sue, and would probably win, since a snare trap is illegal."

"Just kidding," admitted Todd. "I'll run the soaker hose out to the trail as soon as I water the tomatoes."

"You're becoming quite the farmer," teased Liz." How come?"

"My favorite part of summers spent here with our grandmother was helping her in the vegetable garden. You might say I'm replicating a fond memory. It's more work now, for some reason. Lack of Gram's company, I guess."

Liz offered coffee and oatmeal cookies, so they enjoyed their treat before going on with their self-appointed tasks. Then Todd returned to the garden, while Liz and Dan went into the parlor to practice ju-jitsu. Wendy found herself alone, so decided to work on plans for the July Fourth two-day barbecue. The grocery list she was writing had grown to an alarming length when she heard a shout from the back yard. She hurried out the back door and saw Todd facing two rough-looking men. She thought one of them might be Stan Gubinsky, judging from Liz's description. The other was a stranger. They both held what Wendy assumed were blackjacks, which they smacked against their palms. They stood facing Todd, who held a long-handled hoe across his body, gripping it with both hands.

"What do you want here?" Todd asked them.

Both men sneered, and Stan said, "You rich city slickers, thinkin' you're gonna come up here to the mountains an' make even more money. You're such fools, we felt you needed protection. I can supply it, for a reasonable fee. I was thinkin' maybe a thousand a month, startin' now, a'course."

"Protection money! Are you out of your mind?" shouted Todd. "I'll never pay, so you might as well leave now!"

Gubinsky noticed Wendy on the porch and changing his aggressive tone to a wheedling one, he said, "You got your little sister there to protect. You want her to be healthy, you better pay."

"No!" said Wendy. "You'll never get money from us, so you'd better leave."

Dan and Liz came out the door and Liz said, "That's Stan Gubinsky!"

Dan, standing right behind Wendy, asked, "Want me to call the troopers?"

"Not yet," said Wendy. She stepped to the edge of the porch and speaking firmly, she said, "Look, you've got one minute, and if you're not gone, we'll call the troopers and let them take care of you." She held her left arm up so she could easily see her watch and began counting off the seconds. She had reached thirty-three when the man accompanying Gubinsky grabbed his arm and whined, "Look, I don't wanna run into no state troopers. The ones downstate know me too well, an' we don't get along. Let's go!"

Gubinsky snarled and said, "You'll be sorry. You 'specially, little girl. I don't let no woman tell me what to do, an' you're gonna hear from me." Then he turned and stamped from the yard, followed by his companion.

Wendy watched him go with a profound sense of relief, but she realized that she was trembling. Liz came up to her and put her arms around her. Wendy leaned against her friend and immediately felt calmer.

Dan said, "Look, you should report this to the troopers. It's definitely a threat, and I'm sure he meant it. Write up a statement like you did last time, and deliver it as soon as you can."

"Yes," said Liz. "Write it up now!"

Todd said, "I want to finish putting in this row of seeds, but it'll only take a minute. Will you start the statement, Wendy? I'll be right in."

"Okay, but I don't know how to start, since I wasn't here until I heard you yell." When Todd gave her an exasperated look, she said," I'll start from what I heard and saw and you put in the beginning."

"You got it," said Todd as he turned back to the garden and pulled seed packets for carrots, lettuce and radishes from his pocket.

Wendy sat in front of the computer in the tiny office off of the kitchen. It took her only a couple of minutes to write her eyewitness account of the threatening event. Todd came in and she slid out of the chair so he could enter the arrival of the two thugs. When he was finished, Wendy suggested, "Save it and print it so we can run it out to the troopers. They're going to have quite a file on The Greenhouse Bed and Breakfast."

Todd did as she suggested. He picked up the sheet of paper and said, "I'll run this to Raybrook right after lunch."

Wendy had to remove her barbecue shopping list from the table before they could eat. Todd glanced over the list and said, "Looks good. It's going to be a real feast, even if it doesn't deter our would-be firebugs." At Wendy's alarmed expression, he added, "It will. There'll be dozens of people here for two days."

Wendy said, "I invited the women from the Adirondack Community Church when I was there Sunday. Also, they had said they were looking for someplace to hold a big outdoor event, and I said they could hold it here. The front lawn and side lawns would hold the number of people they hoped to attract. It's a mission event, so it should be fun and worthwhile."

"Did you mention Dennehy?" asked Todd.

"Yes, and they seemed to consider him a bully, nothing more. They want to come to look the place over before deciding on whether or not to hold their event here. There'll be about a dozen people coming over, including the pastor's family. The pastor is a really nice woman, and she's looking forward to seeing the greenhouse, because she's a gardener, both indoors and out."

"Good deal. The more people we have and the busier the property is, the less chance there'll be of problems."

Wendy said, "I'm sure you're right, especially with forest rangers and state troopers around. They'll create just the atmosphere we'll need. I've noticed that even out of uniform a police officer still has that police aura about him or her. They always look like they mean business."

Todd said, "You mean the 'Don't mess with me' aura, don't you?"

"Exactly. We've got to develop that aura ourselves, also."

Todd chuckled and said, "You already have, counting down the seconds to make Gubinsky and his chum leave. Boy, were they ticked!"

Liz looked worried as she said, "I hope that doesn't backfire on us. Maybe Gubinsky will think he has to prove something, like how much of a *big man* he is. But we'll be ready for him. He's obviously a bully, and he's not the sharpest marble in the drawer."

When both Wendy and Todd laughed, she said, "Well, you know what I mean, don't you?"

"Absolutely!" exclaimed Wendy. "I agree. He's dumb as a doorpost, as Gram would have said."

Liz looked puzzled, and then asked, "Are doorposts dumb, or just wooden?"

"Both, I think," said Wendy. "But, with God's help, we're more than a match for him."

"You bet!" said Todd. "That jerk didn't know what he was getting into, trying to scare off this family!"

CHAPTER FIFTEEN

"May our Lord Jesus Christ himself, and
God our Father, who has loved us and given
us everlasting consolation and good hope by
grace, comfort your hearts and establish you
in every good word and work."
(2 Thessalonians 2:16-17 NKJV)

After dinner, Wendy and Liz cleaned the kitchen. Wendy complemented Liz on their delicious dinner. "What a great idea to baste Cornish game hens with apple cider and glaze them with apple jelly! That was genius, Liz!" Liz smiled happily.

The phone rang and Wendy answered. Liz, washing the roasting pan, stared when Wendy's voice rose in surprise. She said, "No, we don't offer journalists a discount. Our rates are reasonable. The food is very good. The local farmer's markets carry fresh locally grown produce, which you'll appreciate. When were you planning to come to Lake Placid?" She listened, and then said, "Yes, we'd be pleased to accommodate you."

Wendy wrote on the register and then said, "We look forward to seeing you, Ms. Keyes. Bye"

She turned back to Liz, shook her head and said, "That Keyes woman thinks a lot of herself! She said that she's a highly accredited travel journalist and we should be pleased she's going to stay here. She assumed she'd get a discount, of all things."

"Keyes? Not Natalia Keyes? It must be!" cried Liz.

"Do you know her?" Wendy asked.

"I know *of* her because I read her travel articles. Do you realize what it would do for The Greenhouse B and B if she writes a complementary article on us? What a break!"

Liz jumped up and down, pumping her arms in the air. Wendy laughed at her, but Liz didn't curb her enthusiasm. "What will we serve her? It has to be the greatest food!"

"No, Liz. We'll serve her the same meals we've been serving our guests. Everyone has raved about your food. You couldn't improve it if you tried."

"Well, maybe. But I'm going to think about it. I'll come up with some really delicious meals. When is she coming? What room will you give her?"

Wendy chose to answer Liz's questions in the order in which she asked them. "Next week, Friday through Sunday. A room overlooking the lake, like the Azalea Room would impress her."

"See? You're impressed by Natalia Keyes too. Aren't you?"

Wendy shrugged, but she admitted, "Okay, I'm impressed. A glowing article in a travel magazine could really put us over the top. We wouldn't have to advertise for a year. Wouldn't it be nice to see an article on The Greenhouse in Traveler Magazine?"

"You bet! Who else will be here that weekend?"

"It'll be quiet. There's just Linda and Paul Graham, a young couple with two pre-teen children. When I talked to her on the phone, she said they were looking forward to riding the elevator to the top of the ski jump tower." She glanced at an ORDA schedule by the phone. "What luck! There's going to be a ski jump competition next weekend. Remember, Liz, Patty told us how great it is to see the skiers zoom down that long steep slope, sail through the air and land in the pool at the bottom with a great splash. The Graham's kids will be thrilled."

"I'd like to see it myself," Liz admitted. "I meant to go earlier, but we were too busy, and I just couldn't make it."

Wendy nodded in agreement. "Me too. We'll both go with them. Linda said she wants to attend the nine o'clock service at the Adirondack Community Church because they attend a Methodist church in New

York, and from what I told her, she thinks they'll feel at home at our church. That'll give them the rest of the day to see the sights. I'm pleased that so many professed Christians are coming here. Do you realize that over half of our guests have gone to church with us?"

"I sure do. It's great to share that experience with new people. I wonder what Natalia will be like. From the tone she usually takes in her articles, I think she's quite upbeat. I'm looking forward to meeting her."

The next week was busy as both Wendy and Liz helped Todd with the gardening. In spite of only light rains, which Todd augmented with sprinklers, both weeds and vegetables flourished. Liz harvested lettuce, peas, beans and tomatoes daily. She was thrilled to see the Butter and Sugar sweet corn grow taller by the day. Sweet corn was her favorite food and she anticipated cooking and serving it.

On Friday afternoon, Liz left the garden with a pail full of fresh vegetables. Tom Decker was visiting Wendy, so she had left the garden to sit on the back porch and visit with him. Liz noticed that Tom wasn't discussing the threat implied by Cleary's body appearing on the property, but instead seemed to be exchanging personal information with Wendy. She thought, *I believe the man is smitten with her.*

Before Liz went into the house, she said, "You'd better wash up, Wendy. Your clothes and hands look look like you've been gardening."

Wendy grinned at Liz's motherly attitude and excused herself to Tom. When she got to her feet, he admitted that it was time for him to go to work. Before leaving, he kissed Wendy on the cheek. She blushed and smiled as she entered the house.

Both Wendy and Liz were on the back porch with a pitcher of lemonade and what Wendy had begun calling "Liz's Famous Triple Chocolate Cookies", when a sleek red sports car pulled in the driveway.

"A Jag," whispered Liz. Wendy glanced at her friend and saw a wide-eyed Liz staring at the car in open admiration. "I'm not sure, but I think it's from the sixties."

Then she gasped when a slender brunette slid from the car. She popped the trunk of her car, but only took out a makeup case. She was dressed in a classic chic pencil skirt, a fitted jacket and what appeared to be a silk top. "Guccci," said Liz, still in a whisper. "Just how successful *is* she?"

Wendy whispered, "Maybe she knows some top fashion designers." She walked forward to greet their guest. "Natalia?" she asked. When the other woman nodded, she introduced herself, and introduced Liz as her friend and the B and B's chef. "Would you like to have some lemonade and cookies before going to your room?" Wendy asked.

"Oh, yes. I hate driving, but there are some places that aren't available by any other means." She waved a casual hand at the sports car and admitted. "That's why I have the Jag. If I must drive, I might as well enjoy it."

"I know what you mean," said Wendy and poured lemonade for their guest.

"I don't suppose you have anything stronger than lemonade?"

"No, we don't serve liquor." Wendy passed the cookies to their guest, who enthusiastically took one. "The only exception to our no-liquor practice was late this spring when a couple came here to spend a week for their second honeymoon. It was their fiftieth anniversary. Their honeymoon was spent here when my grandmother was running the place. They brought a bottle of the same kind of wine that was served at their wedding reception. Gram had been pleased to relax her usual no-liquor custom. I could do no less for a couple married fifty years."

"Ah, you're sentimental," said Natalia with a smile.

"True," Wendy admitted.

"Ummm, these cookies are heavenly. Liz, did you make them?"

"I did, and no one has ever complained. In fact, we have friends who always ask if I'll make them, when they're invited here."

"Don't blame them, but how do you two stay so slim? If I had these available to me, I'd eat myself into a size twenty."

"We're too busy to sit down and snack," explained Liz. "I have a personal rule, which Wendy's adopted. I only eat when I can sit down and relax. Between the vegetable garden, preparing meals and my ju-jitsu exercises, I don't often sit down."

"Ju-jitsu! No wonder you're slim. Now, I'd like to go to my room and change."

Wendy and Liz both helped Natalia unload her luggage. It had been a tight squeeze to get four suitcases into the tiny car, but Natalia had done it. Liz carried two and Wendy and Natalia each carried one upstairs.

In the Azalea Room, their guest walked directly to the window and admired the sunny ripples on the lake. "How lovely, and look at that graceful bird flying over there. Look, he's plunging into the lake. Wow! He's caught a fish. It's almost as big as he is. I've never seen anything like that before. How natural all this is. Those hills across the lake are so green. This is beautiful!" She spun around to observe the room. "And this room! The azalea prints on the wall match the bedspread. You must tell me how you found all these pillows and pictures to make the room fit its name."

Wendy explained the history of how the rooms were named by her grandmother. Natalia seemed to be touched by the story, but she said, "It's too bad we can't pop into the bar now and drink a toast to your grandmother's ingenuity." She sprawled into the wing chair by the window, "Don't you think you'd be more successful if you forgot about your grandmother's no-liquor policy? After all, everyone drinks at least a little today."

Wendy heard the shrill cries of children and looked out the window. Two children were running toward the lake, with Todd and a tall man following them.

"It looks like our other guests are here, so I'd better go downstairs. If there's anything I can do for you, just come down and ask." She hurried from the room, relieved not to have to pursue the subject of alcohol. She thought, *a bar, of all things. Is that what she considers necessary to run a successful bed and breakfast? I hope she isn't going to write a bad review on us, just because we don't serve liquor.*

She found Linda Graham removing luggage from their loaded SUV and hurried to help her. After they introduced themselves, Linda removed two large bags of toys and asked, "How can two children need so much to travel for a long weekend? No, they don't need it, they just want it." She and Wendy laughed. Wendy suggested, "Don't try to carry all this in. The men are back, and they can carry it in."

Todd introduced Wendy to Paul Graham and the two children, Pam and Nate. The men carried the luggage up to the Rhododendron Room. The children listened to instructions not to go near the lake alone, then raced downstairs and burned off their excess energy by running around the lawns.

Upstairs, Paul set strode to the window that overlooked the rhododendron bed on a side lawn. "Look, Linda. Those rhodies have blossoms the size of dinner plates."

Linda abandoned the suitcase she was unpacking and joined him at the window. "Wow!" she said. "Mine don't grow that big. Wendy, you must have a green thumb."

Wendy put a bag of toys in a corner and admitted, "That's mostly Todd's doing. He takes care of the gardens. He learned how when we were children visiting our grandmother here. She called him her junior gardener. Would you like to sit down with a glass of lemonade or would you like stroll to get the travel kinks out of your legs?"

Paul said, "I'd like to walk around the house and enjoy the views of the mountains and the lake, then I'd love some lemonade."

"Me too," said Linda.

On the back porch, Todd had brought out enough folding chairs for all of them. The children decided that lemonade was more appealing than running around, so dropped, out of breath, onto the porch.

Natalia and Linda exchanged memories of travels they had taken in Europe during their college years. Linda smiled fondly and said, "I really enjoyed visiting the cathedrals. They're so impressive. Just think, they were built before modern machinery was available. They had nothing but the use of the inclined plane and brute labor. It must have taken such devotion to build them."

"Oh, I don't know about the devotion," Natalia said. "Most of them were ordered built by kings and emperors to impress everyone with their power and their supposed closeness to God." She waved a hand in dismissal. "Such ego!"

Linda admitted, "Yes, ego always plays a role in the actions of kings and emperors, but faith must have been a factor in their actions."

Wendy was concerned that the conversation might become unpleasant. She was relieved when Liz called that dinner would be on the table in five minutes. Linda herded her children to the bathroom to wash their hands, while Wendy joined Liz in the kitchen to help bring dinner to the table. She sniffed appreciatively at the rack of lamb and garlic mashed potatoes. The tossed salad was one of Liz's multi-layered concoctions. Wendy knew this dinner would impress Natalia, which she realized was Liz's intention.

When everyone was seated, Wendy said a short, heartfelt grace, and then picked up her napkin. She noticed Natalia was already serving herself salad, apparently having chosen to ignore the grace. *Oh my, another strike against us. No matter, we'll just carry on as usual. Her dinner's been prayed over, like it or not.*

Everyone enjoyed the dinner and the dessert of lemon meringue pie met with raves from each one, including the children. Nate had claimed he didn't like lemon, but after his first taste, he changed his mind and ate with enthusiasm.

Mosquitoes were buzzing around the porches, so Wendy offered a tour of the greenhouse. The women admired the flowers, especially the orchids, while Paul inspected the construction. Wendy was asked so many questions about growing orchids that she finally had to resort to her small collection of orchid books to answer them. They ended the evening sitting at the greenhouse's small wicker table sipping iced tea and eating tiny sugar cookies. When the children were too tired to keep their eyes open, the Grahams said they would all go to bed. Plans were made for the next day and they said goodnight.

After they had left, Wendy, Todd, Liz and Natalia stayed at the table. Natalia asked them all, "Don't you think having a bar would add to your B and B's ambiance?"

"No, it would take something away," said Todd bluntly. Natalia glanced at Wendy with raised eyebrows. Wendy explained, "We've discussed this before and feel this is a place where people who prefer to avoid alcohol can feel relaxed."

"In other words, a rest home for alcoholics?" asked Natalia.

"No, not really," Wendy answered. "We had a young couple here this winter who were expecting their first child this summer. She didn't drink and neither did her husband. They both appreciated a no-alcohol environment."

"Oh," was Natalia's only comment. She stretched her arms and said, "I'm going to turn in early, also. Good night, everyone." She left the greenhouse and went upstairs.

Liz looked worriedly at Wendy. "Do you think she'll give us a bad review because we don't serve alcohol?"

"If she's the professional I think she is, she won't let it color her article. If she does write one about us, she might mention it, which wouldn't hurt us at all."

Todd stood and said, "It might even help. A lot of people prefer to avoid a drinking atmosphere and the problems it can cause on occasion."

"Yes, we're doing what we were inspired to do," Wendy reminded him. "It just happens to be what Gram did, also. It's in keeping with the history of The Greenhouse. Natalia couldn't change my mind about that, no matter what her article might say. "

The next morning the sun was warm, but not hot as the group left the jump tower elevator and walked to the fenced off area around the pool the ski jumpers would land in. Todd said they were lucky to be there early, as the parking lot was filling rapidly. They watched as a group of slender young men and women started the climb to the top of the tower. They carried skis and ski boots and didn't seem daunted by the steep stairs.

"Why don't they take the elevator like we did?" Nate asked.

A nearby young tourist explained, "The climb gets them warmed up and that gives them better muscle control when they jump."

Nate nodded, impressed by the man's knowledge.

The group from The Greenhouse included Natalia, who to Wendy's surprise, had decided at the last minute to join them. She had remarked that the cold lake water didn't suit her for swimming, so she had nothing else to do.

"He's ready!" Nate shouted, pointing to the figure poised at the top of the jump. There were announcements of the order of the skiers, but a breeze distorted the words and couldn't be understood. There was a shout and the skier shot down the steep slope. The crowd gasped in unison as he soared off the end of the jump and soared high into the air, then landed with a splash. Pam and Nate laughed as water drops hit them.

Someone used a long pole to pull the skier to the edge of the pool and help him out. The crowd applauded enthusiastically as he shook water from his ski suit.

He was followed by ten others. Once the last one had landed, Paul picked up Pam and Linda took Nate's hand. Both children protested, but once in the car, they promptly fell asleep. "See you back at the B and B," Wendy said as she headed for Todd's car.

Natalia had ridden with Wendy, Liz and Todd. Before she got into the car, she took Wendy by the arm and led her several yards away. "Look, Wendy. I'm just trying to be helpful. Think about this. I assume that your success in business is important to you."

Wendy acknowledged that she was correct with a nod, but didn't speak.

"You could expand. For example, if you used one of the big lawns to put up a conference center type building, close to the water, with another twenty rooms, a large dining room and bar, you'd have a wildly successful business."

Wendy didn't bother to explain that the Adirondack Park Agency would never approve such an expansion. She just shook her head and said, "It would spoil The Greenhouse property and the pleasant ambiance we have. There's enough rooms available in Lake Placid. I'm convinced the area couldn't sustain another conference center. Also, I like getting to know my guests individually, going to church with them, taking hikes, and giving them the feeling that while they're here, they're family."

When Natalia started to turn away, Wendy added, "A Christian family, at that." She caught up with Natalia and walked arm in arm with her to the car.

Wendy had invited Tom to join them for a lunch of salads and sandwiches. Then they all piled into their cars to drive to Wilmington to travel up the eight-mile Veterans Memorial Highway and enjoy the view from the top of Whiteface Mountain.

"Oh my!" said Linda, as she held Pam's hand and leaned against one of the gigantic rocks that lined the overlook.

Below them the valley opened like a gift. Billows of evergreens were sprinkled with the sharp blue of lakes. "I see Lake Placid," Liz exclaimed. She pointed it out to Nate, "See, right there." The boy would have climbed on one of the rocks, but his father held him back. "Just look, don't climb. We'll go up to the tower in a few minutes."

Tom watched the delight fill Wendy's face. Her hair danced around her face in a tangle of gold. He had to reach out to touch it and she turned to him. He glanced at the others, absorbed in the view, and pulled her close for a kiss.

That evening, after a dinner of short ribs with Liz's tangy barbecue sauce and wild rice, everyone was so stuffed that they decided to sit on the front porch and enjoy the lake view. A breeze kept mosquitoes away. They enjoyed lemonade and home-made sherbet.

When Natalia's cell phone rang, she looked irritated, but answered. She listened for a moment, then jumped to her feet and paced the porch. "When?" Her staccato questions allowed little time for answers. "How serious is it?" and "Can he speak?" was followed by "I'll come right away." After a brief silence, she said, "But I should be there!…What do you mean, he won't know me?" She listened for a moment, then said, "All right, first thing tomorrow morning. But it's stupid, I won't sleep tonight. Okay, bye." She threw herself back into her chair and covered her face with her hands.

Wendy moved to the chair next to hers and put an arm around Natalia's shoulder. "Can you tell me?" Wendy asked quietly.

"My father had a stroke. My mother said he didn't know her. He was always my hero. He told me I could do and be anything I wanted." Her shoulders shook with sobs and she leaned toward Wendy.

A voice called from the lawn. "Wendy, I stopped by to see if I can help with plans for the fund-raiser. Oh, may I help you?" Carole moved to Natalia's side and looked questioningly at Wendy. Natalia looked up and asked, "Who are you?"

Wendy introduced Carole as the pastor of her church and told Carole that Natalia had just received the shocking news that her father had had a stroke.

Carole knelt in front of Natalia and asked, "May we pray for him?"

"Why?" Natalia asked. "God's never done anything for me. I doubt he exists."

"Carole spoke softly. "He's only waiting to be asked. He loves us all and will help if we ask. May I?"

"Oh, go ahead. It's useless, but who cares."

"God does," Carole said softly. "And we do." She glanced at Todd and Liz They moved next to her and placed their hands on Natalia's hands.

Carole's prayer was eloquent. It moved all those around her to tears. Finally, she sat back and said, "Now we can only continue to pray privately and wait." The small group around her returned to their chairs and bowed their heads in silent prayer. On occasion, one or more of them would stand to stretch, but continued praying. The moon had passed across the sky and stars were twinkling down on them when Natalia's phone rang. She snatched it up and answered. "Yes, Mom, what's happened?

"He did? Wonderful! I'll see you in the morning. Bye, Mom."

She told them, "He opened his eyes and recognized my mom. The doctor said it's a good sign." She threw her arms around Wendy and Carole. "You did it, you pulled off a miracle!"

"No," Carole told her, "God answered your prayer. It may take a long time for him to fully recover. He may need physical therapy and your encouragement."

"Yes, I will. I'll stand by him the way he always stood by me. Thank you, all of you." Natalia dried her tears as the group went indoors to go to bed.

CHAPTER SIXTEEN

"He who dwells in the most secret place of
the Most High shall abide under the shadow
of the Almighty. I will say of the Lord "He
is my refuge and my fortress; my God, in
Him I will trust."" (Psalm 91:1 NKJV)

Wendy stood in the shade of the largest apple tree near the driveway
and greeted people as they arrived for the July Fourth barbecue.
Within an hour, thirty people had parked their cars and greeted her.
Liz brought her a glass of lemonade and lingered to meet the guests.
Tom Decker arrived with a group of people who Wendy thought, from
their easy familiarity with him and each other, must be his family. He
introduced her to his brother Ted, his sister-in-law, Kim, and their
three children.

Kim was very friendly and outgoing. She and Liz hit it off
immediately When Liz mentioned there were jugs of lemonade in
the kitchen, the two women left to carry them out and soon appeared
with the jugs and paper cups. When Kim noticed that Tom and Wendy
were standing close together, she winked at him, and then handed out
sparklers to the children and shooed them onto the lawn to play. Wendy
wondered what the wink meant, but suspected she'd soon find out.

Wendy said to Tom, "I'm glad you could bring family with you.
That makes it so pleasant, to share an event with family."

"Yes, and this is rare. Ted is also a state trooper and we seldom have the same days off. I don't know how he did it, but he said he'd be here today, just to meet you."

"Why? Is it the puzzle of the dead animals, or maybe John Dennehy's threats?"

Kim grinned impishly and said, "No, Tom's talked about you so much that Ted felt he had to meet the woman who's created such interest in his younger brother." She laughed as Tom flushed, then she hugged Wendy and whispered, "He's a keeper."

Wendy sympathized with Tom's embarrassment and excused herself to get food from the house. Minutes later, she staggered out the backdoor carrying a huge bowl of potato salad. She laughed at Liz's remark that the "mother of all salads" was probably a Guinness Book of Records winner. She was greeted by the sight of over a dozen children racing around the lawns waving sparklers in loops and swirls, with tiny sparks trailing after them. She carried the salad toward a table set up in the shade, but Tom appeared to take it from her.

"Let me help, Wendy. You shouldn't carry anything this heavy. Is there more?"

Another trooper remarked, "Decker, you're just trying to get first dibs on the food. Look out for him, he's a champion eater!" His wife tried to shush him, but they all laughed, apparently accustomed to the good-natured ribbing. Wendy joined in their laughter and admitted that there was more food in the house. She said, "The church women brought salads and rolls, and Liz has been cooking up a storm."

Liz left the house with a large aluminum tub full of spareribs. She was ready to place the ribs on the grill. Wendy thought she looked like she meant business as she stood at the grill, holding tongs in one hand and a large mitt in the other. She was wrapped in her favorite apron, which always gave Wendy a laugh. It was bright red and was printed in white with the ju-jitsu gym's logo and the words, "Women Warriors Are Hot Cooks". Dan was with her, watching her fondly. Todd leaned over the aluminum tub, counting the ribs. He was unsure there would be enough, in spite of Liz's assurances that she had planned for large appetites.

More cars arrived, and Wendy walked out to meet them. Another group from the church arrived and Wendy introduced them to the troopers and forest rangers and their families. She noticed that as usual, groups were forming of people who were already familiar with one another. She took Carole around to various groups and introduced her to each of them. Carole caught on right away, and continued to move from group to group, bringing others with her. Before the ribs were ready to eat, people were mingling as if they were a community, rather than strangers only recently met.

Wendy and Todd stood on the back porch and looked over the more than fifty people gathered, some in the shade and others in the sun. Mothers were watching the children with sparklers, ensuring their safety. "This is turning out to be a great event," Todd said.

Wendy answered. "Yes, I'm beginning to feel that The Greenhouse Bed and Breakfast might be intended to be more than just a place to vacation. Carole and I were talking about the mission project she has in mind. It's a few local churches putting their efforts together to build a food pantry and thrift shop. It'll cost a great deal, so a few big events will have to be held. They thought to hold them in the Olympic Regional Development Authority building, but lately, ORDA's been told by the state that they have to charge for any use, even not-for-profits, so they had to think of someplace else. For outdoor events, we can put tents on the lawn, if need be. We can be available spring through fall."

"I had a feeling you'd do something like that. You've always been interested in mission projects." Wendy looked a question at him and he said, "It's a great idea!"

She said, "I was thinking of Gram yesterday, and remembering the kind of giving person she was. I wondered what I could do for others through my good fortune. I'm just beginning to find out what that is."

Todd started to walk toward the grill. He sniffed the air that was ripe with the scent of spare ribs slathered with Liz's apple cider barbecue sauce. Suddenly, he turned and darted toward the hiking trail. Dan and several troopers saw him and ran after him. Wendy followed slowly, unsure of what had caught Todd's attention. She watched as the four men raced along the edge of the trail, skirting damp footprints in the wet soil. They ran out of sight and Wendy stopped and murmured an urgent prayer for their safety.

Then, the ripping sound of an ATV sounded through the quiet mountain air. A few minutes later, the four men returned. A trooper was carrying several cardboard boxes that had red lightning bolts printed on their side. Another trooper carried a battered box, out of which protruded an ugly piece of metal. One trooper pulled out his cell phone, punched in an instant-dial number and began to describe the boxes. Tom joined them, then went to his car and brought back a point-and-shoot camera. He took photos of the footprints on the trail, then asked a trooper to stand on the trail for scale, and then stepped back to get a picture of the position of the trail in relation to the back yard and house. He spoke to the trooper who had made the phone call and returned to an anxious Wendy.

He said, "They had an ATV waiting at the point where the trail widens, at the intersection with the old logging road. The road hasn't been used for decades, but I see there's been some fresh clearing of it. Apparently, they've planned this for some time."

"Planned what?" Wendy asked.

"Some of those boxes have fireworks in them, and one has a home-made version of a grenade launcher. I've never seen one like this, but I've heard of them being used in cities to launch explosives into a building someone wants to destroy without having to be seen approaching it."

Wendy was so shocked that she feared she wouldn't be able to stand up, but Tom saw her start to waiver and put an arm around her. Liz promptly produced a folding chair and pushed it against the back of Wendy's knees. She was reluctant to release herself from Tom's arm, but finally sank into it.

When Todd approached her, she asked him, "Do you think this is one of John Dennehy's tricks?"

Tom answered, "We'll soon know. I called in the position of the ATV and we have troopers ready to pick them up when they try to exit the logging road. They have to exit at the state highway."

One of the troopers explained, "The footprints on the trail don't look like the ones I saw earlier, when we found the body. These are cleated hiking boots. The earlier ones looked like dress shoes. We could be dealing with two different persons or groups."

Wendy groaned, "Oh no. Just what we need, two sets of enemies."

Todd said, "Or two groups hired by one man who's operating behind the scenes."

Wendy said, "John said he'd have an "incendiary specialist" take care of his problem with us. By today, at that!"

Tom said, "That's what I was thinking also." He answered his phone, listened briefly and then said, "I'm on my way."

He spoke to Wendy and Todd, saying, "We've got them. I'm going in now to find out what they have to say for themselves. I suggest you continue your party and have a good time. No point in worrying. We've got it under control."

He bent over Wendy and kissed her cheek, then left.

The party went on, with more food being brought by guests and more from The Greenhouse kitchen. Some children continued to race across the lawns. Others had collapsed onto blankets in the shade and were napping.

Carole and five other women from the Adirondack Community Church approached Wendy with a special request to see the raffia cross that she had mentioned. Wendy was pleased to escort them into the greenhouse and show it to them. Carole noticed the worn raffia chair in front of it. One of the wide arms held a Bible and a Daily Guideposts devotional.

"This is your prayer chair, isn't it?" Carole asked.

"Yes, it's quiet in here, since I take care of the greenhouse myself. It's the perfect spot to read my Bible and devotional. I saw that chair at a local yard sale and knew it was just perfect for here."

"It is, it's just right," said Carole. "Wendy, we're aware that someone has been threatening you and we'd like to pray for your safety, and the safety of your home."

Wendy said, "Thank you, I'd appreciate that."

The six women held hands in a semi-circle in front of the cross. Carole took Wendy's hand and led her into the circle. She began to pray aloud. Wendy recognized that her eloquent prayer was drawn from Psalm 91, one of her favorites. Carole concluded, "When we call on God for protection, He will answer us. When we call on him when we are in trouble, he will rescue us and give us a long, full life. We pray for heavenly protection, in the name of Jesus Christ, our Lord. Amen."

Wendy, touched by Carole's prayer, let her tears flow freely. Carole patted her cheeks with a soft cotton handkerchief, saying, "You're in the hands of God, Wendy."

The women admired the flowers growing on the table and shelves. They particularly loved the Cattleya orchids that grew on bark slabs fastened to the house wall. When they left the greenhouse, Wendy stayed behind for a minute. She looked at the cross and whispered, "Thank you, Lord. I needed someone to pray for me. I appreciate your supplying the answer to my need, as you always do."

Evening approached too slowly for the young guests. They asked parents, "When will the fireworks start?"

Repeatedly, they were told that the sun would set about eight-thirty, and the biggest hotel on Lake Placid had scheduled their fireworks for nine o'clock. The village of Lake Placid would begin their fireworks over Mirror Lake at about nine-thirty.

The children were appeased with slices of watermelon. Pit-spitting contests were held on the front lawn. They began with the children, but soon adults found their competitive spirit aroused and soon over a dozen people were engaged in the fun.

Wendy declined to compete, but both Todd and Liz were persuaded to join in. Wendy laughed so hard at the children that she had to sit in a lawn chair. The littlest children couldn't spit, but their parents and friends encouraged them, so they tried as hard as they could. Finally, red-faced and worn out, they accepted the trinket prizes that Wendy had for them.

Adults continued to enjoy watermelon and several impromptu pit-spitting contest ensued. They ended with the contestants laughing so hard that they had to cancel.

Todd and most of the men continued to eat the ribs that Liz stacked in a cast iron warmer over the dying coals of the grill. Liz teased them about their appetites until Todd and Dan decided to repay her teasing. They grabbed her and to the accompaniment of her screams, threw her off the dock. She emerged from the cold water shivering and laughing, to loud cheers and applause. She dashed inside to dry off and change clothes.

At dusk, most families spread blankets on the front lawn, where the fireworks would reflect in the water. Wendy was pleased that the morning's breeze had kept up just enough to discourage mosquitoes. She spread a blanket near the Decker family and was joined by Liz. Tom Decker joined her, bringing her a glass of lemonade.

He told her that the Ray Brook State Police headquarters had informed him that two men with an ATV had been picked up as they left the old logging road. They were seen loading it into a pick-up truck, and as they sped away, they swerved over the center line several times, and were stopped by the troopers. Both men tested positive for alcohol and were arrested for DWI. They had two boxes of illegal Mexican fireworks, which was another misdemeanor. There was no proof that they intended to use the fireworks to attack The Greenhouse B and B.

Wendy and Tom voluntarily decided not to continue to discuss the threat, but instead enjoyed a pleasant chat. They shared information about their early lives and favorite family anecdotes.

Finally, just as the children thought they couldn't wait another minute, a huge explosion of fireworks from the nearby resort hotel lit the night. "There's fireworks in the lake!" exclaimed Tom's little niece. The reflections weren't quite as dramatic because they were a quarter mile away, but since the fireworks were shot high in the air, the display was impressive.

After the fireworks ended, the tired but happy guests left. Small children were picked up from the lawn while sound asleep and placed in family cars. When everyone else had left, Tom and Wendy sat on the back porch, Liz, Todd and Patty sprawled in deck chairs behind them.

Tom explained that the men with the fireworks would be tried for DWI and for having illegal fireworks, but since both were misdemeanors, they would probably be fined or serve only a short jail time. "Of course," he said, "It depends on whether or not they have prior records and the kind of lawyer they can afford."

Wendy looked up at the sky, watching the sliver of a quarter moon in the star-lit blackness. On the western horizon, a particularly bright star appeared in a gap between mountain peaks. Tom noticed her watching it and said, "That's Venus. Come on, let's walk. You need to relax after the hectic day you've had." He pulled her to her feet and led her from the porch. At the same time, Todd said, "I'm going to hit the sack. It's been a long day. Enjoy your walk." Liz and Patty grinned and Patty said, "Let's go in, I think there's a romance in bud there."

Liz agreed. "Budding romance needs privacy," and followed Patty into the house.

Wendy and Tom walked toward the water, which now glittered sedately with the reflection of stars and faint moon. "I'll do all I can to protect you, Wendy," Tom said, "I've become quite fond of you and I'd like to continue to see you personally, not just as a police officer. If that's what you want, that is."

Wendy tilted her head back to meet his eyes and answered. "Yes, I'd like that very much. I admit you've become very special to me. I'm glad I saw you with your family today and had a chance to talk to you at length. It increased my feelings for you."

When Tom put his arms around her and drew her close to him, she felt as if she was melting into his arms. She welcomed his kiss and was pleased to return it. She didn't notice as the stars moved through their ordained patterns overhead. She only felt as if stars were spinning through her body.

CHAPTER SEVENTEEN

"The sting of death is sin, and the strength
of sin is the law. But thanks be to God,
who gives us the victory through our Lord
Jesus Christ. Therefore, . . . , be steadfast,
immovable, always abounding in the work of
the Lord." (I Corinthians 15:56-58 NKJV)

Wendy awakened early but was groggy and felt as if she was half-asleep through breakfast. Sipping her second cup of coffee, she told Liz, "The party was a lot of fun, but I wouldn't want to do that much work more than once a year."

"I agree. It was a lot of work, but such fun! We should make this an annual event." When Wendy stared at her, she said, "I bet we'd find it easier next year, now that we've had experience under our belts."

"I'm sure you're right. Experience counts."

Todd hurried into the kitchen and handed a printed e-mail to Wendy. "Good news." he said.

Wendy skimmed the message. "It's from Natalia. She says her dad is recovering. He's living at home and a speech therapist and physical therapist come a few times a week. His speech is still slurred, but he's speaking much better, and starting to walk using a walker."

"That's great progress," exclaimed Liz. She took the paper from Wendy's hand and said, "Look how she signs off. 'In God's love, your forever friend, Natalia.' Now if we only knew what she was going to write about The Greenhouse!"

Wendy said, "She might not have had much time for writing. I understand she is close to her father and is probably involved in his therapy."

"She'll write it eventually," Liz said. "She still has to earn a living."

We'll just have to wait and see," said Todd.

After breakfast, Wendy stepped out the front door, and the bright sunlight gave her a charge of joy that she felt right to her toes. She held her arms out to the warmth and wondered how much her joy had to do with the sunlight and how much was due to her knowledge that she was in love for the first time in her life. She looked down the length of Lake Placid as a breeze rippled its surface into sparkles. The lake, the morning sun and breeze all seemed to be in harmony. She smiled to see nature reflecting her joy.

"The lawn looks like it was trampled by a herd of elephants," griped Todd as he bent over to pick up burnt sparklers. Wendy laughed at him and said, "It was a great party, and the grass will recover Give it a day or two, a little rain and you'd never know a herd of elephants was here."

He grinned at her and said, "You look bright and sunny this morning!" She laughed because his remark echoed her feelings. "Any plans for today?" he asked.

"I thought I'd go shopping. Carole told me about a natural food store in the village, and she suggested we should have gluten free food on hand. Lately many people are being diagnosed with gluten intolerance. You might want to include a mention on our website that we can handle gluten free diets. What do you think?"

"What does Liz think?" he immediately asked.

"She says she can cook gluten free, if necessary, but would need to know in advance, so she could be prepared. She wants to buy gluten-free cookbooks, also"

"We'll do it," he agreed.

They were both startled as the sound of children's laughter and voices. They seemed to come from the trail that ran in back of the property. Both walked toward the trail, where through the trees, they saw a boisterous group of young Boy Scouts and two leaders. The boys called greetings and waved, while they and one leader ran ahead toward the uphill portion of the trail. The other leader introduced himself and explained that the local Boy Scouts walked this trail early every summer. Wendy and Todd introduced themselves and explained that they lived in the nearby bed and breakfast.

The hike leader said, "We try to get here around July fourth, before most of the summer tourists arrive and it gets crowded. I notice that this part of the trail is wet. That's unusual. Do you know why that is?"

Todd explained that he had soaked the trail because someone appeared to have been snooping on them from the trail. "We caught someone here last night, so I turned off the soaker hose. It seems we don't need it any more."

Wendy looked at him in surprise, but said nothing. She wasn't sure the threat was gone now that men with fireworks and a grenade launcher had been caught. She decided to talk to him about it later. They wished the Boy Scouts a pleasant hike and left them.

Todd said that he had accepted an invitation from Terry Johns to look at some locally made picnic tables that Terry thought they could use. He said, "It'll take a couple of hours, especially if I buy some, so I won't be back until noon. See you later."

Wendy reminded him to get receipts for any tables he purchased. "Remember, you planned to advance the business up to ten thousand dollars, and I think you're close to that. The Greenhouse B and B must be self-supporting, so don't spend too much. We'll go over the figures tonight." He agreed and left.

Wendy wandered around the lawns, trying to decide where picnic tables would look nice and be reasonably close to the kitchen. She decided on the back lawn, between the porch and the immense white pine trees that bordered the back edge of the property.

Then she knew she had to go indoors and work on the greenhouse plants, which she had put off while preparing for the July Fourth celebration. She went through the kitchen to tell Liz where she would be.

Liz, already dressed in her ju-jitsu exercise clothes, said, "I'm going to practice ju-jitsu in the parlor while this bread is baking." She gently placed two loaves of bread in greased pans and wiped their tops with egg whites. She checked the oven temperature and then placed the bread inside. She picked up a timer and set it for the time the bread needed to bake. Carrying the timer, she followed Wendy to the parlor

In the greenhouse, Wendy set out her watering pot and a box of Miracle-Gro as Liz spread out her mat in the parlor. Liz was bending and twisting her torso in warming up exercises when she heard the back door slam. She walked toward the kitchen and saw a red-faced, irate John Dennehy. Instead of his usual immaculate clothing, he appeared disheveled. He shouted, "What are you creeps trying to do to me? I had the state cops pestering me and my associates yesterday. You're tryin' to drive me out of business, ain't you? Well, you ain't gonna get away with it! Where's that Bailey brat? I'll fix her!"

Liz whirled around and ran to the greenhouse. Once inside, she shoved Wendy toward the hidden staircase, and whispered, "Get upstairs. Dennehy's gonna hurt you!" Wendy obeyed and slipped through the hidden door before Dennehy followed Liz.

Liz left the greenhouse and closed the glass door behind her. Dennehy entered the parlor and approached her with both fists clenched. He peered through the glass wall that separated the parlor from the greenhouse, apparently searching for Wendy. Liz stood firmly on her mat and said, "Get out of here, Dennehy! You'll have to answer to the cops for this, too. You're not welcome here, so go!"

"Tell me where she is! She thinks she's so tough, giving my guys seconds to get off the property. She'll pay for that! Get her in here, or *you'll* pay for it!" He held his fists up and advanced on Liz. She glimpsed a revolver tucked into his waistband and hoped he wouldn't draw it. Her ju-jitsu training had taught her how to defend herself from an unarmed assailant, but an armed one was beyond her capabilities.

She shouted, "Leave now, Dennehy. There's nothing for you here."

He snarled as he took a step closer. "You'll pay for this, you hellish woman!" Suddenly he pulled his gun and lunged toward her. He moved quickly, but she immediately dropped to the floor and used her ju-jitsu training to knock his feet out from under him. His gun dropped as his momentum caused him to fly forward and smash head first into the glass wall in front of him. As glass shattered, Liz sprang to her feet.

Wendy ran down the main staircase and stood by her. Her voice shook as she said, "I called the troopers from upstairs." She glanced at Dennehy's body and drew Liz away from him. "Don't touch him or go near him. The glass cut his throat." Both women saw blood pouring from a gash in Dennehy's throat, from which protruded a huge shard of glass that had dropped guillotine-like, from the narrow frame. They clung to each other, trembling. Wendy muttered a prayer of thanks that they were spared. They heard sirens and then troopers were running in the front and back doors.

Several troopers looked at Dennehy's body as Liz explained his threats and attempted attack. Liz said, "I didn't mean for him to die. I just wanted to keep him from killing us." Her voice trembled and Wendy put her arms around her, hugging her close.

Then a trooper was shoving a man into the parlor, saying, "I found him in the kitchen."

It was Stan Gubinsky, who was shaking and unable to speak as he stared at the lifeless body of his boss. Then Gubinsky stared at Liz and screamed, "You witch! You killed him!" He whirled toward Wendy and screamed, "You put her up to this! This is your fault! You'll pay for this!" He was still screaming curses and threats as a trooper handcuffed him. Two of them gripped him firmly and dragged him from the house. A trooper took statements from both women and then pictures were taken of the scene. Dennehy's gun was bagged as evidence and his body placed in a body bag and removed.

Liz and Wendy collapsed at the kitchen table, but Wendy refused coffee and sipped a glass of water. Liz gulped her coffee and said, "I was sure you'd call the troopers from upstairs. I hoped to stall him long enough for them to get here, but he jumped me and I had to react fast. I've never seen a dead body before. That was gruesome!"

A light tap at the back door made them both jump, then Patty came in, followed by her niece, Kinsey.

Patty said, "We heard the police sirens and thought you were in serious trouble."

"We could have been," Wendy admitted. She explained the events of Dennehy's threat and Liz's effective response.

"Wow!" said Kinsey, her eyes wide in admiration. "I'm gonna to sign up for ju-jitsu classes. I'm good at gymnastics, so I bet I could learn ju-jitsu. Right, Aunt Patty?"

"You talk to your mom about that." Patty looked thoughtful, and then admitted, "You're agile. You'd probably be good at it. Don't know what my sister will say."

"I'll talk her into it, I will."

"Probably," admitted Patty. "Now, Wendy, what do you think the threat is now that Dennehy's dead?"

Liz answered for her, "Gubinsky sounded like he really blamed us for the death and he wants to get even. He's probably out of police custody by now, since all he did was scream and yell threats. I think we still have to be careful, like remembering to set the alarm system every night, and even during the day if we're here alone."

Everyone jumped when Liz's oven timer dinged, but she promptly moved to the oven, pulled on mitts and removed the fragrant brown-topped loaves, placing them on cooling racks that she had ready.

Todd came in the back door, took one look at Wendy's white face and asked, "What happened here?"

Wendy again explained the events of the tumultuous morning, trying to sound as matter-of-fact as she could.

Todd interrupted her when she said that Liz had found Dennehy in the house. "Didn't you have the alarm on?" he asked.

"No, we've been turning it off as soon as we get up, remember?"

"It's my fault," Todd said, rubbing his face with both hands. "I knew the two of you would be here alone when I left. I should have told you to turn it on as soon as you went back into the house. From now on any time the two of you are here, or even when Patty's here, turn the alarm on. We can't take chances. Now, tell me the rest."

As soon as Todd heard of Gubinsky's threats, he emphatically repeated his instructions to keep the alarm on during the day. "That guy could be real ugly. He apparently looked up to Dennehy and he'll want to get even."

The back door had opened quietly and Tom Decker said, "You're right, Todd. We had to let Gubinsky go, since there's no evidence he was tied in to Dennehy's attack. He is tied in, though. We know that, but without evidence, we can't hold him." He looked directly at

Wendy and said, "Be careful. Whatever you do, do it with safety in mind."

She met his tender expression with a look that echoed it and said, "We will. We'll remind each other."

Tom said to Wendy, "Let's go for a short walk."

She started to rise, but then said, "There's a bloody mess in the parlor that has to be cleaned up."

Patty stepped forward. "You go for a walk and calm down. I'll take care of the mess." She gently pushed Wendy toward Tom and then nodded to Kinsey. They both headed for the parlor, Patty looking grim and businesslike.

The woman trooper who had taken Liz's statement came in the back door and said she wanted to go over Liz's statement with her. The trooper requested that they move into the dining room for privacy. Liz knew that it was going to be a long process, so she offered the trooper coffee, which she refused. She filled her own cup before she sat down. The trooper's questions were pointed. She wanted to know about Liz's self-defense training; who had she trained with, did she have a history of having been attacked in the past, who else knew of her ju-jitsu expertise, had her awards been publicized. Liz's brain felt stuffed with cotton wool as she delved into her memories for the data needed.

Finally, the trooper cautioned her not to let Dennehy's death become a personal issue with her. She advised, "When someone dies as a result of self-defense, the person who defended herself mustn't see the death as a personal failing. You did what you had to do to survive, remember that."

Liz thanked her for her advice and said she was going to have to pray about it. The trooper nodded in agreement, and said that was a good idea.

Outdoors, Tom took Wendy's hand and said, "I told you you're special to me, Wendy, but this threat has deepened my concern for you. I'm worried and I don't know what to do to protect you." They walked to the lake and found a large sun-warmed rock to sit on while they talked. Finally, after a long talk in which they confessed their love for one another, they realized they had forgotten to eat lunch and walked back to the house.

Patty met them with the news that the parlor rug would have to be sent out to be cleaned, which she would take care of. She also said that Liz's exercise mat had cleaned up with a brisk hosing and she had hung it from the clothesline

Liz was still answering questions, but the trooper said she was done. Liz made everyone sandwiches with her fresh bread and ham left from a dinner earlier in the week. They all ate with a hearty appetite. Tom reluctantly said that he had to go to work. He made Wendy, Liz and Patty promise to lock the house and turn on the alarm when they were there alone, and left. The female trooper said she would call if she had more questions and she also left.

Wendy was still feeling light-headed and joy-filled. She realized that love was the cause of her feelings and decided to go out of doors, where such an enormous amount of joy seemed to be fitting. She picked up her daily devotions book and walked back to the lake and sat on the rock she had just shared with Tom. She closed her eyes and thanked God for giving her such love. Then she prayed to be worthy of the love that God had entrusted to her and Tom. As she read her book, the time slipped away and before she knew it, dusk was drawing in. She was pleased to see a few fireflies flitting around.

She looked up to see that lights were on in the house and a few stars could already be seen in the still pale sky. She got to her feet and found that she was stiff from sitting so long. She stretched her arms overhead with all the strength she could muster, feeling the stretch from her shoulders to her lower back. *Lord, how wonderful are your works. You have made me the person I am, and I thank you.*

Suddenly, she was seized and a damp cloth clamped over her mouth. A sickly sweet odor filled her nostrils and lungs as she gasped for breath. Then, she collapsed into a dizzying darkness. She was vaguely aware of being carried, then of being dropped onto a hard metal surface. She tried to breathe through her mouth and when she could not, she dragged in air through her nose. Her mind fought to free her from the cloying dizziness, but she could only bring herself to a dim consciousness of being on a hard, rocking surface.

Then, she was aware of motion. The hard object she lay on was moving. She struggled to move her arms, but they were fastened behind her. Thick tape was fastened tightly over her eyes. She kicked her legs and realized that they too were fastened. She heard an ugly laugh. Then a familiar voice said, "You're lucky, you brat. I could only get a little of the stuff to knock you out, but it'll take care of you until I get you stashed."

She tried to open her mouth to scream, but found her mouth was taped closed. As she twisted her arms, she realized that they were taped. *"Please, God, help me. Get me away from this man."* She knew she was in the hands of Stan Gubinsky and that he hated her enough to hurt her, perhaps even enough to kill her.

The movement of the hard surface she lay on was familiar. She was in the rowboat! It was on the water! Did he intend to drown her?

The boat continued to move and she could sense steady pulls on the oars. She prayed desperately, but the movement of the rowboat seemed to go on forever. She heard the familiar screech of the hawks that lived on the islands in the middle of Lake Placid. They would be returning from a day of hunting. *Going home*, she thought. *How I wish I was going home. What will he do to me?* She shuddered as the possibility of being raped crossed her mind. She knew that she had to remain as calm as she could and that could only be done if she firmly put her mind on God. She drew a deep breath through her nose and prayed fervently.

Father, every day I am renewed through the life and power of Jesus Christ in me. Thank you for setting this process in motion when I trusted Jesus as my Lord and Savior. I know you will take care of me in this situation. This evil man is not your match. Only you can turn him away from his evil intent. I am yours, my Lord.

CHAPTER EIGHTEEN

"Therefore strengthen the hands which
hang down, and the feeble knees, and
make straight paths for your feet, so that
what is lame may not be dislocated, but
rather be healed." (Hebrews 12:12 NKJV)

Wendy felt the boat hit something hard, as if it had struck a rock. She heard Gubinsky curse and something coarse like rope fell on her as he scrambled over her, apparently to climb out of the boat. Course rope was dragged over her. She realized that he must have been tying the boat to something. He continued to curse and then she heard him say, "This'll do. I knew this wasn't far. Now I gotta carry the brat." He got back in the boat, roughly picked her up and heaved her over one shoulder.

She felt him scramble out of the boat and up a steep incline. The scent of pine filled her lungs as branches whipped her face and arms. He muttered curses as his feet slipped. She gasped and struggled to get her breath as his stumbling passage bounced her on his heavy shoulder. He increased his pace to a light jog and she was jostled from side to side, the force of the each step driving air from her lungs. She tried to lift herself up so she could breathe better, but when he felt her movement, he pulled her off his back and shook her. Then he threw her back over his shoulder and muttered, "You just stay where I put you, brat!" Gubinsky's familiar voice gave her chills.

When he moved on, there was less bouncing and his gait smoothed, as if he had found a path. She could hear birds singing and a soft breeze sighing through trees. *How strange,* she thought, *though I'm sure my life is in danger, my mind can pick up lovely sounds and enjoy them.* She centered her mind on God and sent him a heartfelt prayer to take care of her. *I trust you to protect me from this evil man, Lord. I am helpless, but he is no match for you.*

She wondered how long they were going to travel through the woods. Both of the islands in Lake Placid were small, but she didn't know if he had rowed to an island. Maybe he had a hideout selected along the shore. That didn't seem likely because except for the few areas that had been cleared for buildings, like the hotel or her home, the shore was very wild and densely wooded. Then he seemed to be moving over a rough rock surface again. When he slipped on occasion, he cursed and slapped her legs. It happened often enough that she was sure her legs were bruised.

He stopped abruptly, bent over and she felt the coolness of shade. She was dropped suddenly and roughly on a rock surface. He snarled, "Not your usual luxury digs, is it, brat? You'll stay here until I'm ready for you. I gotta decide how I'm gonna get even with you guys for wreckin' the only means I got to make any money. Your muscle woman didn't have to kill him! I'm gonna fix you!" Then he moved away and his footsteps faded. She knew he had left and was relieved. She breathed a prayer of thanks to God that as of yet, Gubinsky appeared to have no plan to exact his revenge. She had the impression that he was acting on impulse, and he may not even have decided what to do with her. Again, she prayed intensely and asked God to let her family realize that she was missing, and had been kidnapped.

"Wendy," called Todd. He saw Liz leave the back door and walk toward the lake. He called to her, "Have you seen Wendy? I've looked everywhere." When she shook her head, he turned to the driveway as he heard Patty drive up. She looked at his worried face and asked, "What's the problem?"

"I can't find Wendy. She's not in her room or the greenhouse or anywhere else on the property."

Just then Liz called, "Look, I found her book of devotionals on this rock by the lake. I also found this." Using only two fingers, she held out a torn cloth at arms' length. "What does this smell like, Todd? It seems familiar, but I can't place the scent."

Todd leaned close to the cloth, sniffed, and then jerked his head back in shock. "That's chloroform, I'm sure. I'm calling the troopers. I think Wendy's been kidnapped."

"But who?" Patty started to ask, but Liz interrupted, "Gubinsky! He said he'd get even for Dennehy's death."

Ten minutes later, several troopers' cruisers pulled into the driveway. Tom Decker jumped out of one and asked them, "When did you see her last? And where?"

Liz explained that she had found Wendy's devotional book on a rock near the dock. She showed him the rag that smelled of chloroform. Tom promptly put it in an evidence bag and ordered, "Let's go down there."

They hurried down the slope of the lawn to the rock where the book and rag had been found. Tom looked at the dense forest that edged close to the lake. "It wouldn't be hard for someone to slip up on her. But how would he know she came down here to read and pray?"

"He's been watching us!" said Liz.

"He used the rowboat!" Todd shouted from the dock.

Tom strode the length of the dock to where Todd was kneeling by the post that had the rowboat tied to it.

Todd said, "Jerry Brewster told me to always tie the rowboat to the dock with two double hitches because the storms that whip up the lake could pull out a looser knot and the boat could be lost. This isn't even a knot, the rope was just tossed over the post a couple of times."

"When did you last use the rowboat?" Tom asked.

"This weekend, Sunday, during the party because a few people wanted to watch the fireworks on the lake. I'm sure I tied it securely when we got back. I didn't allow any kids to play in the rowboat during the party, either."

Tom instructed a trooper to use the fingerprint kit on the boat's aluminum oars.

As he worked, they all stood on the dock and stared at the two wooded islands that could be seen in the early evening light. Liz shuddered, as she thought of Wendy out there or hidden in the forest. "Where is she?" she asked, her voice choked with tears.

Tom said, "I'm going to call this in and get a search party organized. We'll also need a motor boat." He hurried back to the cruisers, while another officer interviewed Todd and Liz and took notes. Tom spoke to a trooper, who climbed in a cruiser and left.

When Tom returned, he said, "The CO agrees with me that the kidnapper probably took her to one of the islands, so he approved acquisitioning a motorboat. Both Buck and Moose Island have camps on them, but the terrain is so steep and heavily wooded on each that he could be within yards of a camp and no one would see him."

"How long will it take to get a boat here?" asked Liz in a trembling voice.

"There's one we've leased on occasion that's docked at the marina and my CO is contacting him as we speak. He'll pull up here and we'll cruise the near shoreline, starting with Moose because it's closer. Scanning the shoreline with binoculars isn't ideal, but we may spot disturbed vegetation where he tied up to leave her."

"You think he just left her out there?" Patty asked.

"Unless he has another boat available, he won't be able to get out to her, which might be good because then he couldn't mistreat her." Tom's face was pale and he turned to Todd and asked, "Do you have binoculars?"

Todd said, "Yes, I'll get them." By the time he returned from the house, one of the cruisers had returned and a trooper was handing Tom a pair of high-powered binoculars. There were others in a canvas bag at his feet.

Tom asked Patty, "Could we get some water to carry on the boat?"

"Yes, we have bottled water left from the weekend. I'll get it." She hurried to the house and quickly returned with several six-packs of water, which she handed to Tom.

Then a Forest Ranger vehicle pulled in and Dan Picard was there. He told Liz, "I heard it on the scanner. Was it that Gubinsky character who took Wendy?"

"We think so, and it seems that he used the rowboat to take her somewhere, maybe to one of the islands."

"I'll help," Dan said, and walked to Tom. After a brief conversation, Dan nodded at Liz and remained standing by Tom.

Then the sound of a motorboat was heard and a racy cruiser sped toward them. Tom hurried to the dock and signaled the boat's operator to pull in to the end of the dock. A hurried conversation took place between Tom and the operator. A minute later, the operator climbed off the boat and approached Todd. He introduced himself as Dick Hanks and then said, "Tom can operate the boat. No problem, but I'd like to help."

Todd said, "I think we should let him call the shots. He's the expert, and I just want my sister to be found, safely." Dick stepped back and waited for instructions.

Tom approached Todd and Patty, who stood close together. He said, "I don't believe this is a kidnap for ransom, but someone should stay near the phone, just in case."

"I will," Patty said promptly.

"Good. Now we'll go. Everyone should have a binocular." He led Todd, Dan, Dick, and three troopers to the boat. They were a tight fit, so Tom lined them up on the rails. He backed the boat from the dock and steered it toward the closest point of Moose Island, which was a rough promontory called Rocky Point. From there, he hugged the shore and instructed everyone to train their binoculars on the shoreline. "I have to watch for underwater rocks, so the rest of you be sure to note any tree braches that are bent or broken, because that could indicate where he might have tied up."

The searchers watched the shoreline, taking drinks of water in turn. Tom frowned as he looked at storm clouds that were moving across the sky. Finally, Dan pointed to a rock that shelved into the water. "There, the white pine that's bending over the tock. One limb is scraped."

"Good job," said Tom. He threw an anchor over the rock and pulled the boat as close as possible. He instructed Dick and Todd to stay with the boat, while he and the other troopers, accompanied by Dan, climbed onto the rock.

Dan whispered briefly to Tom, who waved him forward. Dan

dropped to his knees and went over the earth that bordered the rock, inch by inch. "Here's the trail," he finally said to Tom. "He slipped climbing up this rock. See where the pine needles are disturbed? One set of footprints. He's probably carrying her. I'll find out where he went from here." He moved forward cautiously, his eyes perusing every inch. The others crept after him, trying to remain as silent as possible.

"Here." His penetrating whisper alerted Tom and the troopers that he had found the trail. "Yes, he's carrying her. His footprints left a distinct mark But look, there's another set of lighter footprints coming this way. He hid her and left. That's why the rowboat was back at the dock."

He peered ahead at the trail as it wandered into the dense forest. He looked at Tom and said, "He must have a hiding place that he picked out in advance."

Tom said, "An old summer camp? But no, property is too valuable out here. Anyone who couldn't keep up a camp would have sold it. Any caves around here?"

"No, not on a granite island. Some overhangs, but they wouldn't be deep. I think we should follow his trail and hope we can find her. We have extra water, don't we?"

"Yes, plenty." Tom followed Dan as he led them along the trail.

Suddenly, the air was rent with the crash of thunder and rain fell heavily. Dan stood up and cried, "Please God, let the trail be plain! We have to find Wendy!" He went back on his knees and peered at the now soaked trail. He moved ahead in a slight crouch, unwilling to take his eyes off the trail. After a few minutes, he stood and turned back to Tom. "I've lost the trail. The footprints are washed out. All we can do now is follow the path of least resistance."

"Yes, far as I know, he's had no country experience. All his past has been in the city, so he'll walk in any direction that'll give him the least trouble."

"He seemed to be heading toward that cliff." Dan pointed to a large outcropping that could be seen beyond the trees. "Maybe he found a hiding place there. The trees are a little thinner here, so I'll go in that direction."

"Good, we're right behind you."

All the men were soaked, but no one hesitated to follow Dan. Tom said a quick prayer of thanks that lightning hadn't accompanied the rain, so far. He knew that it would be too dangerous to stay among the trees if lightning struck. If that happened, they would have no choice but to abandon the search until later.

Suddenly, as if brought on by his fears, a bolt of lightning struck a nearby tree. Everyone threw an arm over his face, as splinters shot by them. Only one trooper had to pick splinters from his arms.

"We're going back, fast!" said Tom. They all ran for the relative safety of the boat as fast as the terrain permitted. Once on board, Tom said to Todd, "I didn't want to wait for a bigger boat to be brought from Saranac Lake, so there's not much shelter here. I'll get us back as fast as possible to your house."

Wendy stretched out as much as she could. She felt rock under her and as she shifted around in a futile effort to get comfortable, she bumped her head on rock. She felt rock with both shoulders, but her feet were in open space. When she moved her legs forward, she felt rain on her feet. She decided that she was either in a small cave, or under an overhang. She thought, *"Where am I, Lord? Will anyone find me?"*

She remembered several stories that Dan had shared at the Fourth of July picnic. Apparently, Dan had considerable expertise as a tracker. Even experienced trackers like Clive DuBois had called on him to assist them with a difficult trail, such as following a wounded deer over rough terrain. She hoped that the rain would not interfere with his efforts to follow Gubinsky's trail. She knew all she could do was pray, so she thought of one of the psalms that her grandmother had asked her to memorize.

At the time, twelve years old, she had asked, "Why memorize Bible passages, Gram? All I have to do is look them up in my Bible."

Her grandmother had replied, "You never know when you might feel you want to recite one of them, and you won't have a Bible available, or can't read it."

She thought, *"You're right, Gram. Having my eyes taped over certainly does fit that scenario."* She tried to rub the tape off her mouth by rubbing her chin against her shoulder, but it wouldn't give. Then she began to recite Psalm twenty-seven in her mind. *The Lord is my light and salvation; whom shall I fear? The Lord is the strength of my life; Of whom shall I be afraid?* Suddenly, remembering that the next verse referred to the wicked eating one's flesh, she shuddered and switched to her favorite psalm, the twenty-third; *The Lord is my shepherd; I shall not want, He makes me to lie down in green pastures; He leads me beside the still waters. He restores my soul; He leads me in the paths of righteousness for His name's sake. Yea, though I walk through the valley of the shadow of death, I will fear no evil; for you are with me; Your rod and Your staff they comfort me. You prepare a table before me in the presence of my enemies; You anoint my head with oil; my cup runs over. Surely goodness and mercy shall follow me all the days of my life and I will dwell in the house of the Lord forever.*

Yes, please Lord, show me your goodness and mercy. Let me be rescued!

Then she was aware that she had to urinate, and clenched her muscles so she wouldn't wet herself and wondered how long she could hold it.

A rumble of thunder sounded, echoing in the small chamber. She hoped that lightning would not accompany the storm. Lightning would make it too dangerous for searchers to move through the forest. She thought, *I wonder if I'm on one of the islands. Probably I am, because the lakeshore is too built up with camps to risk hiding me there. I'm probably on Moose Island. It's closest and the biggest, so less chance he'd run into someone while carrying me here. What can I do to let searchers know I'm here?* She couldn't think of any means of making noise, or doing anything that would indicate where she was. She thought of slipping out of the cave so she would be seen by anyone on the trail. The rain was still falling, and the idea of getting soaked didn't appeal to her. *I'll stay healthier if I'm dry. If only I could find a sharp rock to cut this tape.* She squirmed around; trying to feel the walls with her arms and hands, but couldn't get herself into the right position. Everything she could touch was smooth.

Her thoughts were interrupted by an enormous crash of thunder, followed by the crack of lightning. She caught a whiff of scorched wood and wondered if the lightning had set a tree on fire. The rain continued to pound the ground, so she was sure a forest fire couldn't start. The next roar of thunder seemed to shake the ground and the lightning was so close that she could hear it crackle.

She knew that if any searchers had been in the forest, they would have left by now. She had read that the most dangerous place to be in a lightning storm was under a tree. She prayed for the safety of anyone searching for her.

Tom led the group from the boat to the house on a dead run. Liz was waiting for them with coffee and sticky buns that she had made early that morning. She had turned the dining room into Search Central, with a topo map of the Lake Placid area in the middle of the table. She pushed it aside to make room for the snacks, and then asked, "When will it be safe for you to go out to the island again?"

"As early as we have enough light tomorrow morning," Dan explained.

Tom explained, "Dan marked the trail where we stopped. We'll pick it up from there. We'll split up, since there seems to be two paths to that rock overhang we were heading for. They're each looking like the path of least resistance." He helped himself to coffee and a sticky bun. When Liz turned to Dan with a puzzled expression, Dan explained what Tom meant by "the path of least resistance."

"You think she's on Moose Island, but you don't know where?" she asked.

"We think so, but other than a bruised branch where he could have tied the boat and some footprints, we don't have much to go on. The rain washed out the footprints, so now we have to rely on experience, hunches and prayer."

Patty said, "You supply the experience and hunches, we'll do the praying. I called Carole at the church and she's lining up a prayer team who will pray around the clock until Wendy's found."

"Thanks, Patty," said Todd, Liz, Dan and Tom in near unison.

The troopers had finished the sticky buns and Liz was making another pot of coffee when Tom announced, "It's stopped raining and the thunder and lightning are moving east. With the wind coming from the west, it won't come back. I think we can get back to the island early in the morning."

No one was willing to leave The Greenhouse for the night. Liz and Patty sorted out the troopers, two men and one woman, into rooms.

Dan offered to sleep on the couch, but Liz insisted that he had to take a room. Finally, everyone was settled in for the night, which included Liz, Patty, Dan, Todd and Tom staying up to pray. They prayed with Carole by phone, then realized they needed sleep and went to their rooms.

At dawn, coffee mugs clattered onto the table after Liz had made a hearty breakfast. Todd led the way to the boat. He asked Tom, "Will you let me go with you on the search?"

"Yes, because we'll have to split up. Dan will take one group, and I'll take the other. You can take orders from him, can't you?"

"You bet, I've been told what a great tracker he is, and I have no experience beyond Boy Scouts."

On the island, when they reached the fork in the trail, Tom divided his group. Dan took Todd and Dick. The three troopers stayed with Tom. He handed each one a whistle. Dan looked surprised, and Tom told him, "This is our best way to communicate if we get split up. Do you know Morse Code?"

"Only SOS, I don't know the rest."

"That's enough, in case someone falls and breaks a leg. If you find her, sound three long whistles. If you hear three whistles from us, move fast to the rock we're aiming for."

They started on their separate trails. The water dripping from the trees soaked them in moments. Todd consistently prayed in silence, feeling that his prayers were linking with those from the prayer team at the church.

In a half hour, Dan signaled them to stop for a water break. "We're almost there," he said. He pointed ahead, and said, "That rock has a lot of shatter grooves from glacial action, so it may have overhangs. I'm hoping that Gubinsky used one to hide Wendy."

He held up a hand, as they all heard a whistle. With Dan in the lead, they hurried toward the rock, plunging through underbrush and ignoring the trail. Hope built as they ran forward, not even noticing branches slashing their faces. When they found Tom and the troopers, without sign of Wendy, they drooped in disappointment.

Tom said, "We're going over the base of this outcrop, foot by foot. If you see anything like branches leaning against the rock, pull it away and look for a hiding place."

He handed Dan a heavy-duty flashlight and turned on one himself. "It's so overcast, we'd better use flashlights. We're sure Gubinsky isn't here because the rowboat is back at the dock. Proceed carefully, anyway. The last guy in line, glance back frequently, in case he has another boat he can use. We don't want to be caught by surprise. He'll have to use a flashlight, too, so we'll see him."

CHAPTER NINETEEN

"These things I have spoken to you, that in
Me you may have peace. In the world you
will have tribulation; but be of good cheer, I
have overcome the world."(John 16:33 NKJV)

Todd jogged close to Tom and asked him, "Are you sure we're looking in the right place?"

"No," he admitted. "This is just the logical place for a non-woodsman like Gubinsky. If she's not here, we'll widen our search area. For now, we'll search around this rock, and check every overhang, no matter how small."

Todd observed, "Wendy's a small person. She could be hidden in a small place."

Wendy heard a whistle and then she thought she heard a voice. She thought, "Is it Gubinsky, talking to himself again?" Then she was aware that it was several voices. Her hopes soared as she recognized Todd and Tom's voices. She hitched as far forward as she could and thrust her feet forward the opening.

She heard Tom shout, "Look! I see her feet. Over there, under the overhang!" Then he was sprawled beside her, whispering assurances as he held her in one arm and pulled the tape from her eyes and mouth. Dan pulled tape from her feet.

Tom ordered, "Careful with the tape. Put it in evidence bags. It should have his fingerprints on it and I want to be sure he goes to jail for this." Tom and Dan slid her out, helped her to her feet and unbound her arms. She couldn't stand unsupported, so Tom held her against him as she sobbed in relief.

Then she became aware that other troopers were there. "Thank you all. Thank you, God." Tom held a bottle of water to her lips and cautioned her to drink slowly.

Then, flushing in embarrassment, she whispered in Tom's ear, "I have to go to the bathroom."

He said, "Okay. Penny, can you find a private bush for her?"

The female trooper separated from the others and took Wendy by an arm. "Come this way," she said quietly, and led Wendy into the trees. The other troopers looked away or turned their backs, as Penny helped Wendy to squat behind a thick blueberry bush. Wendy was relieved that the stress of holding her urine was over. She was surprised to realize that her relief was as strong as her gratitude at being rescued. She thought, *The embarrassment of wetting my pants before anyone found me was actually my worst fear.*

When she returned and had had enough to drink to appease her thirst, Tom picked her up in his arms, and Dan led the way through the dripping forest to the boat.

Once on the boat, Todd wrapped her in a dry blanket. "Are you okay, little sister? He didn't hurt you, did he?"

"Not really, but he hit my legs and I think they're bruised. I'm very stiff from being tied in a cramped position for so long." She stretched both arms out in front and flexed her legs, trying to work the circulation back into them.

Todd slid her slacks legs up and looked at her bruises. He said, "Not too bad, but they're turning black and blue. Did he give you any clue as to what he wanted from you or from us?"

"He didn't seem to have made his mind up about what he was going to do. Apparently, he was going to decide that after he kidnapped me. He's angry because Dennehy is dead, but I guess only because Dennehy paid him to be his muscle man."

"Yes, Liz said that Dennehy had introduced him as his long-term associate. Which means that Gubinsky was out of a job as soon as Dennehy died. Also, there may have been people who resented

Gubinsky for things he did at his boss's command, and he could be in danger. Never mind, you're safe now."

"I had time to do some serious thinking while I was waiting. I decided that I'm going to give the gold away, but I haven't decided just how. Carole and I were talking about a missions project recently, and it may work out to be that's where it should go."

"Think about it later," Todd said. "Just allow yourself time to recuperate from this ordeal first."

Wendy peered through the dusk toward her home. "Thank God we're almost at the dock. Who's there? There seems to be a crowd on the lawn."

"Yes, it looks like Carole brought the church's prayer team here to pray for you. Patty called Carole and they said they'd pray around the clock until you were rescued."

"Thank God, and thank all of you!" Wendy was so happy to see them that she was in tears, but they were tears of joy. She saw tears and smiles on the faces of many of those who waited for her on the dock and the lawn.

A cheer went up before the boat reached the dock.

Todd said, "Tom's brother and sister-in-law rounded up a few more people to join Carole, so you had a two-tiered prayer team, church and troopers."

"In other words, I was prayed to my safety." She stepped off the boat right into the arms of those waiting.

Carole asked Tom, "You're running her to the hospital to be checked out, right?"

Wendy started to shake her head in the negative, but she was immediately outvoted. After Patty and Liz hugged her, both of them insisted that she should allow a quick trip to the emergency room.

Patty said, "It should go on record because it may be necessary when Gubinsky goes on trial for kidnapping."

Wendy knew that she was right. Neither Tom nor Todd wanted to be separated from her, so Tom drove her in a trooper cruiser and Todd accompanied her to the Lake Placid Medical Center. She was diagnosed with dehydration and the doctor told her how much she should drink and when. "Remember," he said, "Don't think you can catch up on your bodily fluids all at once. Take your time, and you'll recover quicker."

Wendy refused to stay in the hospital, because, she said, "I'm just slightly dehydrated, and really, really hungry." The emergency room doctor filled out a form for the state police, which, to Wendy's embarrassment, included photos of her bruised legs.

At The Greenhouse, Liz produced a large pot of chicken soup. Patty insisted on setting up a padded lounge chair in the dining room, so Wendy could lie stretched out while eating. Wendy insisted that everyone stop fussing over her. She said, "I'll sip soup and water and nibble on these goodies that Liz keeps producing. By the way, Liz, this chicken soup is really delicious."

"It is," agreed Tom. "Tell me, what led you to make soup on such a warm day?"

Liz answered, "Cooking is how I cope with stress, and there's nothing more stress-relieving than a bowl of soup."

"With the best cheese crackers I've ever had," said Todd.

Dan agreed, "The best ever!"

Patty said, "I think you should plan on taking a few days off, Wendy." She glanced at the open guest book on the counter and said, "You don't have guests coming until next weekend, so you have a few days to relax. It's supposed to be sunny tomorrow, so you could lay out and get a suntan."

"I'll try," said Wendy. "But I'm not good at laying around doing nothing."

Todd said, "The veggies are coming up in the garden, so you could lay out there and watch them grow."

Tom said, "I'll take some time off and watch them with you, okay?"

Once she had stopped laughing, Wendy agreed that she'd do as Todd suggested.

Then Patty returned from using the kitchen phone and announced, "I've arranged for Ellie, a masseuse to come here tomorrow at ten to give you a massage. She's a local woman who has done massages for some time, and she knows what she's doing. You said you were stiff, so a massage should help."

"Thanks, Patty, a massage sounds wonderful. I look forward to it."

The next morning, Wendy found that Tom hadn't been joking about watching the vegetables grow with her. They spent the morning sprawled on lawn chairs, with only an occasional stroll around the lawn when Wendy insisted that she had to move.

Tom's two-way radio wasn't far away from him, and at mid-morning, he took a call that provided good news. He sat up in his lawn chair and leaned toward her. "Gubinsky's been picked up. Of course, he's insisting that he knows nothing about a kidnapping, but the fingerprints we took from the rowboat and tape clearly mark him as the perpetrator. Will you be up to testifying?" he asked.

"You bet! I recognized his voice, and I'll say so in court."

"It may take a few weeks, even months, but kidnap cases usually come up fairly quickly. Judges don't look favorably on attempts by defense attorneys to delay trials like this. Now, Wendy, there's something else I have to talk to you about." He swung his legs off the chair so he could be closer to her. He reached in his pocket and took out a small velvet-covered box.

He handed her the box and asked, "Wendy, will you marry me?"

She opened the box and took out a lovely gold ring that was set with a small, perfect emerald-cut diamond. "Yes, Tom, I will."

He took the ring from her and slid it on her ring finger. "I'm relieved. I guessed at the size and it's a perfect fit." They held hands and could only look at one another, both too happy for words.

Then they were interrupted by Liz's voice calling, "Hey, we have news!"

Liz and Dan walked toward them from the house. Wendy noticed that Liz was more light-footed than usual. In fact she was almost dancing. Initially Wendy thought that Liz was only waving to them, but then she noticed the gleam of a ring on Liz's left hand, which she was waving overhead.

A half-hour later, Todd and Patty were told that The Greenhouse Bed and Breakfast was going to be the site of a double wedding in the spring.

"As soon as the snow melts enough to get everyone here," Dan said.

"That won't be too early," reminded Todd. "You'll be lucky if you can get married in late May. Remember the snow we had laying under the trees around here until early June this year?"

"That won't stop us!" declared Liz. "The roads will be clear, and the greenhouse will be full of flowers, even if only crocuses and snowdrops are blooming through the snow outdoors."

"Right!" agreed Wendy. "The Greenhouse Bed and Breakfast will host its first wedding in late May. I bet it'll be the first of many. What a perfect setting!"

Everyone agreed with her statement. Patty produced a pitcher of lemonade and glasses. They all drank a toast to the first of many weddings to be held at The Greenhouse.

When Ellie, the masseuse arrived, she set up her portable massage table in the parlor. As Wendy stretched out on the table, she reminded herself that she had to shop for a new rug for the room. The dry cleaner had declared the old rug a total loss, saying that the amount of blood staining it couldn't be removed without damaging the fabric. She had heard of a rug store in Albany that carried Oriental-style rugs and hoped to find one that was similar to the original, with its pattern of birds, flowers and fruit. Then she relaxed into the massage, as Ellie's strong, gentle hands soothed her still aching muscles.

An hour later, Wendy rose from the massage table, feeling much refreshed. As Ellie was packing up her equipment, Wendy interrupted her by asking, "Ellie, would you be willing to be on call for our guests when someone might want a massage?"

"Oh, yes, I'd be pleased to do that. In fact, when the skiers come back after a day at Whiteface, they might need a massage. Some of the trails at Whiteface can be strenuous. I drive a Jeep Patriot, so with four wheel drive, so I can be here no matter what the weather." Then she laughed, and said, "Maybe I shouldn't be so sure of that. I've seen some snowstorms that kept me and everyone else in Lake Placid housebound for days. But I'll try to get here, no matter what the weather. Here's a couple of my cards."

Wendy tried to pay Ellie for her services, but she refused payment.

She said, "Patty's an old friend and I came today as a favor for her. She sure thinks a lot of you." She waved goodbye and left. Wendy was sure that Ellie's expertise would add to the enjoyment of The Greenhouse Bed and Breakfast's guests.

CHAPTER TWENTY

"I will praise you, O Lord, with my whole
heart; I will tell of all your marvelous works,
I will be glad and rejoice in You; I will send
praise to your name, O Most High."
(Psalms 9:1-3 NKJV)

Wendy ran across the lawn to the edge of the lake. She felt that the joy of being free and in love was almost more than she could contain in her own body. She wanted to scream her joy to the bright morning sky above her. She laughed at the thought of the reaction such wild behavior would cause in the household. She glanced back at the house and saw Todd pushing the lawnmower to the top edge of the front lawn. She returned his wave and walked out on the dock. The cool, clear water enticed her to sit on the end of the dock, kick off her sandals and dangle her feet in the water.

The water was much colder than it looked, and she pulled them out quickly. August in Lake Placid did not include warm water, except for a tiny beach area to the left of the dock where Todd had cleared out the water plants and carted in a small amount of sand. She suspected that even that minute beach was illegal, according to the Adirondack Park Agency. They required that all lakefront areas be left wild, or "pristine" as some preferred to call it. She and Todd had noticed that guests with young children had no place for the children to enter the water where it would be shallow enough for safety and free of entangling plants, so Todd risked the ire of the APA, and hoped no one would turn him in.

The warmth of love she felt for her considerate brother led her to dip her feet in the water again. This time she splashed vigorously to keep her circulation going.

"Having some fun in the water?" Liz asked as she dropped onto the deck beside Wendy. "Isn't it too cold?"

"Try it, you'll get used to it after a minute," said Wendy. She saw Liz remove her sandals and put her feet in the water. She promptly pulled them out and said, "No, it's too cold for me! When will it warm up?"

"It'll be a little warmer by Labor Day, but not much. You might as well get used to it. If you swim strongly for a few minutes, you'll be warm enough. And you like to swim."

"In indoor pools, like the one at the gym I belonged to in New York. That's my idea of a swim. Not in ice-cold water."

Wendy protested, "You swam during the party on the Fourth of July, but not for long, I admit."

"No! I was thrown in! I swam because I had to. Fully clothed at that! And it wasn't easy. Did you notice how fast I changed my clothes when I got out?"

Wendy laughed. "Of course I did. But you teased Todd and Dan about how much they were eating, they couldn't resist throwing you in."

"That's right, stick up for your brother! Okay, I admit I asked for it, teasing them like that. But did you notice how much they ate?"

"Of course, but they didn't eat much more than most of the men. I'm glad they enjoyed it. You know, the party was so much fun that your suggestion that we should do it every year was right on target. Don't you still think so?"

"Naturally. In fact, I think Todd should include it in our advertising. Her fingers carved quotes in the air. "The Greenhouse Bed and Breakfast Annual Summer Barbecue." How does that sound?"

"I love it! We'll invite all the locals who were here this year, and include any guests we have at the time. It sounds like a community event, which tourist guests will enjoy."

"I heard you and Carole on the phone last night. Did you finalize the plans for the fund-raising event?"

"No, there's a lot to plan yet. The local churches have to get together to decide what each one can contribute in the way of talent and food. So far, only the pastors and a few teens with a Christian soft-rock band are ready to step in. Oh, and the church ladies who cook, which is most of them."

"That doesn't sound promising," Liz said with a grimace." Anything decided by committee or in this case by committees, plural, is chaos in motion."

"They'll do it, wait and see. It's such a worthwhile effort to find a place to set up a food pantry and thrift shop. It won't be easy, but I'm sure they'll do it. We can help by holding fund-raising events here on the lawns.

"I'm waiting to hear about Stan Gubinsky's trial date. I'll have to testify, and while that's going on, I can't imagine I'll be much good around here."

Liz hugged her and said, "You'll do great. Just tell what happened in the sequence in which it happened. The lawyer, the DA, I mean, will lead you through it anyway. You'll just have to answer questions, for the most part."

"You realize I never saw his face, but only heard his voice, right?"

"His fingerprints were on the duct tape he put on you, and on the towboat oars, so don't worry about it. That's evidence enough. The lawyer that Mr. Powers lined up for you will walk you through it ahead of time. He's supposed to be very good."

"So I heard. What's this?" She looked across the driveway where Patty had just parked. Patty's niece Kinsey hopped out of the car and called, "Hey, Liz, I got my sister's bridal magazines for you like I promised. I'll put them here." She dropped an armload of magazines on the porch steps. Patty intercepted her, and insisted, "Put them in the house, on the dining room table."

Kinsey sulkily picked up the magazines and flounced into the house.

Wendy stared at Liz and said; "I thought you wanted a plain, simple wedding in the greenhouse, just like I do. What's with the bridal magazines?"

Liz didn't meet her eyes, but said, "I thought that since we talked about getting married in a double ceremony, we should do it up right. I know a photographer and editor of a bridal magazine because I used to cook for the magazine's annual banquet. They'll cover the weddings and write it up as a feature. Can you imagine the publicity the B and B will get from that?"

Wendy gasped. She didn't know if she was more pleased at the idea of the free publicity or appalled at the thought of her wedding becoming a publicity event. "Do you really want a public show for our weddings?" she asked.

"The photographer and editor won't get in the way. They've done this sort of thing before, and we'll get the pictures for free. Do you know what a professional wedding photographer charges? We can choose the pictures we like and make up our wedding albums ourselves. Come on, you know we can do it."

"Yes, of course we can, but do we want our weddings in a nationally published bridal magazine? That's the ultimate in invasion of privacy."

"Let's talk about it later. They'll need to know by February because they plan the magazine stories months in advance. We have time to decide."

"What will Tom and Dan think? In fact, I wonder if Tom would be allowed to have a magazine spread about his personal life. I thought troopers were supposed to safeguard their privacy."

"Oh yes, I hadn't thought of that. Guess it wasn't such a good idea. I'll tell them we decided not to do it, due to the privacy issue. They'll understand."

Wendy breathed a sigh of relief. She had hated the publicity that had resulted from her kidnapping, and the thought of turning her wedding into a public spectacle gave her the cold shivers. She did shiver, and Liz noticed.

"What is it? Are you cold?" Liz asked.

"No, it's just the thought of all the publicity, past publicity from my kidnapping, future publicity from testifying at the trial, then your idea of a publicly published wedding. It's too much, that's all."

"I see what you mean. The idea is now officially dead in the water. I'll never mention it again, I promise. But, we should look at the bridal magazines that Kinsey brought. We might find some ideas we like. Can't tell, right?"

"Right. I have no female siblings or even cousins, so I've had no experience in helping to plan family weddings. Any of my girlfriends who got married either did it all themselves or hired a professional wedding planner. We're starting from scratch, but I suppose that's good. We can just do it our way."

Patty called from the house, "Wendy, Olga's on the phone." Wendy ran up the hill and picked up the phone in the kitchen. She enjoyed Olga's lively chatter about the new opera season that she was helping to plan. Then, Olga asked, "Tell me, Wendy, are you all right? That evil man who kidnapped you didn't hurt you, did he?"

Wendy assured her that she was fine, and had suffered only bruises and strained muscles. Then she asked, "Tell me, how did you know about the kidnapping?"

"It was on the national news! Didn't you know?"

"Oh no! I was just saying to Liz that I dread the publicity of Gubinsky's trial, but I had no idea there was so much publicity that you would hear about it in New Orleans."

"It wasn't front page news, dear, just a second page story, which emphasized how your friends teamed up to find you. You sounded very brave."

"Thank you, Olga. I appreciate that. But I must tell you our important news. I'm getting married to Tom Decker, the trooper who helped to rescue me. Liz is marrying Dan Picard, a forest ranger who also helped in the rescue. We're talking about a double wedding in the greenhouse on the fourth Saturday in May. We considered the last Saturday, but that's Memorial Day weekend, and I expect we'll have a full house. May we send you a wedding invitation?"

"By all means! You couldn't keep me away. How wonderful! Tell me all about your young men."

It took Wendy a half hour to describe Tom and Dan to Olga's satisfaction. The diva was thrilled to hear all the details, and promised to attend the wedding. She asked Wendy to reserve a room for her for the entire week prior to the wedding.

After Wendy hung up, she discovered that Liz had returned to the house. The scent of frying bacon drew Wendy to the kitchen where Liz had just finished frying bacon in order to make a potato-bacon salad for supper. The bacon was placed between layers of paper towels on a plate and then put in the refrigerator.

While they were eating lunch, they heard the deep throaty roar of a high-powered car and went outdoors to see who had arrived. A gleaming black Mercedes was in the driveway. A tall, slender young woman got out of the car. Wendy noticed that she was dressed in an expensive silk dress and wearing what Wendy thought to be an excess of diamond jewelry for an early summer afternoon. The woman was attractive, but a beaky nose prevented her from being beautiful. She approached them, walking unsteadily on very high heels. She looked the two of them over with a cold, calculating gaze.

She stared at Wendy and said, "You're a lot smaller than I thought you'd be. But *you*," she pointed a finger at Liz, "You look like an athlete. I guess that's how you got the best of John Dennehy. Amazing, really, but you shouldn't of done it."

"He gave me no choice," Liz said. "He threatened me, and he had a gun."

"I guess you don't know what you did to the family. His grandfather is near death, grieving over John's death. John was named after him, you know. But my cousin, Otis Cleary, he paid the price for letting John down. Dumping him here was inappro…p…p, I mean," her voice stumbled and Wendy decided that the woman wasn't sober.

"May we help you, ma'am?" Wendy asked. She pulled several light lawn chairs forward and asked, "Would you like to sit down?"

The woman staggered to a chair and sank into it. She said, "You've done too much already, defying John over the gold. Too bad he had so much going on in the city, he couldn't take care of you himself. But, sometimes he liked to have strong-arm types like Otis do things like that for him, made him feel important. But Otis never had the violent streak that John had. We're all family, you know, cousins, at a remove, of course. My part of the family never had the money the Dennehy's used to set up John's grandfather's empire. But the old man's dying now, so that's over. But," she shrugged, "He's been dying for years, and he keeps rallying. Guess you can't keep a bad man down."

Liz said, "I'll get lemonade and cookies." She hurried into the house.

After the woman had drunk a glass of lemonade and demolished most of the plate of cookies, Wendy said, "You haven't introduced yourself. I mean, other than as Otis Cleary's cousin."

"Yeah, I'm Clarissa Cleary." She looked around the neat, sun-drenched lawn and said, "You got a real nice place here. Inherited from your grandmother, John said. People like you have all the luck. Nobody in my family never inherited nothin'"

"My grandparents worked hard to buy this place, and then worked hard to run it. It was, and is now, a hands-on operation. My brother and I, and my friend Liz, have to work hard to keep it going. Did you notice the vegetable garden?" Wendy waved one hand at the neat rows of vegetables growing behind what Todd called "the rabbit fence". "That's my brother's work, and it's paying off. We've eaten vegetables, mostly tomatoes, lettuce and beans from it for several weeks."

Clarissa shrugged and said, "I'm a city gal. Diggin' in the dirt ain't for me." She held out her hands, showing off her long red fingernails, then shrugged and picked up her glass of lemonade, which Liz had refilled.

Clarissa pointed to a chart that lay on the small table. "This stuff looks confusing." Carole had left it for Wendy. It designated where the various fund-raising booths and musical groups might be set up on the wide lawns surrounding the bed and breakfast. Wendy was sure that once the churches made their final decisions on who would participate, there would be many changes, but the chart was a place to start. Carole believed copies of the chart she sent to each church would create impetus for them to make decisions.

Wendy and Carole had decided that only the musical groups would need to be near the house in order not to have to run electrical lines to the outskirts of the property. Most participants would want to set up in the shade, but since the shade would move as the sun crossed the sky during the daylong event, Wendy knew that changes would occur all day.

Wendy explained to Clarissa, "We've offered use of the property to run a fund-raiser in early August for the local ecumenical charity group, to support their thrift shop and food pantry. They desperately need a central place to run the shop and pantry under one roof."

"What's your percentage?" asked Clarissa. "Take my advice, if they offer ten, insist on twenty."

"We're not taking a percentage," Wendy said. "Everything they make here is for them. It's our way of contributing to the community."

"You're gettin' nothin'? What are you, some kind of do-gooders?"

Clarissa stared at Wendy, then glanced at Liz. Both just nodded to indicate that their guest had heard Wendy correctly.

"If you want to put it that way, I guess so," Wendy answered. "Would you like to attend? Here's a ticket." She handed a bright green card to Clarissa, and explained, "It's free. We thought giving out tickets would serve as a reminder to people to attend."

Clarissa took the ticket between two perfectly manicured fingers, and tucked it into her purse.

"Well, this puts a different slant on things." She paused, and resting a finger on her chin, she stared at Wendy. "I was supposed to come here to make you see the light. Y'know, the family felt that John's share of the gold should go to them. He'd been talkin' about it for such a long time, we got used to it, thinkin' that sooner or later, he'd get it."

Liz sat forward on her chair and asked, "You mean you were supposed to threaten Wendy into giving you the gold found on her property?"

"Yeah, but it looks like your friend here ain't so hot on money, so maybe you wouldn't understand."

Wendy spoke up firmly, "For your information, I no longer have the gold. It's been sold. In fact, that's one of the first things I did after I was rescued from being kidnapped. I realized that I didn't want money from illegal sources, and I'd already talked to our minister about this event. I sold the gold to set up a matching fund as a part of the fund-raiser."

Clarissa's mouth dropped open. "You gave it away? Don't tell me nothin' that crazy. I convinced the men in the family that only a woman could persuade you to give up the gold. That's why I'm here, and my reputation as a mover and shaker depends on you turnin' the money over!"

Wendy stood up, and leaning over Clarissa, she took the woman's right hand. She shook it and said, "It's been nice meeting you, Clarissa. Here, let me give you a few more tickets. Maybe some of your family would like to attend the event."

Clarissa seemed frozen to the chair for a moment. Then she accepted the tickets that Wendy held out to her.

"Well, we'll see. I'd like to see this place again. I'll see what the family says. Maybe…well, thanks." She got to her feet and walked to her car.

Wendy sat down and she and Liz stared at one another. Then as Clarissa's car pulled from the driveway, they burst into laughter. They laughed until tears ran from their eyes. Finally, Wendy wiped her eyes and said, "Thank you, Lord, for letting "the family" send Clarissa to threaten me. She's a character, but I'm sure you knew that. Please let her persuade some of "the family" to attend the fund-raiser. I'm sure they have lots of money, even without the gold, and maybe this is your way of helping us to raise sufficient money for this worthy cause."

CHAPTER TWENTY-ONE

"But I say to you who hear: Love your
enemies, do good to those who hate you, bless
those who curse you, and pray for those who
spitefully use you." (Luke 6:27-28 NKJV)

At eight o'clock in the morning, a few people arrived to set up
booths for the Ecumenical Charities' fund-raiser. Some booths had
been set up on the front and side lawns the previous evening, right after
the local weather reporter had predicted a clear, sunny day. By nine,
two dozen more people had arrived. Wendy looked up at the warm
morning sun peeking through fluffy cumulus clouds. She had checked
the forecast earlier and was pleased to know that a warm, sunny day
was still predicted. She hoped that the changeable Adirondack weather
would remain stable today. There were already thirty people busy
arranging booths and tents. Their children were in high spirits. One
young mother tried to apologize to Wendy for her noisy helpers. Wendy
told her that the children's enjoyment was setting the right mood for
the day.

High-pitched shrieks rang out as children trailing balloons on strings
raced down the lawns. The younger ones splashed into the lake at the
little beach alongside the dock. Three eight to ten year old boys ran the
length of the dock and jumped into the lake. They emerged dripping
and shivering. Mothers ran to them with towels and the boys played up
their dilemma by chattering their teeth as though they were freezing.

Their mothers weren't deceived, even as they rubbed them dry. They knew that the water was cold, but not *that* cold. Wendy and other adults enjoyed watching the horseplay. Wendy laughed and suggested that the children be brought into the house where they could change into dry clothes. The mothers had dry clothes ready. "Boys and lake water," muttered one. "That's an irresistible combination."

Both corners of the front porch were busy with teens setting up amplifiers and unpacking instruments. "Where's Tony and Art?' one of them yelled.

"It's early morning, they aren't up yet, I bet," answered another. "They'll turn up by noon, as usual."

Centrally located on the front porch was the Adirondack Community Church's donut making machine and a table where various implements were laid ready for the donut-making process.

A volunteer for the quilt booth asked Carole, "Should we hang the quilts now?" The pastor glanced at the lake and surrounding forest and said, "Yes, the fog has completely burned off. They won't get damp now."

Carole took Wendy by one arm and said, "There's a young couple I'd like you to meet." She led Wendy to one of the baked goods booths and introduced her to a young woman and man named Jennifer and Ryan. Jennifer was a slender, bright-eyed pixie and at five foot ten Ryan towered over her.

Jennifer said, "Carole tells me that you and your chef are both planning on being married here at the B and B. Do you think you'll have other weddings here?"

Wendy said, "I wouldn't be surprised. Word gets around and one such event leads to another. We believe this is a perfect setting, especially for an outdoor wedding."

Ryan said, "We'd like to talk to you about being married here." He glanced at Carole, who nodded encouragingly. "You see, Jen and I wanted a church wedding, but both our parents are of the Woodstock hippie generation and they disapprove of church weddings. We want them to participate in our wedding, but they won't if we have it in a church." He drew a deep breath and looked at Jennifer.

She said, "Carole said your greenhouse reminded her of a cathedral, with all the glass and the prisms reflecting the light. She heard you even have a cross, though its made of raffia." Her eyes glittered with emotion and she said, "It sounds like it would meet our needs, something like a church, but not a church, if you follow me."

Wendy said, "I know just what you mean, and we'd be pleased to have your wedding here. Do you have a date in mind?"

"Probably around Thanksgiving, since we'd both have time off from our local teaching jobs then. Of course, we wouldn't have much time for a honeymoon, but we really can't afford one, anyway."

Wendy asked, "Why not honeymoon here? We could give you a package deal, wedding and honeymoon, all here at The Greenhouse Bed and Breakfast."

Jennifer burst into happy tears and Ryan clasped her in his arms. He looked at Wendy over Jennifer's head and said, "Thank you, that's a great idea!"

Carole hugged Wendy and whispered, "Thank you, Wendy. This is going to be a wonderful wedding! The wedding and honeymoon package is just what they needed."

Wendy told the young couple that they would talk about the details later and jotted down Jen's phone number and email address.

Then she excused herself and wandered from one booth to the next. She was delighted and pleased by the crafts and variety of foods available. She stopped to help at the quilt booth. She had carried her checkbook with her as she had planned to make purchases today. She saw a quilt she liked, pulled out her checkbook and asked the volunteer to wrap up the dahlia embroidered quilt for her. She knew it would match one of the B and B's guest rooms. Her grandmother hadn't been able to find a quilt for the Dahlia Room; Wendy was pleased that she was able to continue her grandmother's quest.

"Hey," said Todd. "You're not supposed to buy the place out before it opens."

Wendy just smiled at him and said, "If only one of the local artists has a dahlia picture I could hang in the Dahlia Room, it'll be complete. Look at this quilt. I'll put it in the room. Isn't it perfect?" She held up the bag so he could see the design on the quilt.

"You're right. It'll fit in that room." He said, "It's nine-thirty, and we don't open for a half hour, but people are arriving already. All these," he glanced at the about thirty people bustling around the lawns, "they can't all be volunteers."

"I bet they are," said Wendy. Then, out of the corner of her eye, she saw Liz waving frantically at her and she hurried up to the driveway. "What is it?" she asked.

"Look there," Liz jerked her head toward the end of the driveway, where a long, antique yellow automobile was slowly entering.

"Tell Todd that 'the family' is here." Wendy told Liz. Her friend nervously hurried off to deliver the message.

Wendy cautiously approached the car. Parking had been arranged near the highway, but the driver of the antique vehicle apparently intended to drive right up to the event. The car stopped in the driveway and a uniformed chauffeur got out. He was an enormous grim-faced man, built like a professional wrestler. He opened the back of the car and removed a folded-up wheelchair. He set it up and wheeled it to the side of the car. Then he opened a rear passenger door and leaned in. He emerged carrying a thin, frail, elderly man in his arms. The man's few strands of white hair moved limply in the slight breeze of his passage. The chauffeur carefully set the man in the wheelchair and then hurried to the front passenger door. He opened the door and Clarissa Cleary stepped out. She was dressed in a light, bright green silk dress. Diamonds sparkled at her ears and throat. Wendy noticed that she bore a resemblance to the elderly man.

Clarissa carried a light blanket over one arm, which she wrapped over the elderly man's lap, tucking it in carefully. She smiled into his wrinkled face and he smiled back. The chauffeur stepped back, allowing her to wheel the chair up to Wendy.

Wendy realized that the old man was dressed in 1920's fashion. He wore a trim black suit that was shiny with age. She saw one knee that slipped out from the blanket that was almost worn through. His neat white spats were worn over gleaming black shoes.

Then Clarissa cleared her throat, and Wendy turned to look at her. "Good morning, Clarissa. I'm glad to see you here," Wendy said warmly.

Clarissa half-heartedly returned her smile and said, "I'd like you to meet my grandfather, John Dennehy."

The old man peered at her through thick-lensed glasses and held out a thin arm. When Wendy took his cold hand, she felt as if she was holding a fragile bird's claw. "I'm pleased to meet you, Mr. Dennehy. Welcome to The Greenhouse Bed and Breakfast and welcome to the fundraiser for The Lake Placid Ecumenical Charities Group."

"These the folks you're givin' your money to, I hear," Mr. Dennehy said in a weak, quavering voice. "Mind if I ask why?"

Wendy drew a deep breath. "Lake Placid has an unusual economy. There's no manufacturing, so we depend on tourists for economic support. During the ski season, if we get a warm spell and the snow melts, the skiers leave. That means that waitpersons and chambermaids have no jobs. They're paid by the hour and when there are no tourists in town, the hotels and restaurants have to tell them not to come in to work.

"They need a food pantry to get them through those times and a group like Ecumenical Charities to pay their heating and electric bills. Bad weather in the summer is unusual, but it's happened that we've had rain for weeks. Few people will golf or sail in a downpour. Of course, the mountain trails can be dangerous then, so the hikers leave." Wendy suddenly felt as if she'd been talking for too long, and began to step back.

Mr. Dennehy held up his right hand, palm out, and said, "You know what you're talkin' about, missy. Some folks can't get through hard times like the rest of us. I got some family I have to help out, now and then." He drew a deep, rasping breath, then said, "A'course, they're family, not like the folks you're tryin' to help."

"Jesus said we're all family," said Wendy. "He told us to help one another."

"Yeah, guess you're right, but I always had to take care of myself first. Taught Jackie the same thing, an' now he's dead. Nuthin's worse than buryin' family younger than you, I tell you. Don't know what else I coulda done for him, 'cept bring him into the family business, like I did." He cleared his throat, then said, "That's all changed, now. I don't understand all these new recreational drugs. There's nothin' like good likker, far as I'm concerned. But, you gotta sell what the people want, like it or not. Understand?"

"Uh, I guess I see where you're coming from, but I can't say I like it." Wendy was confused. She was beginning to like the old man, but didn't want to give the impression that she approved of his family's way of life.

"Would you like to get out of the sun?" Wendy asked. "I think your chair will go over the lawn to the nearest shade trees."

The chauffeur walked onto the lawn, then bent and pressed one hand several times onto the surface. "Yeah, this is firm as a golf course. The chair will ride on it okay." He straightened and waited for instructions from his boss.

"Yeah. Over by that maple tree. It looks good there. It'll give me a good view of who's comin' and goin." The chauffeur wheeled the chair under the tree and Clarissa followed. Wendy detoured to the back porch and picked up several folding chairs, which she placed near the wheelchair for Clarissa and the chauffeur. Clarissa smiled and introduced the chauffeur as her cousin, Ryan. Wendy shook hands with him and told him where the food booths were located. He smiled in response and headed toward the donuts being dispensed from the front porch.

Mr. Dennehy pulled Clarissa close to him and whispered in her ear. After she responded with a whisper in his ear, she stepped back to speak to Wendy. "I don't suppose there's any liquor served here," she said. When Wendy shook her head, Clarissa dropped her voice to a whisper and said, "He ain't supposed to drink, but he does. I know he has a stash in the car, but I persuaded him it would be rude to drink here."

"Thanks for thinking of that," Wendy said. "Will he be comfortable here? There's a lemonade stand right there." Wendy pointed to a colorfully decorated booth manned by several local Boy Scout troops.

"I'll see if he wants any. As for being comfortable, as long as he's sittin' where he can see anyone comin', he's fine." She left for the lemonade stand.

For the first time, Wendy noticed that Mr. Dennehy's wheelchair was placed so he had a good view of the people coming and going. His narrowed eyes never left the procession of people who arrived. Although the event had just started, Wendy saw early shoppers leaving, carrying their purchases in green bags with the Ecumenical Charities logo of four clasped hands forming a square cross.

The p.a. system popped and screeched a few times. Then Carole's voice could be heard. "We would like to officially open this event with a few words of dedication. I'll start with a short reading from Matthew twenty-two, verses thirty-seven through thirty-nine. 'Jesus said, You shall love the Lord your God with all your heart, with all your soul, and with all your mind. This is the first and great commandment. And the second is like it: You shall love your neighbor as yourself.'

We are here today to emulate Jesus' example. He gave up everything he had for us so that we might share in everything that He has. We cannot out-give God, but by sharing today, we can participate in God's ongoing cycle of generosity. The forms to donate to the matching grant are here on the table at the foot of the steps."

Then she laughed and said, "We're right under the donut stand so you can't miss us. How's that for good planning? Now, enjoy the day and God bless you!"

One of the bands began to play a very upbeat version of "Amazing Grace." The crowd, now grown to several hundred people, flowed from one booth to another. As the morning grew warmer, the lemonade stand did a brisk business. Wendy exchanged a delighted smile with Carole, who was helping people fill out forms at the matching fund table. Although a beach umbrella shaded her, Carole was waving a fan at her face in a vain effort to cool off.

Liz caught Wendy's arm and said, "You'll never guess what Carole wants—she wants me to lead a teen Bible study group, studying the women of the Bible. Me!"

"I'm sure you can, Liz. You read the Bible daily and I'm sure you've picked up a lot of knowledge on the women of the Bible without realizing it."

"She gave me the study book and it looks interesting." Liz held up a brightly covered book titled, "Women of The Bible."

Wendy encouraged Liz on teaching the study, and then felt a pang of sympathy as she saw Todd remove a full bag from a garbage can and replace it with a clean liner. She knew he would continue that task all day.

Suddenly Clarissa was at her elbow, saying, "My grandfather would like to speak to you." Wendy followed Clarissa across the lawn, only waving when people started to speak to her.

Once she reached the shade where Mr. Dennehy was seated with Ryan by his side, the old man told Clarissa, "Get my wallet from the car, please."

When she returned with a leather-bound folder, he ordered, "Get a chair for Miss Bailey." As Clarissa went to search for another folding chair, Wendy said, "Please, Mr. Dennehy, call me Wendy."

"Yeah, our families have known each other long enough. Here, Wendy, sit down." Clarissa set a chair behind Wendy, so she sat.

Mr. Dennehy took a deep breath and leaned slightly forward in his chair. Looking Wendy right in the eyes, he said, "You shoulda got about forty thousand for them gold coins. Did you do any better than that?"

Wendy answered, "Our friend, Sty Powers, found a numismatist who specializes in old gold coins. He offered us forty-six thousand dollars and we accepted his offer."

The old man peered at a xeroxed form in his hand. "I had Clarissa ask that preacher woman, Carole Cody, and she said that's what you put up as your end of the matching funds." He cleared his throat and stared at her with red-veined brown eyes. Then he raised his voice and said, "The whole thing? What possessed you? You can't be makin' a whole lot here, runnin' a B and B!"

"It wasn't mine to keep, Mr. Dennehy. My grandfather obtained it through illegal means, so I felt it should be used to help others." When the old man shook his head, Wendy continued, "When I thought of how much injury and family harm that alcohol consumption has caused, I knew money earned from that source had to be used to help people who were seriously in need."

"Yeah, we kinda figured that." He exchanged a grin with Clarissa, and then opened the wallet. Clarissa handed him a pen, but he pointed toward Carole's booth and told Clarissa, "Ask her now."

Clarissa walked briskly to the booth and spoke briefly to Carole. The pastor looked surprised, and then spoke to her. Clarissa nodded and returned to the group in the shade. "She said it's about twenty thousand, but it's early yet, and there'll be more from the booths. Most of them are staffed by not-for-profits, but they'll split their take with Ecumenical Charities."

"Good! I like to see that everyone's pitchin' in. Makes me feel it's worthwhile." He wrote a check, then pulled it from his book and handed it to Wendy. To Wendy's surprise, the check written to Ecumenical Charities was in the amount of twenty thousand dollars.

"Thank you, Mr. Dennehy, We really appreciate this."

"You're welcome, Wendy. Now, I think it's time this old man left." As Ryan got up from his chair, Jack Dennehy took Wendy by the hand and said, "You should know, there's no bad feelings between our families, from now on. There's been enough harm caused by the way we carried on, back in my day, so it's over. And," he gently shook Wendy's hand, "if you ever need help, you call me, and I'll see to it that my family takes care of you." His eyes gleamed with sincerity and Wendy was touched. "Thank you, Mr. Dennehy. I appreciate that." She glanced at Clarissa, who was opening the car door. Clarissa nodded and smiled warmly at her.

The early evening sun was losing its luster by the time the cleanup was done. When everyone finally had a chance to relax and talk, they sat on the front porch eating donuts. Liz and Todd were sprawled on the lawn. Liz said, "Todd, I already told Wendy that Carole talked me into teaching a teen girl Bible Study on women of the Bible."

"Good idea!" said Todd. "I saw you carrying a book with that title, so I know you're interested. Are those the girls you were talking to today?"

"Yes, I hope they know what they're getting into, with me as their teacher."

Carole said, "They know you and look up to you. I'm sure you'll get along."

Wendy sat on the porch steps wearing a bemused, contented smile.

She said, "It's over, the dangerous animosity that's been hurting our families for three generations. It's over and oddly, it ended with a generous gesture. Not only the money, but also the offer of help, if we needed it. Frankly, I see God's hand in this."

Carole nodded in agreement, "Only God could have pulled that off. Changing the heart of a tough old hoodlum like Jack Dennehy. Thank you, God!"

"What on earth would we need his help with?" asked Liz. Laughing, she suggested, "Maybe if we want someone rubbed out?"

Todd howled with laughter and as Dan and Tom approached them, he suggested, "Tell them what the old man offered."

More laughter greeted Liz' announcement, but Tom whistled in appreciation when he learned how much Dennehy had donated. He shook Carole's hand and said, "You did good, all of you. Even without Dennehy's donation, you did good."

He sat next to Wendy and slid an arm over her shoulder. "You're a genius, my girl. You really are!"

Wendy blushed in pleasure, but waved a hand at the rest of the group on the porch. "Everyone did it, not just me."

"It takes one good idea, and one generous person to get the ball rolling. You're that person, and I'm proud of you. About Jack, remember the story of the scorpion who stings someone who helps him, explaining, 'I'm a scorpion, what else could you expect?'"

Wendy looked thoughtful, and then said, "In other words, he might be setting me up so I'm not looking for some nasty trick he might pull?"

"Exactly," said Tom. He hugged her close to him

CHAPTER TWENTY-TWO

"He who is of God hears God's words;
therefore you do not hear, because you
are not of God." (John 8:47 (NKJV)

The morning of Stan Gubinsky's trial dawned bright and clear, but a few narrow pink clouds on the horizon threatened rain before the day was over.

Wendy was pleased that Tom, Todd, Liz and Dan were in the courtroom to give her moral support as she testified.

She had to keep praying in her mind in order not to tremble as the defendant's lawyer aggressively questioned her. He tried to imply that she had been hung over the day that she had disappeared, claiming that the party of the Fourth of July the day before was a "drunken debauch." That brought an objection from the district attorney. The judge informed Gubinsky's attorney that such "reckless speculation" would not be permitted.

Under the guidance of the D.A., Wendy summarized being drugged unconscious, awakening bound and gagged in the boat that was being rowed by an unseen person. She stated that she had heard Gubinsky's voice often enough to recognize it. Her time spent concealed on Moose Island took only minutes to describe.

Tom Decker and two other troopers who had both attended the party and participated in the search testified. They made it clear that there had been no liquor served the day of the barbecue, debunking Gubinsky's attorney's claims.

Wendy had dreaded the trial and testifying before the judge and jury. Once started, she was surprised at how quickly it went. After the forensics experts had testified to finding Gubinsky's fingerprints on the rowboat, oars and the duct tape used to bind and gag Wendy, there seemed to be little to add to the proceedings.

However, Gubinsky's attorney lamely tried to claim that the fingerprints on the rowboat could have gotten there by some other means, which he couldn't identify. Finally, he gave up. Gubinsky sat slumped at the defendant's table and did not testify.

The jury's guilty verdict came in within several hours, and Wendy felt as if she could collapse in relief.

The little coffee shop near the courthouse was filled, but Todd had found a table by arriving before the jury verdict came in. He admitted he had been so certain that Gubinsky would be found guilty that he felt it was a waste of time to wait.

"Besides, I think this coffee shop must have a direct conduit to the courthouse. I'm told that a verdict is reported here as soon as it's reported in the courthouse."

Wendy had to agree with him, because as she walked in the door, a waitress said, "Congratulations, I hope the judge puts him away for decades! Too bad you'll have to wait until next month to find out what his sentence is."

Wendy sat with Todd, Tom, Liz and Dan, who were all finishing off a platter of homemade muffins.

Dan said, "These aren't as good as yours, Liz, but then again, I'm biased."

Liz grinned and said, "The advantage to these muffins is that I didn't have to spend time in a hot kitchen to make them."

They all laughed, knowing that her love of cooking kept her in the kitchen on much hotter days than this warm early August day.

Suddenly Liz said, "Look who's here!" They all looked at the door and saw Clarissa Cleary glancing around the room. She saw them and walked directly to them, ignoring the waitress who was offering to find her a seat.

Clarissa leaned over the table and hugged Wendy. "I was so proud of you on the stand," she said. "You did a great job."

Dan pulled a chair from another table and Clarissa sat near them. "I wanted you to know that my grandfather kept his word, Wendy. That dumbnuts lawyer that Gubinsky found really blew his case. Grandpa told the family lawyer that he wasn't to touch the case, that Gubinsky had to get his own lawyer."

Clarissa's dangling diamond earrings jiggled as she laughed. "He did, all right. Not that a good lawyer could have gotten him off! There was too much evidence against him. But like I said, you did a great job. You're an inspiration to me.

"Oh, that reminds me, I'm going to college evenings to get a business degree. Looking after Grandpa takes up most of my daytime hours, but he encouraged me to "do something with my mind", was the way he put it. He named you as a good example. So, you're my ideal, Wendy." She hugged Wendy again, and then said, "Grandpa's waiting for me to call him and let him know the verdict. I'd better go."

After one more hug, she asked, "When's the wedding?"

"Last Saturday in May," said Wendy.

Wendy added, "You're invited, of course. Please give us your address so we know where to send the invitation." Clarissa happily scribbled her address on a napkin. It was a post office box in Manhattan. Then she waved goodbye and stared to leave.

She suddenly turned back and pulled a magazine from her enormous purse. "I brought this because I knew you'd like to see it." She opened the magazine to a full page picture of The Greenhouse, taken from the lake edge. Wendy seized it and avidly began to read. "Oh, Liz! Your meals are wonderful, she says, and the rooms are unbelievably lovely and comfortable." She continued to skim the article until she got to the last paragraph. "This is interesting; she says that if you weren't a believer before you stayed at The Greenhouse, you might be one by the time you leave. She says no one pushes faith, but practical evidence is evident. Isn't that marvelous!"

Clarissa said, "I knew that would *really* make your day. Bye now." She waved and left the coffee shop.

"Whew!" said Dan. "I thought she was never going to leave."

"She likes to talk, doesn't she?" said Liz.

Wendy said, "I think she's become happier than she was the first time we saw her. She's finding that she can be her own person, not just an insignificant member of a crime family. Her grandfather is cutting the apron strings by letting her go to college."

Todd said, "Want to bet who she'll work for when she graduates? Old man Dennehy isn't going to let her get too far away. He's letting the string out only far enough to keep her happy, but not enough for her to be independent."

"I think you're right," said Wendy thoughtfully. "Now that you guys have eaten all the muffins, I guess we can go home."

The trip from the county seat in Elizabethtown to Lake Placid took about a half hour, with Tom driving. In the bright sunlight, daylilies ran riot through the ditches. Fields were throbbing with butterflies. The road was dry until they reached the outskirts of Lake Placid, where they saw it had rained.

Dan said, "Typical Adirondack weather, dry in one village, rain in the next." The road was wet all the way to The Greenhouse.

As the car entered the driveway near the house, Wendy leaned forward in her seat. "Look," she cried out, "Over the lake. What a rainbow!" Tom stopped the car and everyone piled out. They all walked quickly toward the lake, as if drawn by a powerful magnet. A double rainbow curved from over the mountains to the east to a hazy end somewhere in the forest to the west. The colors shifted and changed as they watched. Dan ducked into his car, which he had left at the B and B, and pulled out his camera. He took one picture after another. He walked along the lakeshore, seeking interesting and different angles. But then, he stood still and just let the light surround him.

Wendy walked to the edge of the lake, then out onto the dock. She stood with her head tipped back. Her face glowed in the reflection of the lovely lights overhead. As the others approached her, they could hear her soft prayer, "Thank you, Lord, for this perfect ending to an excellent day. I praise you and bless you, my Lord and my God."

The group that gathered at the dinner table that evening was cheerful and boisterous. Liz's pot roast received high praise.

Liz and Dan exchanged a glance and Liz said, "We want you all to know that we're getting married in mid-October. Dan is house-hunting in Ray Brook, so we didn't want to wait. We hoped we could have an outdoor wedding here."

Wendy said, "That's short notice, but we can do it!"

As Liz served apple pie a la mode, Todd said he wanted to propose a toast.

He stood up and holding his glass of apple cider high, he said, "To the Greenhouse family! Especially to the future brides and the two guys who were smart enough to get themselves engaged into this family. Here's to all of us!"

"Hear, hear! To the family! To the family!" shouted Dan and Tom.

CHAPTER TWENTY-THREE

"By this we know love, because He laid
down His life for us. And we also ought
to lay down our lives for our brethren
But whoever has this world's goods, and
sees his brother in need, and shuts up his
heart from him, how does the love of God
abide in him." (I John 4:16-17 NKJV)

Wendy smiled at Tom as they left Carole's office after the last
session of their premarital counseling. They had both been comfortable
in Carole's book-lined office that overlooked Mirror Lake. Carole's
approach had led them to think deeply about their convictions in their
Christian life and upcoming marriage.

As they walked out of the church into the morning sunlight, Tom
squeezed Wendy's hand and said, "Carole's statement that Christian
premarital counseling has Godly intent really opened my eyes. Though
both you and I committed our lives to Christ years ago, these sessions
deepened my commitment. I had the impression you felt the same way."

"I did." She returned the grasp of his hand and said, "I find that
I've made Jesus Christ not only my personal Savior, but also an integral
partner in our marriage."

Tom was scheduled to work in the afternoon, so when he they
returned to the B and B, he shed his uniform jacket and grabbed a rake
to join Todd in raking the lawns.

It was only mid-morning and Wendy didn't want to go indoors and miss any of the lovely mid-August day. She strolled to the lake and then the length of the dock. She looked across the lake. Most of the trees surrounding Lake Placid were evergreens, but the occasional splash of autumn color from birch and aspen could already be seen on the lakeshore. The trees were reflected mirror-perfect in the still morning water.

Although the air was warm, she knew that summer was almost gone. She thought, *Only eight weeks to Liz's wedding!* Liz approached and Wendy waited for her.

Liz said, "I'm glad Carole insisted we have pre-marital counseling I thought of myself as a Christian, but I skirted the idea of commitment, and felt I had to take care of myself first. As long as I was self-reliant, I was sure I'd be okay. In fact, I'm sure that's why I took up ju-jitsu. That was part of my self-reliance thing. Now Dan and I know better. We're both entrenched in self-sufficiency, and that could have troubled our marriage. Without counseling, both of us could have put ourselves first, which might have resulted in a very brief marriage."

They walked up the lawn to the house. Wendy thought *I love having another committed woman to share my thoughts and prayers with.*

They saw a gleaming black BMW enter the driveway. Wendy was puzzled, as their next guests were not due for several days. Liz entered the house and Wendy waited on the porch for the driver to get out of the car. A tall, heavyset, blond man wearing aviator sunglasses approached. He coolly glanced at her, but did not return her friendly greeting.

Instead, he looked around at the lawn and the back of the house. His face drew into a contemptuous sneer. "Much too plain," he said, in a sarcastic tone. "Considering how much you stole from my family, you could've dressed the place up better than this. Tennis courts, at least."

Wendy observed his sharp profile and recognized Jack Dennehy's features. She asked, "Are you related to Jack Dennehy?"

"You bet. I'm the grandson you *didn't* kill." He stamped onto the porch and Wendy stepped back to distance herself from his anger. "I'm Rolf Dennehy and I'm a lot smarter than Jackie ever hoped to be. That jerk! Trying to deal with a woman. Even Grandpa Jack didn't have it in him to get rid of you!"

Wendy asked, "What do you want here?"

"Want?" He voice rose to a shout. "I want what you owe us – that's what I want. Never mind that religious crap you fed Grandpa Jack. You owe us! I'm gonna be running the family's business from now on and I mean to collect!"

The back door opened and as Todd stepped out, he said, "Forget it, Dennehy, that's all behind us now. Your grandfather put an end to it, and that's that!"

"No way! You people owe us and I'm collecting." He suddenly stopped speaking and stared at the door through which Tom had appeared. Dennehy stared, first at the uniform, then at the tall man wearing it.

"You're leaving now," Tom said firmly. He moved toward Dennehy and asked, "Do you want me to escort you off the property?"

Dennehy gulped, and then said, "You can't make me leave." His voice sounded weaker than earlier.

"You're on private property, so yes, I can make you leave." Tom dropped one strong hand on the other man's shoulder and its weight forced him to step back. Then Tom turned Dennehy around, and gripping him by his shoulders, he forced him off the porch and to his car.

"Now go and don't come back," he said firmly.

Dennehy slipped into his car and glared uselessly at them. He turned the car on the lawn and, gunning the motor so the tires churned up the grass, he left.

"Wow!" breathed Liz from the doorway. "Nothing like having a cop on the premises. Thanks, Tom!"

Wendy took Tom's hands and squeezed them in hers. She said, "Yes, thanks. That guy scared me. I had no idea what he might do."

Tom shook his head, "I don't think *he* knew what he might do. He apparently hoped to bully you and see where it would take him. I don't think he'll be back."

Wendy's cell phone rang and she answered it. She listened for a moment, then said, "Clarissa, what's the matter? You sound upset." She listened again, and apparently interrupting Clarissa, she said, "He was here, and Tom sent him packing. It seems that a uniformed state trooper was more than he bargained for. Don't worry, he's gone. Thank you and God bless you."

After she ended the call, she explained, "Clarissa knew that Rolf Dennehy was bragging that he could make me hand over enough money to make up for what the family thought they should have gotten from my grandfather. He apparently saw himself as his grandfather's heir, but the rest of the family do not. Clarissa promised that the family would keep Rolf from bothering us again. I hope that's true. I thought we'd seen the last of this Dennehy problem."

The family left the porch and sank into lawn chairs. They breathed sighs of relief.

Wendy looked up to the brilliant blue sky, and lifting both arms overhead, she said, "Thank you, God, for helping us cope with Rolf Dennehy."

Liz echoed her with a fervent, "Thank you, God."

Tom looked at Wendy with a fond smile, and reaching across the space between their chairs, he grasped her hand and squeezed it.

At lunch, Liz told Wendy that she had asked the four teen girls in the Bible study she was teaching to serve as her bridesmaids, but one of them wanted to know if she and her mother could make her own dress. Liz agreed, explaining that she had chosen a simple style, and would use locally available hand-woven cloth, with full skirts and plain, fitted short-sleeved bodices.

Wendy asked, "You've gotten to know these girls well, haven't you?"

"Yes, we worked together at the fundraiser, and I've enjoyed teaching them. Actually, I've learned as much as they have, which is a major reason why I wanted them to be a part of the wedding."

Wendy couldn't resist asking, "Are you going to have them dance across the lawn, like the wedding video we saw on TV? You mentioned that you loved the idea."

"They'd love to do it, but I don't know what Dan's friends will think. Actually, Dan's brother, Karl, is only a couple of years older than the girls. They know him, and they're going to ask him if he'd participate. The dancing bridal party may be for real!"

Wendy laughed at the idea. "Now you have to sell Dan on it. Good luck." On their return to the house they shared their news with Patty, who found it amusing

It was the next day when Dan heard the news about the dancing bridal party from Karl. He laughed and said that if his friends who had agreed to be his groomsmen were willing to dance, he'd go along with it. He called Liz and asked if Karl was correct. Liz told him, "Yes, the girls want to do it, and I love the idea. What a great way to launch a wedding!" Finally, much to everyone else's surprise, it was decided that the wedding party would dance across the lawn.

Several nights later, Tom and Wendy went out to dinner. Across a candle-lit table, Tom asked her, "What kind of surprises do you have in store for me for our wedding?"

"None, I promise. According to Liz, I'm conventional, so of course I'm looking forward to a traditional wedding." Then she laughed and admitted, "As if a wedding in a greenhouse can be considered conventional! But I promise there will be no dancing bridesmaids. Although I suspect Liz will skip on her way to the altar as my matron of honor, and I think Kim will also. She's *that* pleased that we're getting married. I really like your family, Tom. I consider myself very lucky. Just think, I'm going from a family of two to," she paused and laughed. *"How many people are in your family?"*

Tom chuckled. "Locally there's just my brother's family of four, but if you want to count cousins, you'll need the fingers on both hands to count. Some of them might come up from New Jersey to the wedding, probably about a dozen. We'll see.

"I consider myself lucky, too. You know, since both of our parents died when we were young, we're both orphans. I think we're meant for each other. By the way, I really like the idea of being married in the greenhouse. I'm glad you and Liz took Terry Johns up on his offer to make a birch-bark altar to be used at the weddings."

"Carole told us what size it should be, and Terry said he'd have it ready in plenty of time for the wedding in October. I told Terry that I'll save the altar for future weddings here, starting with the one on Thanksgiving weekend. He was pleased."

Tom said, "Isn't it wonderful that for a couple of orphans, we have so many friends who are willing to help us with our wedding?"

"Wonderful doesn't begin to describe how I'm feeling," Wendy replied. Tom reached across the table and took her hands in both of his. Wendy was filled with such love and warmth that she had to blink to keep tears of happiness from falling.

"That reminds me," Tom said, "Somehow my niece Susie got the idea that because her uncle is getting married, she's entitled to be a flower girl. But," he ducked his head in embarrassment, "you probably don't intend to have a flower girl. You said you wanted to keep it simple."

"I'd love that! I wish I'd thought of it myself. Please ask Kim if Susie can be my flower girl. Maybe Sam would like to be a ring bearer. He's such a confident little guy, for eight years old. I'm sure he'd do a good job."

"I'll ask, and I'm sure the answer will be yes. At this rate, my whole family will be in the wedding. With Ted as my best man, Kim as a bridesmaid and both kids involved, you'll have more Deckers than non-family guests at this rate."

They were both pleased at the idea of the extensive Decker family filling the greenhouse.

A waiter hovered in the background, but after noting their delight in each other and the obvious love they were expressing, he sighed sentimentally, and stepped back.

Tom said, "You know, Wendy, there's one of Carole's questions we haven't followed up on. We haven't decided where we'll live, once we're married."

Wendy flushed in embarrassment. "How could I have forgotten that?"

Tom admitted, "Me too. I've been so concerned about your safety that it slipped my mind. Do you have any ideas?"

"Would you be willing to live at the B and B until we can buy or build a house? My room is the largest and we could use the box room next to it to store your stuff, especially all the out-of-season gear I know you have."

"That's a good idea. I wouldn't mind living at the B and B for a while, but I'm sure we'll need a place of our own before long. But," he squeezed her hands," there's something else we should consider. I didn't want to bring it up with Carole, because I wanted to hear it straight from you. I know how committed you are to using the B and B as a means to bring others to Christ. I approve of that, but will that mission of yours come before our marriage?" He looked worried and asked, "Do you have energy for, first, our marriage, second, your mission *and third, running the business*? Or is that a matter of taking on too much?"

"My mission, as you call it, seems to fit into the running of the B and B. An example of that mission is Jen and Ryan's wedding there over Thanksgiving. A young bride whose parents are antagonistic to Christianity is a challenge. But, give her a Christian wedding in the greenhouse, and her former hippie parents will hardly notice. *Unless, of course*, I can persuade them to see the light.

"I'm trying to fit my mission into my favorite quote from Philippians. Paul wrote, 'Whatever things are true, whatever things are noble, whatever things are just, whatever things are pure, whatever things are lovely, whatever things are of good report, if there is any virtue and if there is anything praiseworthy—meditate on these things. The things which you learned and received and heard and saw in me, these do, and the God of peace will be with you.'"

When Tom nodded in approval, she went on, "As to where we might live later on, the property has lots of acreage. We could request a zoning waiver on an acre, and have it rezoned residential and build there."

"Good idea. You'll be close to your business, and I can drive to headquarters in ten or fifteen minutes. Is Todd ready for a housemate?"

"He loves having you around. While we're on our honeymoon in Canada, he'll miss both of us. Oh, thanks for helping him with the yard work this week. Todd is so pleased to have some of the work taken off his hands."

Tom laughed and said, "It sounds like I'm a member of the family already. Sharing the work is part of that. I only hope I can share your mission."

Wendy smiled and squeezed his hand. "I know you will. Your faith is strong and you set a good example, which is the best way to express Christianity." Suddenly, she noticed the waiter and suggested, "Don't you think it's time we ordered?"

Tom waved the young waiter forward and after apologizing for making his wait so long, they placed their order.

CHAPTER TWENTY-FOUR

"For I know the thoughts that I think toward you, says the Lord, thoughts of peace and not of evil, to give you a future and a hope. Then you will call upon Me and go and pray to Me, and I will listen to you. (Jeremiah 29:11-12 NKJV)

"How are you doing on plans for Jennifer and Ryan's wedding?" asked Patty as she arrived for work on Monday. She headed for the laundry room; sure that Wendy would have stripped the beds as soon as the weekend's guests had left.

"Everything's set. Jen wants to keep costs down, so instead of her having to buy flowers, we're leaving all the flowers in the greenhouse that are there now. Her wedding colors are pink and light green. That's what will be blooming in the greenhouse on Thanksgiving. The pink orchids will still be in bloom. The bridesmaid's dresses have been selected. Carole says that everything will work out well."

Patty asked, "Will you leave the raffia cross up on the wall?"

"Oh yes, that's important to both Jen and Ryan. It looks lovely with the swag of light green silk over the horizontal bars extending to the Cattleya orchids on either side of it. I'm so glad Liz thought of that! Her parents will just have to put up with the cross on the wall. After all, it's Jen and Ryan's wedding, not theirs."

Patty hugged Wendy. "Good for you! Let me know if there's

anything I can do to help that young couple. I like them and I'm looking forward to seeing this wedding come off as they've planned."

When Liz entered the room, Wendy asked her, "About your wedding music, would you like me to ask Ted Decker to play his keyboard so you could walk to the altar to the music you want? You'll have to tell him what you've chosen, so he can get the music and practice. He could set up on the porch like the musicians did for the fund-raiser. I've only heard him play once at a benefit in Saranac Lake, but I think he's a terrific musician and I'm sure he'd do a good job."

"Yeah, Ted would do a good job, but," Liz held a hand up, "about the greenhouse as a site for your wedding, how many people could we seat in there? Probably not enough, considering the number of people we've become friends with since moving here, and old friends from New York, I mean *really old*, like Mr. and Mrs. Powers."

"You have a point there. We'd better think about that." Wendy caught at Todd's sleeve as he was slipping through the room. He was trying to ignore the "whole wedding mess" as he called it. She asked him, "Can we remove the table in the middle of the greenhouse? I don't use it. You don't even start your veggies there." He didn't meet her eyes, so she demanded, "Give me some help. Can we move it out for my wedding?"

"It weighs a ton, but I suppose we could get some help and move it. The water pipe isn't hooked up, so that won't interfere." Warming to his subject, he suggested, "We could empty the parlor of furniture and put up folding chairs in there. They'd have a good view through the glass wall and a microphone could carry the music and wedding vows. That guy who did the audio for the concert Ted played at might be willing to do it. It seems he's friends with the Deckers, so maybe he wouldn't charge much."

Wendy sighed and opened the three-ring binder that she felt had become attached to her right arm. She made notes of Todd's suggestions, and thanked him.

The next morning, both Tom and Dan were at the B and B for breakfast. Immediately after they ate, Dan said to Liz, "There's something I want to show you."

Liz exchanged a puzzled look with Wendy, then followed Dan out the door. Wendy was also puzzled and she couldn't imagine what Dan had to show Liz at eight in the morning.

She told Todd, "I'm just beginning to realize that I don't know Dan very well. "What could he be up to?"

"Nothing nasty, I'm sure," he answered. "Dan's a good guy, a real straight arrow, as Terry Johns would say. We'll just have to wait and see."

Their puzzle was answered when Liz and Dan returned before lunch. To Wendy's practiced eye, Liz looked excited and happy. Wendy took Liz by both hands, and said, "Come on, tell me, what's the secret?"

"Dan's been looking at houses, and he likes one in Ray Brook. It has a marvelous kitchen and though it's small, it's just right for us for now. It's only a ten-minute drive from here. Only problem I have with it is the plain yard. I love it here with flowers in every yard, and those beautiful rhodies! I'd really miss them."

Todd interrupted, saying, "I have to trim the rhododendrons back this week. I noticed that some of the branches have developed roots where they touch the ground. If you want them for your new home, I'll be glad to save them when I cut them off. "

"I'd love that." Liz said enthusiastically. "How wonderful, that I could bring plants from this property, where Dan and I met, to our new home."

Wendy suggested, "You wanted the wedding outdoors, but hadn't decided where. How about holding it on the side lawn near the rhododendrons? They'll still be green and we can wind colored ribbons through them. Pick your colors right away, so we can shop."

Liz exclaimed, "Fall colors, deep red and yellow, to match the colors on the maple trees. They will have changed color by then, won't they?"

"Probably, but we won't know until October. Oh, this is so exciting! Our first wedding at The Greenhouse Bed and Breakfast!"

When Patty arrived early the next morning, ready to help set up for a weekend of ten guests, she was greeted by two excited young women who only wanted to talk about the fall wedding. It took her almost an hour to bring them down from their wedding planning high so they could plan menus for the weekend. Finally, Patty's practicality broke through their euphoria. Before the guests began to arrive, Liz and Wendy were back in business mode. Last minute grocery shopping distracted them until it was time to greet the guests and start cooking.

Much to Todd's relief, the wedding planning took a back seat to entertaining their guests. The men wanted to fish and the women preferred shopping, so Todd and Wendy accommodated them. Wendy found that when the guests left and Liz reverted back to her wedding planning mode, she had to make an effort to bring her mind back to that subject.

Liz asked, "Patty! Where can we find dresses in fall colors? Anyplace local?"

Patty laughed at Liz's excitement and told her, "You'll have to go to Plattsburgh. That's the closest bridal shop. The biggest is in Albany, but you probably don't want to take the time to drive there."

"Right. Wendy, let's go shopping next week. We can take a day off in the middle of the week, can't we?"

"Of course we can. Are your bridesmaids ready to shop?"

Todd slipped out the back door, as it appeared that the two women were just getting warmed up to their subject.

"Yes, but I don't want them to have to buy dresses they'd never wear again. I told them about the simple design I have in mind, something practical. They like what I described to them, and they're looking forward to being a dancing bridal party."

"I can picture that," said Wendy, laughing. "Four Forest Rangers dancing across the lawn with Dan!"

Liz broke up laughing, and they decided that they would share their humor with Patty. When she was told about the dancing bridal party, she shook her head and said, "You'd better hope Dan keeps his sense of humor. He'll need it!"

Todd entered the room with a pile of mail. He asked Wendy if she had time to sort the mail, as he had work to do out doors. She agreed, and sorted the mail into piles for Todd, Liz and herself.

She picked up a plain white envelope with a Manhattan postmark, addressed to her and said, "Wonder who this is from? I don't know anyone in Manhattan but Clarissa."

Liz said, "Well, open it!"

Wendy opened the envelope and removed a bright orange flyer that advertised the Lake Placid Annual Olympic Antique Car Show the next weekend. "How odd," she said, "Why would someone in Manhattan send me this flyer? Oh look. There's a note on it."

"What kind of note?" Liz asked.

"It says, "Be here by two o'clock, OR ELSE". What on earth?"

"Let me see," said Liz as she snatched the flyer from Wendy's hand. "That sounds like a threat! Do you suppose it's that crazy old Dennehy?"

"He's into antique cars, or has one. Maybe he's going to make me another offer."

"What kind of offer?' Tom asked as he and Todd joined them.

Wendy handed Tom the flyer and he glanced at it, and then gave it to Todd.

"This sounds like more of a threat than an offer," said Todd. He looked at Wendy and asked, "Are you going?"

"Yes, I'm curious to know what it's about."

"I'm going with you," said Tom.

"Me too," said Todd and Liz in unison.

Tom said, "It sounds like we're going to have an expedition. Might as well show up in force, in case that old man intends to make trouble."

The Olympic Antique Car Show had drawn hundreds of tourists to the village of Lake Placid. Tom knew that parking would be allowed on a back lot of the Lake Placid Club property. He parked the car in one of the last slots available. Then Wendy, Liz, Tom, Todd and Dan walked the several blocks to the show. It was nearly two o'clock and over a hundred antique cars were on display on and around the skating oval in front of the high school. A large crowd, encouraged by the bright, sunny day, eddied around the cars and refreshment booths.

The program they were given on paying their minimal entry fee explained that cars were grouped according to the decades in which they were manufactured. The 1920's cars were lined up on the far side of the property.

Jack Dennehy's bright yellow Hispano-Suiza glittered in the warm sun. It stood out among the others, larger and flashier than most. Jack sat beside it in his wheelchair, attended by his burly chauffeur and Clarissa.

Wendy was not surprised to see that Jack was dressed in his antique black suit, complete with white spats on his narrow, black shoes.

Liz whispered, "I see Clarissa hasn't cut her ties to her grandfather."

Jeff muttered, "Not as long as the old man is as rich as he is. I bet she's counting on collecting in the long run."

"Hush," whispered Wendy. "Good to see you," she called to Clarissa.

The young woman came forward to greet them, "It's good to see you," she said as she hugged both women.

Wendy showed her the flyer and asked, "Did your grandfather send this to me?"

Clarissa read the message and looked puzzled. She said, "You'll have to ask him. I haven't seen this before."

Wendy approached the elderly man, shook his hand and said, "It's good to see you, Jack. You're looking well."

"Thanks. I'm not feeling bad for an old man. Clarissa, pull up a chair for Wendy so I can talk to her."

Clarissa did as she was told, then stepped back to give them some privacy.

Wendy held the flyer so he could see it and said, "Did you want to see me?"

He leaned toward her and spoke quietly. "I decided that I have enough time left to make one more big killing." When she widened her eyes, he amended his remark, saying, "A big splash, one more chance to show these young folks that the old man's still got what it takes. Also, nobody ever has enough money, not even me, so I intend to add to my stash while I can." He sat up as tall as he could in his wheelchair and grinned at Wendy's puzzled expression.

He said, "I know you realize that I specialized in illegal booze, never got into Jackie's specialty of pharmaceuticals. But now it's time I caught up with the latest fad. I intend to use your place in the woods as a warehouse and distribution point for both fake pharmaceuticals and the real ones that are hot on the underground market."

"You are not!" said Wendy. "My home is not available for your drug trade, so don't even think about it."

When Wendy raised her voice, Todd and Tom stepped forward, but she waved them back to indicate that everything was okay. Both men stepped back, but kept their eyes on Wendy and Jack. Tom was tense and stood leaning forward. He appeared to be listening to every word that each said.

Jack narrowed his eyes, and said, "I don't ask, missy. I tell others what they'll do. I don't like to threaten you, but I can send people to call on you and they'll make it plain that you'll do just what I say you'll do. I'm not past it as far as my people are concerned. They'll work for me as long as I'm alive."

Wendy leaned close to him and said, "My home is a legitimate business and I won't allow anyone to use it for illegal purposes." She took one of his thin hands and, holding it gently, she said, "Now listen to me carefully, Jack. You told me that the animosity between our families was over. It doesn't look like you meant what you said." He opened his mouth, but she went on, "You know I can't allow you to do what you want, and no amount of threats will change my mind."

Tom stepped forward and said, "I'll back her on that, Jack. If I and my fellow troopers have to spend all our free time protecting Wendy's home, we'll do it."

Jack snarled and said, "I might have known that you having a cop in the family would get in the way."

Wendy said, "Jack, you made me an offer. You said that if I needed *anything,* you'd get it or do it for me. I'm asking you to live up to your word. All I want from you is to forget this scheme and stay on the straight and narrow. You don't need more money. At ninety-six, you have more than you can spend in the rest of your life. As for your reputation as a mover and a shaker, okay, it's in the past. You should leave it there. Don't try to top your success from back in the Prohibition era."

She slid forward in her chair and took both of Jack's hands in hers. "There's one thing you can do for yourself, something that will benefit you for eternity."

When Jack's eyebrows rose, she explained, "If you read the Bible every day, and learn from it, you can make yourself good with God. After all, God loves you, his Word is full of proclamations of his love. You can hear him tell you he loves you every time you open his Word."

Jack looked down, shook his head and said, "You don't know all I've done, or ordered done. It's unforgivable."

Wendy tightened her grip on his hands and said, "I forgive you for killing my grandfather." When he gasped, she went on, "My grandmother told me that the hardest thing she ever had to do was to ask God to forgive you, but she did. She knew she had to forgive you in order for her to live fully as a Christian. Now, let's pray together."

She leaned as close to him as she could, and said, "Lord Jesus, you bore our sins in your body on the cross, so we might die to our sins and live for righteousness. We have been healed through your suffering." She heard Jack sob and then quickly catch his breath. She continued, "Lord Jesus, cause our hearts, souls and minds to be so overtaken by your grace that we share the testimony of those you cured by the mere touch of your hand. Lord God, help us to love you as you love us. Amen."

Jack removed his hands from her grip and pulled a handkerchief from his suit jacket pocket. He wiped his face before he turned to look at her. "He'll forgive me, in spite of all I done for all those years?"

"Yes, you only have to ask. First, confess your sins to him, then, *if* you truly love him, tell him you love him and intend to follow his Word for the rest of your life. That's all it takes, but it'll be easier for you if you read your Bible every day. You do have a Bible, don't you?"

"How did you know?" He glanced at Clarissa, who had drawn near during Wendy's prayer, but she shook her head and said, "I didn't tell her, I guess she just knew."

Jack reached for Wendy's hands and grasped them firmly. "It really isn't too late for an old reprobate like me?"

Wendy said, "No, it isn't too late."

"My grandmother gave me a King James Bible when I was confirmed. It just sits on my bureau, collecting dust." Then he glanced at Clarissa, and said, "No, somebody always dusts it, and maybe we could read it together."

Clarissa said, "We could, Grandpa. We both should read it, so we'll do it together."

Wendy released Jack's hands and stood up. "I'll be going now, Jack. I'll pray for you." She glanced at Clarissa and said, "I'll pray for both of you, our whole family will." She glanced back at Todd, Liz and Tom who were grouped in back of her. She met Todd's eyes and he said, "We *will* pray for you, Jack, for your whole family."

Jack met his eyes, and said, "Thank you, all of you."

When the younger people left, Jack said to Clarissa, "I've been here long enough. Let's go home. We have to catch up on our reading."

CHAPTER TWENTY-FIVE

"He has shown you, O man, what is good;
And what does the Lord require of you
but to do justly, to love mercy, and to walk
humbly with your God?" (Micah 6:8 NKJV)

The October morning of Liz and Dan's wedding dawned bright and sunny. Family and friends had watched the weather report closely for days, but a threatened storm had moved south and no longer concerned them.

Todd announced that Indian summer was his favorite time of year, not only because it was so beautiful, but also because it usually arrived only every few years.

Wendy, Liz and Patty strung bright ribbons of red, gold and yellow through the rhododendron bushes. More ribbons hung from the branches of trees that draped their green leaves over the birch-bark altar. When Terry Johns had delivered the altar, both Wendy and Liz were delighted with its finely crafted beauty and had declared it a work of art. It was placed in front of a white birch that Liz had strung with multicolored ribbons. A white unity candle stood on a hand-made ceramic plate in the center of the white altar top. More colorful ribbons draped across the top and down both sides, contrasting gaily with the white bark.

Liz inspected the area and made a few minor adjustments in the bouquets of ferns and chrysanthemums that circled the area where the bridal party would stand. The wedding was scheduled for eleven o'clock. Dan had only his wedding day off; since the local New York State Rangers' recent need to answer several emergencies had caused injuries to a few of his fellow rangers, which left them short-handed. Dan felt he was fortunate that neither he nor any of his groomsmen had been among the injured.

Guests arrived promptly and some accepted folding chairs offered on the lawn, but others preferred to stand in order to stroll around and visit. The bridal couple's fellow teachers were introduced to the church members who attended. To Liz's delight, the event was becoming a festive lawn party.

Since Dan's work schedule called for him to report for work the next morning, he and Liz had decided to put off their wedding trip to Barbados until February. Dan said, "We'll be glad to get out of the North Country for a while by then. Winter always seems to be lasting too long by that time. We'll be sick of seeing snow."

Liz had supervised the preparation of the wedding luncheon/reception, but Wendy had insisted on bringing in help to prepare it, in order to give Liz a break from the kitchen on her wedding day.

One of the bridesmaid's mothers, Mary Abbott, had offered to help the girls get dressed and fix their hair. The girls dressed promptly, but it took Mary an hour to weave the ribbons and flowers into each girl's hair. Her work was expert, but the girl's giggling and hi-jinks slowed her down. Finally, they were ready, and Liz, who had been ready for over an hour, told them that they were beautiful, and she was pleased to have them participate in her wedding.

"Now, let's dance!" she exclaimed and told the musicians that everyone was ready. They enthusiastically said that they were also ready.

Carole stood under the gently dipping branches of the white birch tree, her white chasuble contrasting brightly against the dark green ferns and evergreens that grew behind her.

The music of a keyboard and several guitars played a light rock version of Liz's favorite hymn, "Amazing Grace", from the end of the porch nearest the altar area. The four bridesmaids, wearing light cotton dresses in bright autumn colors, stepped lightly down the stairs and danced to meet the groomsmen, who waited for them on the lawn. The groomsmen picked up the beat of the music and they danced together to the altar. Wendy followed. Her dark red dress, made from a light gauzy fabric, floated around her. She wore a shawl in a matching material over her shoulders. She gaily danced to the beat of the music, and smiled to see that the young bridesmaids were the best dancers.

Liz, who was wearing a spaghetti-strap dress made in a hand-woven fabric striped in bright autumn colors, followed them. A sheer shawl in a matching material was fastened at her shoulder straps and floated to her hemline. She carried a bouquet of yellow orchids and white babies-breath. To Todd's disappointment, she had declined to allow anyone to escort her to the altar, so she walked alone. She did not quite dance, but walked with a light bouncing step in time to the music.

The dancing bridesmaids and groomsmen brought applause from the crowd on the lawn. The applause heightened when smiling Liz appeared. Carole waited behind the altar, knowing that the rehearsal the day before had established where everyone was to stand. They lined up, with Liz in the center.

She handed her bouquet to Wendy. Dan stepped forward, his wide smile indicating his joy. Wedding vows and rings were exchanged and the unity candle was lit. Liz picked up the unity candle, Dan grasped her wrist and escorted her indoors.

The greenhouse had been set up with rented chairs and tables. Although it was a snug fit, there was room for everyone. The luncheon was slightly delayed while Dan's friends all toasted the bride and groom with raucous and affectionate toasts. Finally, the luncheon was underway and everyone agreed that it was a tribute to Liz's culinary skills.

It started with a cold cucumber soup, each bowl centered with a single strawberry. That was followed by a salmon salad, drizzled with an apple-cider vinaigrette of Liz's invention. The three-tiered wedding cake was large, but Liz had made an extra cake, iced with elaborate white icing. She felt it was important that everyone share in the cake. It was served with Liz's favorite Brazilian coffee.

Liz and Wendy had discussed the throwing of the bouquet and Liz had agreed that it should be thrown out of doors, because the enthusiasm of the bridesmaids might send it crashing through the greenhouse windows. On the lawn outside the greenhouse, Liz threw the bouquet over her shoulder. The tallest bridesmaid caught it and received her friends' congratulations amid speculations on whether she would be married next.

After the cake and coffee was finished, Liz and Dan retreated to hearty applause. They planned to spend the night at a local resort, in order to accommodate Dan's early morning schedule.

Dinner was lively the night that Liz and Dan returned from their "quickie honeymoon" as Liz called it. Although Wendy had made one of Liz's favorite crock-pot recipes, they all spent as much time listening to Liz's plans for the redecoration of her new home in Ray Brook as they did eating.

Wendy had noticed that a number of home decorating books and magazines had arrived for Liz within the last several weeks. She was amused to think that Liz had morphed into an enthusiastic homemaker almost overnight.

She mentioned that over coffee and dessert, and Liz admitted that she was having a wonderful time planning the redecorating.

She said, "This is the first time I've had an entire house to work on and I love it .She smiled at Dan and said, "I have someone to work with, too. That's great fun!"

Dan admitted that he was enjoying helping Liz work on the house, but admitted that he often had to curb what he called her "extravagant ideas."

Liz vehemently denied being extravagant, but claimed that she had discovered her "inner artist" and wanted to express that newfound side of herself.

Dan nodded his head in agreement and laughed.

Wendy looked at the papers piled on the dining room table and raised both hands in despair. "Where are we going to put all this wedding planning stuff? We have eight guests coming this weekend. It's too cool to eat out of doors."

Patty said, "Get out your grandmother's card table. We'll move all this into the parlor for now. The Thanksgiving wedding stuff should be separate from yours. That's the only way we'll keep track."

"Yes, that's it. Jen's coming over tomorrow so we can wrap up the final details. She's been very helpful and I appreciate it. I was afraid I'd end up being the wedding planner as well as the hostess, but she's really pitched in and so has Ryan."

"As she should," Patty said. "I admit she's had to do a lot more than most brides since her mother doesn't want to help."

Liz demanded, "What's with her mother, anyway? Most mothers want a lot to do with their daughter's wedding."

Wendy said, "She's angry that neither Jen nor Ryan will accept her agnosticism. Jen thinks her father isn't happy about her mother's harsh attitude, but nothing he says seems to be able to change Mrs. Horne's mind. Fortunately, Ryan's parents are more mellow, and because they love Jen, they're no problem."

Jennifer arrived at the B and B with a shoebox of wedding notes and snapshots of her wedding dress and her two bridesmaid's dresses.

"We took these in the bridal shop. The staff thought it was great fun and they even found a fake bouquet for me to hold. I love my dress! I chose one that's very simple because Ryan doesn't want to wear a tux. His gray suit will do nicely."

Wendy looked at the photos and admired the dresses. "Now," she said, "We have to talk about the rehearsal. Will your parents be here?"

"My Dad and I talked this weekend. He told my mother that since I was his only daughter, he was going to give me away. My brother Jeff will be one of Ryan's groomsmen and Mom didn't want to be totally left out, so she's coming." She laughed and said, "Apparently being anti-Christian has its limits. Thank God!"

Liz entered the parlor to find out what all the laughter was about and stayed to admire the dress photos. "I like these!" she said. "They're much like the ones I had for my wedding, only different colors. They'll look great with the pink flowers in the greenhouse."

Wendy and Jen organized the remaining details for Jen's wedding. Then Wendy said, "You know, since you're being married here the day after Thanksgiving, you and Ryan should eat Thanksgiving dinner with us. I'd love to have you meet our old friends, the Powers, and they'd be delighted to attend a wedding here." She told Jen about the history shared by the Powers and her grandparents.

Jen was impressed by the way Styvesant Powers had stood up to young John Dennehy when he had confronted the Powers and Wendy. She exclaimed, "I look forward to meeting them. You know such interesting people!"

Wendy glanced over Carole's shoulder at her wedding planning book. She was impressed that Carole was organizing Jen's wedding rehearsal as efficiently as she had the one for Liz's wedding. She told the pastor, "You did this so well at Liz's wedding, Carole, you got everyone to go through their routine as you expected, and coaxed them to ignore all the extraneous details. How do you do that?"

"Practice, practice, practice," said Carole. "I find that it helps if I remind everyone in the wedding party up front that they are rehearsing for a ceremony that asks for God's blessings on the couple getting married. That seems to bring their minds into focus, and the small stuff gets put aside. Now, I want to have a word with Mrs. Horne today, so we know what to expect at both the rehearsal and the wedding."

Wendy withdrew and made sure that the soft-voiced conversation between Carole and Mrs. Horne would not be interrupted. When the two women slipped from the greenhouse and continued their conversation in a quiet corner of the parlor, Wendy thought a brief prayer that Mrs. Horne would listen to Carole with an open mind. She talked to Jen, Ryan, Mr. Horne and the two bridesmaids about the flowers that decorated the shelves lining the greenhouse walls. They had been talking for about a half hour when Carole and Mrs. Horne returned. Mrs. Horne carried a Billy Graham book, *Peace with God*, that Carole had given her.

Mrs. Horne approached Jen and said, "I want to apologize to you, Jen, for being so difficult about your wanting a religious wedding. I realize that I was wrong about a lot of things." She looked at her husband, and continued, "I think we were both wrong to turn our backs on God and I'd like us to reconsider. This may help." She held out the book to her husband. Wendy thought he looked relieved and took the book.

He glanced at the book and said, "Billy Graham. This should be a good read."

Wendy exchanged a grateful look with Carole and mouthed a thank you. The pastor nodded and reminded the wedding party of the time they were expected to arrive at the B and B on the day after Thanksgiving. She said, "See you then. Goodbye for now."

The rest of the wedding party left and Liz cornered Wendy. Liz asked, "How did Carole get 'the mother of the bride from hell' to agree to read a book by Billy Graham?"

"The same way she runs an efficient rehearsal, practice, practice, practice."

"Wow, I knew that she's good, but I didn't know she's *that good!*"

CHAPTER TWENTY-SIX

"He has shown you, O man, what is good;
And what does the Lord require of you
but to do justly, to love mercy, and to walk
humbly with your God?" (Micah 6:8 NKJV)

Styvesant and Eleanor Powers arrived in the morning three days before Thanksgiving, Wendy settled them in and apologized for being too busy to visit.

Sty said, "It's still early and I'd like to get out on the lake. No sense in being indoors on such a lovely day." He turned to his wife and asked, "Would you allow me to give you a ride in the boat, just to enjoy the sunshine?"

Eleanor smiled and said, "I'd love that." She borrowed an umbrella to protect her delicate skin from the bright light that reflected from the lake and they both left.

Todd turned to Wendy and Liz. "Now, both of you, we have leaves to rake up!"

'Who me?" cried Liz. "I'm a cook, not a yard person." When Todd's face fell, she relented and said, "Well, like Sty said, it's a lovely day, and I've been sitting too much today. As a member of the family, I should rake for a while." She led them out of doors.

"What a beautiful day!" exclaimed Liz as she spun around the lawn. "Just look at all that sunshine! I haven't seen a day like this since I was in college."

"That's because in New York we spent so much time indoors that we just never noticed how beautiful a fall day could be," said Wendy.

After they had spent an hour raking, Liz watched Todd as he paced the rows in the vegetable garden.

"What do you have for us, Todd? Something delicious, I hope. Are those Brussels Sprouts ready?"

"They were planted late in spring, and are almost ready to pick. I'd like to wait until we've had colder weather, which according to the forecast, we'll have next week. Gram always said that Brussels Sprouts tasted better after they'd had a touch of frost."

"What a farmer you've become, Todd."

Liz was laughing at him, but he was comfortable with their new-found closeness, so he admitted, "Yes, I paid attention when Gram taught me what she knew about vegetable gardening. Anything I forgot I looked up in a gardening book."

Wendy's cell phone rang. "Hello, Clarissa. How are you?... He did? When?" She stared at the others and they picked up on her intensity. She listened for a moment. "My sympathies are with you, Clarissa. I know how close you were to your grandfather. If you feel you should get away from Manhattan after the funeral, please come up here. You're welcome any time that we don't have a full house."

After a moment's silence, she said, "I'm glad he did, Clarissa. God loves us all and I'm pleased Jack was able to discover that before he died."

Then she said, "You don't need to thank me. I did nothing. God spoke to Jack. All he had to do was to listen and I'm glad he did."

Wendy's face lit up as Clarissa spoke again. "You did? Wonderful! Giving yourself to Christ will change your life. I look forward to seeing you again. Bye"

She told the others, "Jack Dennehy died in his sleep yesterday, clutching his Bible, according to Clarissa. Odd, I thought of that old man as almost immortal. He just seemed to go on and on, coming up with new schemes as he got older Ninety six is a late age to find God, but not too late. Clarissa changed, also."

She watched Todd as he pulled a few weeds from the garden and then she leaned on the fence to observe Liz pull up a large handful of carrots. Liz said, "I'm glad the veggies grew so well. After all, we might have other guests like that Naomi woman. Imagine anyone deciding on her way up here from New York City that she wanted to become a vegetarian! Jumping horses in mid-river! What did she expect?"

Wendy choked back a laugh and said, "A last minute change in our menus, obviously. You pulled it off, Liz. You did a great job."

The compliment distracted Liz from her glare at Todd, who was laughing at her mixed metaphor.

Wendy walked away from the fence and said, "Excuse me, I'm going for a walk. See you later." The others realized that she wanted to be alone, so continued their tasks.

Wendy entered the densely shaded path that led up the trail toward Mount Colburn. At first she briskly walked the gradually rising trail, but was distracted by bright red leaves fallen from maples near the trail. She picked up a few and admired their brilliant color. As the ascent became steeper, she was forced to slow her pace. Within ten minutes she reached the destination she remembered from her childhood. She was among sparse cedar trees when she stepped off the trail to scramble up a sloping gray rock that towered fifteen feet above her. She could see the rooftop of The Greenhouse below. Sunlight reflected off the rippled surface of Lake Placid. The bright sails of a few sailboats caught the wind and swept down the lake. Her eyes widened as she turned around to get a panoramic view of the gently rounded mountains surrounding her. They were dark green, except for the occasional splash of bright red, yellow or orange where aspen or maples grew.

She exclaimed, "How beautiful your world is, Lord! Thank you for putting me in such a lovely place." Then her voice dropped into a conversational tone and she said, "I knew it was lovely here when I visited Gram as a child. I didn't see the big picture then. I suppose it was because I wanted to stay so close to my family that I didn't look much beyond them. Now you've shown me the big picture.

"What do you want me to do with it? Is it your will that I use my home and business to try to lead others to you?"

She stretched both arms overhead and prayed aloud, "Father God, thank you for Jack Dennehy's turning back to you. I know he didn't do it by himself. You were nudging him along the way, because you wanted to finish the job his grandmother had started by giving him that Bible. One more soul saved! Two more! Clarissa's turned to you, and has accepted the love of Christ." She dropped to her knees on the rock and her prayer continued to pour out.

"Father, I pray for those you are putting in my path. Thank you that I could help Jack and Clarissa. I pray that I will be strong enough to help any others you may send to me. I pray for their protection from the evil one, as well as my own family's protection. I pray that you will help me to be completely alert so I do not fail you. I am awed that you have trusted me with this task. I fearfully and yet gladly accept it. In the name of Jesus Christ I pray. Amen." She trembled as a feeling of awesome responsibility swept over her. She felt the warmth of the sun pouring down on her and was suddenly wrapped within a presence so powerful that it was all she could do not to fall on her face. She cried out, "Thank you, Father. Please stay with my family and me and protect us as we try to do your will. Amen."

Her legs were trembling and she didn't think she could stand, so she slid down the side of the rock and leaned against it for a moment before she regained the trail. Her slow descent to the B and B seemed to take a long time, but when she stepped into the sunshine, Liz and Todd were still in the garden. The only difference was the full basket of weeds that Todd was carrying and a bucket of fresh vegetables that Liz had at her feet.

"What a couple of farmers you are" she cried. "I'm impressed."

Liz said, "These veggies are for the stew I'm making for our dinner."

Tom spoke from a chaise lawn chair where he was sprawled in the shade. "Not just veggies, Liz. I'm a growing boy, I need my meat."

"You're a carnivore, Tom Decker. Yes, I'm planning on using stew beef. After all, there's two voracious carnivores in this household, and I know how to cook for you."

Wendy joined Tom on the lawn chair. "You always get enough to eat, don't you?" she asked as she cuddled close to him.

Tom grinned and said, "I do, and Liz takes care of that just fine, but she needs a little tease now and then so we can sneak in a compliment."

He raised his voice so Liz could hear him and said, "We carnivores appreciate her. She really knows how to cook for us."

Liz laughed and asked, "Are you staying for dinner, Tom?"

Wendy answered, "Yes, he is." Tom tickled her. "Hey, you didn't even ask me. Aren't you being presumptuous?"

Through her giggles, Wendy said, 'I'm claiming dinner rights to you tonight. Besides, Sty and Eleanor Powers want to meet you, so you have to stay."

Liz went into the house to wash the vegetables and remove some stew beef from the freezer. She had already removed the Thanksgiving turkey from the freezer and left it to defrost in the refrigerator. "I have to check that bird," she muttered to herself. "It should have had enough time to defrost. I'd better make time after dinner to whip up a couple of pumpkin pies." She glanced at her watch and quickened her pace. Like Wendy, she loved Thanksgiving and wanted to produce a dinner that was worthy of the holiday.

Wendy smiled to see that Jen and her bridesmaids, Sarah and Helen were taking turns looking out the windows to the driveway. Sarah said, "I'm sure your parents will be here for your wedding rehearsal. How can they resist?"

Jen shrugged, "You don't know how my mother has been. I told her we were having it here instead of a church, and she seemed to relent when she was here last."

"Will your dad give you away?"

"Yes. I know he wants to, and he says my mom's coming around."

"They're here!" squealed Sarah. "Your brothers here and they're with him."

Jen hurried out to greet her family. Wendy and Liz exchanged glances of relief. They were concerned about Jen's state of mind during her rehearsal. The Hornes entered through the kitchen because Wendy had suggested to Jen that the kitchen was the friendliest room in the house and they might feel more at ease if they came in that way.

Mrs. Horne expressed her admiration of the décor of the bed and breakfast, so Wendy offered her a tour. Jen's father stayed in the kitchen, talking to Jen. Mrs. Horne enjoyed the tour and was very enthusiastic about the flowers blooming in the greenhouse.

"How lovely! I've always loved greenhouses. We used to live on a commune that had one and we grew our own marijuana in it." She noticed Wendy's surprised expression and said. "That was back in our wild days. We don't indulge any more:"

Jen, Ryan, the bridesmaids, groomsmen and Jen's father entered the greenhouse, followed by Carole, who had just arrived. She was pleased to see that the birch-bark covered altar had been brought in and placed in front of the raffia cross. "Now, are we ready for the rehearsal?" she asked.

Mr. Horne said, "I guess we're ready, if all of you are." He glanced at the young people and missed the pleased expression on his wife's face.

Carole had a take charge tone in her voice as she said, "The groomsmen can wait here to my left and the bridesmaids in the parlor. Wendy, if you will start the tape, we may begin. Bridesmaids, you enter, one at a time, as soon as you hear the music."

When Mrs. Horne saw her husband stand next to Jen and offer her his arm, she found a chair, and watched while dabbing her eyes with a handkerchief. Under Carole's direction, the rehearsal moved smoothly. They finished in only twenty minutes. Carole concluded with a prayer.

Once they were finished, Liz entered and told them that refreshments were in the dining room. Everyone left for the food, except for Mrs. Horne, who appeared to be looking for something. Wendy invited her to join them and mentioned the lovely cake Liz had made for the occasion. Mrs. Horne accompanied her to the table, but after being served, she turned to Jen and Ryan and said, "I see your wedding is just as religious as it would be in a church. You've made your convictions clear and I will respect them."

"Mom, my faith is important to me, and to Ryan as well. We avoided a church wedding to try to meet you halfway. You'll be here for the wedding, won't you?"

Mr. Horne said, "I'm not missing the chance to give my daughter away, so I hope you'll come with me. This is an important family milestone."

Jen's brother Jeff said, "Mom, remember when I was a little kid, I always asked you for a brother?"

Mrs. Horne blushed and said, "How could I forget, you embarrassed me so much."

"Well, now I'm going to have a brother." He playfully punched Ryan on his shoulder and said, "It took longer than I thought, but here he is!"

Ryan said, "Better late than never, right?"

"You're right," said Mrs. Horne, smiling at her husband.

The refreshments and coffee seemed to encourage Mrs. Horne to relax, and she talked to Jen about her wedding dress and the plans Jen and Ryan had for trying to buy a house locally.

Wendy breathed a prayerful sigh of relief. She had been worried that Jen's mother would create a problem when she realized that her daughter's wedding would be a religious one. "Thank you, God, you've answered my prayer. I might have known you'd come through, but I worry through habit, I suppose. That's a bad habit I must work on."

CHAPTER TWENTY-SEVEN

"Give ear to my words, O Lord, consider
my meditation. Take heed to the voice
of my cry, my King and my God, for to
You I will pray. (Psalm 5:1-2 MKJV)

It was Thanksgiving Day. Gathered around the dining room table were Sty and Eleanor Powers, Wendy, Tom, Dan, Jen, Ryan and Todd. An empty chair awaited Liz who, having removed the turkey from the oven, was putting finishing touches on the gravy. They all breathed in the delectable scents drifting their way from the kitchen

Then Liz pushed in a wheeled teacart laden with dishes of vegetables and a tossed salad. She placed the serving dishes on the table and then called out, "Ta-da!" She dramatically waved one hand in the air. Todd carried in an enormous platter on which a twenty-five pound turkey rested in gleaming browned splendor.

Sty said a heartfelt grace that thanked God for the past year in which in spite of dangers, they were all well and happy. He asked for the food to be blessed and that each person at the table be willing and able to follow God's desires for them in the coming year.

"How lovely, Liz," said Wendy. "It smells heavenly and looks beautiful. What a work of art!"

"Come on, that's enough admiration, let's eat!" exclaimed Tom.

Todd carved the turkey according to explicit instructions that Liz had given him earlier. Everyone ate their fill and complimented Liz profusely on the dinner.

Liz blushed as she accepted the praise. After everyone had eaten their fill, the dinner remains was removed from the table. All except Liz decided that they had to take a short walk before they could eat dessert. Their walk amounted to no more than a stroll on the lawns surrounding the house.

Wendy said, "I'm glad we're having a warm day. I remember one year we spent Thanksgiving here with our grandmother, and we had almost a foot of snow."

Eleanor shivered dramatically and admitted, "It's lovely today, and I'm grateful for that. Each year it takes me a little longer to acclimate myself to winter weather, so the more gradual the drop in temperature, the better."

Todd turned back to the house. "I'm ready for pumpkin pie. How about the rest of you?" He and Tom led the return to the house. Both pumpkin pies, heaped with whipped cream, were soon demolished and Liz was praised again for her cooking. They lingered over their coffee and talked about Jen and Ryan's upcoming wedding.

"Just think, tomorrow! After all the rush to get ready, I can't believe the time has gone by so quickly," said Jen.

"It can't get here soon enough for me," said Ryan. "It took me a while to convince Jen that her parents wouldn't start another world war if she had a religious wedding. Look how it turned out, Jen. Your father will give you away!"

Jen added, "I think my mother is changing, especially since she doesn't want to be the only family member who won't be here." She chucked and said, "Apparently, agnosticism has its limits. Especially within a family."

Jen had to promise Ryan that she'd ask Liz for the pumpkin pie recipe. Liz insisted that she just used the recipe in her favorite cookbook, Joy of Cooking.

Jen admitted, "I've lived on fast food since college, so I might have to come to you for cooking lessons."

Liz smiled and said, "I might do that, talk to me later."

The next day, in Wendy's bedroom, Wendy helped Jen into her wedding dress. The bridesmaids could be heard in Liz's room laughing and joking. One of the girls' mothers had insisted on helping the girls to dress. In an aside, she had whispered to Wendy, "I know they can dress themselves. I just want them to be ready *on time*."

Wendy asked, "Are you all right, Jen? You're very quiet."

Jen sighed and said, "I've been praying for a miracle. I want my parents to come to accept Jesus as their savior. Dad has been listening to me lately, even before the rehearsal. And Mom said she's reading the book that Carole gave her, and even marked parts that she wanted to talk to Carole about, but it's too early to say anything about her reaction."

Wendy took Jen's hands in hers and said, "Then let's pray for them." They prayed, one after the other, for both Mr. and Mrs. Horne to accept Jesus as their Savior.

Sarah poked her head in the bedroom and said, "They're here! Both your mother and father are here. And your Mom's wearing a killer dress!"

"What? Mom doesn't dress up. She says it's against nature to wear bright colors. Did you notice that dingy wrap dress she wore to the rehearsal? Let me see!" Jen ran from the room to peek down the stairs. Her mother was starting upstairs and called out, "Jen, your dress is lovely. It's even nicer than I imagined from your description. The simplicity is so elegant!"

When Mrs. Horne reached the landing, Jen hugged her and said, "Mom, I love your dress. I've never seen you wearing rose before."

"I wanted to look like I was a part of your wedding, so I chose a color that would relate to the colors of the orchids you said were the shade of your bridesmaids' dresses. I got this in Albany last night. Your father didn't even complain about going shopping with me. Do you think the bugle beads on the bodice are too much?"

"Not at all, you look lovely as the mother of the bride. Our wedding pictures will be stunning!"

"Your father bought four more rolls of film. Let me escort you downstairs. Your father can take over from there." She adjusted Jen's short veil and took her daughter's arm. They walked downstairs together.

The sun shone brightly into the greenhouse, reflecting all the colors of the rainbow from the prisms dangling from the ceiling. The delicate scent of orchids filled the room, causing the guests to breathe in the scent with their eyes closed in delight.

When the music started, Mr. Horne escorted Jen down the aisle between the folding chairs. He blinked his eyes to keep tears from falling. He stopped before the altar in front of the raffia cross and stared up at the cross. An expression of awe and delight crossed his face. Then he kissed Jen on the cheek, briefly hugged her and stepped aside.

Traditional wedding vows were exchanged and Jen stepped outside to throw her bouquet. Sarah caught it, to the cheers of the crowd. Everyone was invited into the dining room, where the white-frosted cake was waiting to be served with punch and coffee.

While the cheerful din from the dining room echoed through the house, Wendy stepped out onto the porch. She looked up at the bright blue sky, studded with fluffy white clouds. She clasped her hands to her breasts and prayed silently, *"Thank you, God. Jen's mother is not only here, but she cried through the wedding. And she bought a new dress for the occasion! It's a dress suitable for the mother of the bride, not for a hippy chick."* She threw her arms out wide. *"Thank you!"*

As she entered the house to rejoin the wedding party, she heard a horn blare from the driveway in back. She continued through the house to the back door. Todd followed.

Out of doors, she was surprised to see a beat up old Chevy. Four or five unkempt young men piled out of it. One of them staggered toward her and yelled, "You stole from our family, you Baileys! Our cousin J-J-Jackie d-died here t-trying to g-get the g-gold that belongs to us. Now hand it over!"

"They're drunk," said Todd indignantly. He stepped .forward and said, "We're having a wedding here. Get off the property!"

"Not till we g-get what we c-come for!" the man shouted.

Suddenly there was the roar of a powerful engine and a bright yellow Hispano-Suiza pulled into the yard. The vehicle swerved in front of the Chevy, facing it, forcing the young men to jump back. The driver's door opened slowly and a person dressed in a dapper black 1920's suit stepped out. The person's black shoes and white spats echoed the '20's aura, as did the billed driver's cap. The person strolled around the front of the car and, raising one arm, leveled a long finger at the young men. Then the finger pointed down the driveway and the hand waved them away.

The men shrieked and piled back into the Chevy. With tires screeching, the driver pulled the car into a tight circle and left.

The person laughed and turned to the porch. The Powers and Liz had joined Wendy and Todd. The cap was removed and blond curls appeared. Clarissa stood before them dressed in her grandfather's suit. "That scared those creeps, didn't it?" she said.

Wendy rushed forward to hug Clarissa. The young woman returned her hug and said, "I love my cousins, but some of them are dumb, dumb, dumb. Please forgive them, Wendy, they don't know any better. The gold has been in our family history too long."

"Oh yes, I forgive them. It was worth it to see you dressed as Jack, and seeing them run off, scared out of their wits!"

"As soon as I heard what they planned, I knew what I had to do. They won't ever come back to bother you, now that they believe Grandpa's ghost is protecting you."

Wendy invited Clarissa to come in, but Clarissa detoured to the car and grabbed a bag. She asked permission to change into her own clothes before joining the party. Wendy showed her to a guest room and told her to come down when she was ready.

The wedding party had to be told of what had happened and all enjoyed the story. Jen said, "What an interesting life you lead, Wendy!"

Wendy laughed and said, "I'm thankful that I have God's protection, or I couldn't put up with it. I don't *need* a life this interesting, believe me!"

CHAPTER TWENTY-EIGHT

"I have come into my garden, my sister,
my bride: I have gathered my myrrh with
my spice, I have eaten my honeycomb
and my honey; I have drunk my wine
and my milk. (Song of Solomon 5:1)

Spring arrived in timely fashion for the Adirondacks. Wendy watched the weather forecasts diligently for a month before her wedding. Spring snows were light and the occasional cold weather wasn't severe. The dreaded "mud season" that Wendy had been concerned about only lasted for three weeks into April.

Wendy turned around in front of the mirror in the bridal shop, the white gown gleaming in the overhead lights. "I love it, Liz. Just look how it drapes gracefully in the back. Although it's not train length, it looks like a train. It's perfect."

Liz, who had tried on her matron of honor dress, lavender silk trimmed with green piping, agreed with her. "It's lovely. It shows off your tiny waist. It looks great on you!"

Kim, wearing her bridesmaid's tress in pale green trimmed in lavender, agreed, "Wendy, you're going to be the loveliest bride. Tom will just fall over at the sight of you!"

Wendy laughed and said, 'Oh, I hope not. I want a conscious groom during the wedding ceremony. That's a necessity!"

She had thought the winter before her wedding was going to seem so long that she'd be in a hurry for it to end. Instead, she was so busy taking care of the B and B and her wedding plans that the months seemed to fly past her before she was aware of them.

An adult ski touring group had discovered The Greenhouse and made several weeklong stays. Todd had found it necessary to construct a ski shed near the back door, so skis could be kept outside, instead of being carried dripping, into the house. The winter was cold with no unseasonable warm spell to drive off the skiers. That created a fine winter season for The Greenhouse and the village of Lake Placid.

In May, snow remained under the trees around the property, but the days were sunny and warm enough to ensure that the access road was clear and dry. The greenhouse was ready for the wedding. Wendy had decorated the large glass room with white chrysanthemums and more orchids in lavender, green and white. Lavender and green ribbons hung from the ceiling. Green dendrobium orchids, in lavender pots, were placed in front of the outside wall of the greenhouse to give them the maximum sunlight.

As Todd had predicted, some guests would have to be seated in the parlor, but with glass panes forming part of one wall, they would have a good view of the wedding. A microphone would allow them to hear the exchange of vows.

The day before the wedding, rented chairs filled the greenhouse and parlor. Wendy would make her entrance down the main stairs, then would be led on Sty's arm through an aisle in the parlor and into the greenhouse.

The morning of the wedding was bright and clear. The remaining elongated piles of snow under the trees reflected the sun, giving the property a wedding day glow.

Madame Olga Stravizinky arrived two days before the wedding and on the morning of the wedding, she insisted on helping Wendy to dress. The opera diva skillfully wound white satin ribbons through Wendy's gently waved hair and applied her makeup with a light professional touch

Wendy sat in front of her bedroom mirror and observed her

transformation from a merely pretty girl to a beautiful woman. She was pleased and slightly in awe of Olga's artistry.

She looked at her sparkling eyes, enhanced by Olga's magic. "Olga, I've never looked this beautiful before."

Olga added a touch of blush. "You are naturally beautiful! I am only complimenting your natural beauty. I must admit that the bridal aura gives you a special glow, which is as it should be. Every happy bride has this radiance and since you are so pretty to begin with, this happiness makes you glow from within. There is nothing in the world you can purchase that can enhance that glow. It is as natural as the sun that shines overhead." She stepped back and asked Wendy to stand. Wendy did so and arranged the folds of her gown as best she could. Olga walked around her, observing her from all sides. Then she clapped her hands and said, "It is complete. You are ready to be married! Now I will help Kim to dress the children. You stay here and think lovely thoughts, so your face is full of beauty when you see your groom." Wendy smiled and thought, *"I'll have no problems thinking lovely thoughts today."*

Olga then helped Kim to dress Susie and Sam. The children were awed by Olga and thrilled to be part of the wedding. They were impressed with their responsibilities. Both children had behaved well during the rehearsal, and promised to do the same during the wedding. Finally, the musicians, set up in the dining room, sounded the opening chord to Wendy's entrance music--an upbeat chamber piece by Handel. She held her bouquet of white orchids at her waist and whispered encouraging words to Susie and Sam as they began their solemn walk down the stairs and entered the parlor, then the greenhouse. Wendy kept her eyes fixed on the pale green silk draped over the cross's arms as it swooped gracefully to the bark slabs to which the petite white Cattleya orchids clung, embracing them in their delicate spring-like aura. She thought, *Lord, this is the life you planned for me. Let me be worthy of it.*

Liz and Kim followed the children, as Susie's small hands scattered lavender and white silk petals onto the gleaming wood floor of the parlor and then onto the woven grass mats in the greenhouse. The little girl stopped at the foot of the raffia cross, gave Carole a lovely smile and then stepped to one side. Sam looked admiringly up into his uncle's eyes as Tom stood at one side of the cross in his dress uniform. The boy proudly gripped the pillow that held twin gold rings fastened with white ribbons. Tom smiled at him and whispered, "Good job, Sam."

When Wendy stepped up to the altar and Tom moved to her side, he looked into her heart-stopping blue eyes and knew he was happier than he had ever been in his life.

Wendy floated through her wedding on a dizzying wave of happiness. When she and Tom had recited their vows and were declared husband and wife, she didn't know if she would cry or laugh. When Tom put his arms around her and kissed her, she knew she could only laugh with joy.

When it was time for her to throw the bouquet, like Liz, Wendy announced that she would do so out of doors. Outside, the bouquet sailed through the sunlight, right into the hands of one of her single friends from church. Cheers echoed across the lawns and the young people applauded the lucky young woman. In the thick of an exuberant crowd, Wendy and Tom were hugged and kissed by dozens of people. Then they returned to the greenhouse where Patty's nieces and nephews had quickly and efficiently arranged it into a dining hall.

Finally, she and Tom were served their meal. Everyone declared that Liz's tasty gruyere-stuffed chicken breasts, wrapped in phyllo dough were delicious and a few asked for the recipe, which Liz promised to deliver. After everyone was seated in the greenhouse, servers passed out a delicious sparkling fruit punch that Liz had concocted.

Tom's trooper friends toasted the couple and told stories of Tom's prowess as a trooper. The family made touching, sentimental toasts, each of which left Wendy in tears.

Wendy was pleased to see that Clarissa Cleary had arrived. She found a moment to talk to Clarissa and the young woman said she was now a full time college student, majoring in business administration.

"In spite of his complaint at the antique car show, my grandfather was pleased to know that you were marrying a state trooper. He once asked that I repeat his offer, that if you ever need help, just call on the family. I'm sure that still holds." She blushed, and then admitted, "I really do have some nice relatives, not just those goons who showed up here earlier."

Wendy thanked Clarissa politely. Then she made an excuse that she had to talk to other guests and put Clarissa's comments out of her mind. She knew that both she and Tom would call on God before they turned to the Dennehy-Cleary family.

After everyone had eaten, Ted's musicians set up on the front porch and played dance music for the guests. Wendy and Ted danced their first dance together as husband and wife. Tom held her closely and whispered to her, "I know I have to share you with God and your mission to bring others to him. I hope I'm worthy of being your helper in fulfilling that mission."

"You are, Tom. I *know you are*, or I'd never have dared to marry you."

He laughed as he swirled her around the other dancers on the porch. "What a team we'll make, you and me!"

A short time later, as Wendy was danced the length of the porch by Styvesant Powers, he said, "Wendy, I can't tell you how proud I am of you. You're just like your grandmother, smart, successful and beautiful."

"Thank you," she said. "I have to give a lot of the credit to you, Todd, Liz and other friends for the success of The Greenhouse Bed and Breakfast. To think that all this," she waved a hand at the dozens of happy people on the porch. "All this started with a murder–and my brave grandmother. It just shows what can be accomplished by people who love one another and rely on their strong faith in God!"

THE END